AN AUTHOR'S SECRET

AN AUTHOR'S SECRET

SANTOSH VISHWANATH

NU VOICE
PRESS

First published by NU VOICE PRESS 2024
An imprint of Hubhawks Pvt. Ltd
www.nuvoicepress.com

This is a work of fiction. Space and time have been rearranged to suit the convenience of the book. Except for public figures, hotels, and institution names, any resemblance to persons living or dead or the real events are purely coincidental. The opinions expressed in the book are those of the characters, and should not be confused with that of the Author.

ISBN: 978-81-980376-6-4
Typeset by Saanvi Graphics, Noida
Printed at Nutech Print Services - India
Published by Nu Voice Press

To those few who always believe in my dreams more than I do,
no matter how audacious those dreams are.

Author's Note

Years ago, in a moment of epiphany, a theme occurred to me where an individual is bestowed the responsibility to complete someone else's unfinished novel. I made up my mind to write this story. As I spent more time playing around with the thought, the title 'The Unfinished Mystery' seemed apt. Thus, I decided to write my first mystery novel. Having only experimented with some humour and a little romance for a decade, I wasn't sure how venturing into the mystery genre would unfold. Let me say that, in the end, it unfolded more beautifully than I had earlier imagined.

Also, the book was never planned to be in first-person female narration. Yet, it only seemed right when I started to write, and I chose the protagonist Ankana's voice as the narrator.

You will encounter a partially completed novel within the main story. It might have been simpler and easier to include a brief summary. However, the more I contemplated it, the more I felt it was important to give my readers the real feel of another story.

When Nu Voice approached me recently about publishing *The Unfinished Mystery*, now *An Author's Secret*, under their banner, I was glad that what I had considered a good story for years would finally reach people.

This last point may apply to all my stories. I hope you enjoy reading it as much as I enjoyed writing it.

Chapter 1

I had trouble sleeping on the moving bus, even though it was an early morning trip to Bangalore. While the roads were surprisingly good and the journey smooth, you have to understand that for a girl my age—well, for a lady my age—having a handsome hunk seated next to her made it a tad difficult to take a casual nap.

Being the queen of reveries, I'd already imagined growing close to him and celebrating Valentine's Day at a Malpe Beach resort with 'Cheeku', as I'd nicknamed him, to mark our second anniversary of being in love. I'd always wanted to be caught in such a situation where a good-looking guy would be seated next to me on a train or flight, or stuck together in an elevator. Luck had never presented me with such an opportunity, and when it did present on this day, I was tongue-tied to start a conversation.

Every time I turned to him, expecting – or rather hoping – that he'd be eyeing me, I was met with disappointment. He was deep into a book. I noticed that he'd just started with it when the journey began, and to see that he'd completed a good number of pages made me think that he must be an avid reader. I tried to look at the book's title, but I was taken aback when it read *Two and a Quarter Murders.* I mean, I'd have thought it was a match made in heaven if the title were to read *Two and a Quarter Love Stories.* But the violent title reduced my appetite for flirting to some extent.

Here is where I should tell you that I'm into love stories. I'm not referring to reading them much. I am an aspiring author of romance! I say 'aspiring' because even though I have completed two manuscripts and started working on my third one, none of these have made it through to the publishing houses, at least not yet. I hope it's only a matter of time before I crack it.

If I think of it, I can say that I've completed two and a quarter manuscripts, and this guy was reading *Two and a Quarter Murders*! That might count for something like a sign from above, right?

"So, has the murderer completed with the second murder?" I realised I'd spoken up.

"Huh!" The guy jumped.

"Hey, sorry. I didn't mean to intrude."

"Oh! My bad. I was just…" He shrugged, looking at the book. "Never mind, and yes, the second murder was just committed, which is why I was surprised when you said what you said."

"Ah! It must be a good story. You seemed to be really involved."

"Yes, ma'am, this is…"

"Uh… please call me Ankana."

"Right… Ankana. That is the magic of Rāghavānka." He smiled with all his teeth visible, including a good portion of his gums. It turned me off, as this was much different from the smile I'd imagined him to have during my daydreaming episode. Only now did I realise that he seemed way too young for me. I was not fond of the age difference.

"Sorry, who?" I asked.

He seemed shocked, as if I were his girlfriend of two years who had forgotten his birthday.

"You don't know… okay… this author is quite good and almost has a cult following."

"That's a strange… ahem… unique name – Rāghavānka."

"I am sorry. I assumed that you are into books as well."

"You are right on that! I am into books." Without waiting for him to react, I pushed in my trump card, "I have written a couple of novels."

Using that line has always helped me get the same expression I desire from the other person. He was awestruck, and it showed in his eyes. Somewhere, I must admit that this is one of the reasons why I wanted to become a well-known author.

"You mean, you write mysteries?"

"No, damn it!" I wanted to say, but refrained and just said, "No. I write beautiful love stories."

"That's wonderful, Ms. Ankana!" He was thrilled.

"Just Ankana is fine." I nodded with practised efficacy. My late mother used to tell me that one has to behave according to what one wants to become, and I took her suggestion seriously.

He pulled his smartphone out and asked me, "Can you tell me the names of your books?"

Oh shit! This guy wanted to check if I was bluffing. No, I think I am being paranoid. But thanks to the internet, he will learn that my books haven't seen the light of the day yet.

"They're still with the publishers, you know… going through the final edits. You won't find them in online bookstores for now," I lied.

"Yes, sure. But don't you intend to try writing anything in mystery or thriller? There are many writers into romance already, no?"

"That's true. There are a lot of folks writing romance. But it's also true that more people read romance than the other genres, no?" Looking at his expression, I knew I got right back at him.

"I am personally not into love stories that much. No offence, Ankana. I am sure it takes a lot of effort to write anything for that matter."

It was a typical guy's response, with their chauvinistic side unwilling to show that they love reading romance in the candlelight when everyone sleeps. However, I felt that his intention wasn't to put me down, and he only voiced his opinion fairly.

"Same way, even I am not into mystery novels." I shrugged.

He smiled and said, "To each his own, I guess," and was about to get back to his book.

"What is it that you dislike about romance, anyway?" I probed.

He seemed to give it some thought, or at least pretended to, so that it appeared genuine, and said, "I have read some of them. It is not that I am against romance novels. I do believe some love stories are written very well. But in more than a few instances, I found the authors trying to evoke some extreme and unwarranted emotions from the readers rather than just narrating a good story, you know?"

"That's possible. Some writers may do that. But then, if you think about it, every mystery story has one or the other person getting killed, right? I mean, what's the fun in reading about someone getting murdered? That's very brutal of us." I countered.

"Hey, wait a minute." He seemed offended, as if I punched his Rāghavānka in the guts when he was not looking. "At least there is a reason for mysteries to have murders in them so that some intelligent investigator finds the criminal. But nowadays, most love stories also have deaths, right?"

"Sorry?" I was confused.

"My friends read a lot of romance, and I believe, in some stories, the girlfriend dies, in some, the spouse dies, and in some, the one whom the protagonist is having an affair with dies, and..."

"Okay, okay, I got that." I was irritated with this guy.

"Sorry, amidst all this, I've not even introduced myself. My name's Dev."

"Good to meet you, Dev." I tried to avoid him and looked away. However, I could see from my peripheral vision that he continued looking at me blankly with a smile, indicating he wanted to speak more.

I turned to him and smiled a fake one. It was all my fault that I invited him for a conversation earlier. I asked, "What do you do, Dev?"

"I'm about to begin the next semester of my MBA. I was returning from my internship with one of the conglomerates in Mangalore."

"Oh, okay!" I'm not sure if he caught the disappointment in my voice. This guy is still studying!

Perhaps he sensed something and continued, "I've received PPO from this firm."

"Eh, what's a PPO?" One more thing that puts me off is jargon. My dream was shattering minute by minute. However, the dream was hardly as old as a few hours.

"Pre-placement offer. Based on my internship, the firm has offered me a permanent job." He was back to showing his teeth and gums.

"That's good to hear, Dev. Congrats!" I smiled politely and tried to withdraw from the conversation.

It looked like he wanted to chat more. The miseries I bring upon myself, I tell you.

"So, you are going to Bangalore to meet up with one of the agents regarding your books?"

"Huh… yeah… right… good guess." I was putting up a fake smile. "I think it's time to find out who's murdered the two people and wonder why the third one was quite unsuccessful, managing to murder only a quarter of the person," I said, maybe slightly bluntly, indicating to him to return to his book.

I don't think he understood my intent, but he literally returned to the mystery at hand. "Oh yes! I will do that."

I returned his smile and turned away from him to look at the cloudy weather outside, pulling my shawl tighter around myself. Of course, I had lied to him that I was going to Bangalore to meet with people regarding my books. It surely would have been awkward had I told him that amidst all the flirting with him, I was actually on my way to attend my brother's funeral.

Chapter 2

I got off the bus after wishing Dev all the best in his future endeavours. The cold, dry Bangalore winds hit me. I was not fond of this weather. How much I've avoided coming to this city, as if it were someone I hated. I relocated to Mangalore with my mother, Ragini, during my early school years. The circumstances under which we left were quite dire, leaving a wound that remained raw and never healed.

Looking up, I could see it was a matter of time before it began to rain. It was not the season, but what else would one expect in Bangalore? "Typical," I said aloud, almost mocking the city, knowing there would be no retort.

I felt it was less of a hassle to get cabs, unlike in Mangalore. The message I'd received last night indicated I needed to be at the cemetery by afternoon, and I looked like I would be on time for the final rites. I requested the cabbie to halt momentarily, not to pick up a bouquet but to get something to eat. No good has happened to anyone by attending cremations on an empty stomach.

"Ma'am, we are near TR Mill. Where do I drop you?"

"Can you please drop me to the cemetery here?"

"Oh, sure, ma'am. I didn't realise you were attending a funeral."

"That's okay."

"Some distant relative, ma'am?" he said, perhaps observing my indifference.

"Eh… yes. Sort of." I nodded, and he got back to his job.

On reaching, I saw that there were many people at the spot. I'd not anticipated there would be so many of them. I realised then that only my mother and I had cut off our relations with everyone. That wasn't the case with my half-brother and father.

I hardly knew anyone around and felt slightly anxious to have come. I felt out of my comfort zone and out of place as random people stared at me for that extra second, perhaps registering who I was. I wanted to make it matter-of-fact and get away from here as soon as possible. I only wanted to visit for courtesy, or that's what I'd told myself. I was questioning even that in the present instance. Did I have to come?

When I was grappling with this, someone approached me. "Ahem… Ankana?"

"Yes?" Finally, a neutral face that didn't seem to judge me, I thought to myself, as my lips curled into a hesitant smile.

"I am Rakesh. I was the one who called you."

He tried to smile back at me, but the sadness on his face overshadowed it. I couldn't help but notice; even with all that sorrow, his face looked strangely attractive.

"Ah yes, I recollect. You said you are Havish's brother-in-law, right?"

"Yes, sort of. I am Rupa's first cousin."

Havish was my half-brother's name, who was no more, and Rupa was his widow. Rakesh showed me the way so that we could find a less crowded space to speak, away from people who let their emotions out standing near Havish's corpse due to his untimely demise.

"Sorry, before that, do you want to see your brother for one last…"

"No." My response was too ready for him to react.

"Sure…" He paused. "It's… too sudden for all of us." His voice was serious and sad.

I nodded diplomatically.

"I… I had heard that you weren't… close to Havish. But I thought it was right to call you and at least inform you. It was not easy getting your contact details." He tried to chuckle nervously.

"Thanks for making an effort, Rakesh. That was very nice of you."

He looked around, unsure of what else to talk about. Then I thought about the obvious question I hadn't asked him and felt like kicking myself. "Sorry, what about Rupa? She must be devastated. She must be here, right?" I considered for a moment whether I should meet and express my condolences to Havish's widow. That was the least human thing I could do.

He stared at me for a moment, "Oh! Of course, you don't know the details. Havish and Rupa were travelling to Madikeri the other night to spend the long weekend when the car met with an accide..."

"Oh god! You mean even Rupa…" I was unable to say anything.

"No, no. Havish… died on the spot. Rupa has been severely injured. Presently, she is in… a coma due to injury to her brai... brain." His voice squeaked slightly at the end, struggling to finish the sentence.

"I am so very sorry, Rakesh. I didn't realise this must be very difficult for you." I felt I should have been more sensitive about this. I might have had a different relationship with Havish, but it need not be true with Rakesh. Apart from that, his close cousin Rupa was still in a coma.

"Wish Rupa recovers soon."

"Yes, I am quite worried about that. But then, it looks like I am the one who has got to tell Rupa about her husband once she comes out of her coma," he gulped.

"Oh shit! She still doesn't know!" My heart went out for him. Somewhere, I'd taken all this too lightly, being too indifferent. While I still didn't feel anything different for Havish, I sincerely wished Rupa recovered soon and hoped she would deal well with her husband's demise.

Rakesh had to return to the larger group, as he seemed to be in charge of the situation. While I had no plans to mingle with people, I felt I should stay for a few more moments before departing. After all, technically speaking, Havish was my last close relative. It began to drizzle, and the crowd scattered away. Havish's body was being buried, as per our caste's rituals. Staying there made me feel nauseous, so I stepped away to remain at a distance.

"Hello, Ankana," said someone while I wasn't paying attention.

"Yes?" I looked at the man, who perhaps was around my age.

"I am Krishav. I am… I was… Havish's friend," he said.

"Oh, hello, Krishav." I didn't know what else to say. I just thought that many others might come to me to sympathise with me, not knowing that I perhaps was the only indifferent person towards Havish in the whole cemetery. The thought made my stomach churn, as I hadn't planned on dealing with such uncomfortable conversations.

I continued looking at this guy, Krishav, who seemed to be struggling to speak. Ultimately, he just shook his head while I raised my eyebrow, wondering what he wanted to say. "I am sorry for your loss." Then he left the cemetery.

"Poor guy." My eyes followed him as he left.

The rain got heavier, and many began to leave the place. I got under an extended shed to avoid getting drenched as Rakesh jogged towards me.

"Ankana, do you want to stay at Havish's place for a few days till all the rituals are done? I can arrange for someone to drop you off now."

"Oh no, no, sorry, Rakesh. I… I will be leaving for Mangalore right away."

He was visibly taken aback and continued to get drenched.

I needed to explain to this guy, who was trying harder than necessary to make me feel like I belonged. "Listen, Rakesh, I think you seem to know I was not on good terms with Havish. I just thought it was the right thing to show my face today. You've been quite helpful, and I hope Rupa recovers soon. But I don't want to stay any further. I just… won't be comfortable. I don't expect you to understand, but I…"

"No, that's… eh… fine, Ankana. I do understand. Fine then, I will keep in touch if there's something, and you, too, can do the same."

"And again, thank you." I nodded as he left to get into a waiting car, the last one to leave.

"Hmmm…" I said to myself as I leaned on a small patch of drywall, lost in thought and now indifferent to the heavy downpour.

My father worked in an investigation department for the government. He always maintained secrecy from the family, and I guess my mother was used to that, as it was his job, and it demanded discretion. I was born to them quite late in their marriage, as I understood vaguely from my mother in the later years that some complications with her health led to the delay.

Immediately after my fifth birthday, my father brought home a boy a few years older than me. He explained to my mother that the boy was an orphan of a colleague who'd just lost his life. Thus, he'd decided to adopt the kid, Havish. My mother got used to the idea after a few months, and after all, Havish was a well-disciplined kid who quickly won over my mother. While we all stayed together for the next few years, which were perhaps my best childhood years, with time, my mother began to realise that my father was very attached to Havish. Call it a woman's instinct, she confronted my father, and soon it was disclosed that Havish was my father's child from an affair he had. The single woman who'd birthed him passed away, and thus, my father had decided to adopt him formally.

My mother went through a deep trauma, and my father's audacity in defending his actions, especially his casual attitude towards the affair, wasn't something she could forgive. The divorce was quick, and since then, it was a matter of weeks before she cut all connections with my father as she went back to her roots in Mangalore, taking me with her.

I have seen my mother go through a lot throughout my growing years. My father did not attempt to meet her or even me after that. That made me hate my father and Havish more and more, to the extent that I became immune to all of it, or indifferent, if I can call it that. I felt a strange sense of closure the day I heard about my father's death in my college days. It was so satisfying that a part of my brain told me I was insane.

It was almost four years ago that my mother breathed her last. Hers was a medical condition, and it was known that she had been on borrowed time for a few years. I wasn't shattered as such when she was gone, but it was at that time it sunk in how lonely I was. Now that I think about it, I vaguely recall that Havish had come to Mangalore to visit me then. It was funny because he'd never attempted to come to us all those years. I had refused to meet him and asked one of our distant relatives to send him off.

That's some number of deaths in my family. I never expected my behaviour or indifference to be validated or understood by anyone. I guess everyone has flaws in their character.

Chapter 3

Hardly a week had passed since my visit to Bangalore, and I was back to my normal routine as if it were all a distant dream. My full-time job was as a store manager in one of the company-managed electronics showrooms, which mostly sold televisions, refrigerators, washing machines, and other accessories. As Dasara and Deepawali approached, we geared up for our peak season, with tough sales targets being decided and customers beginning to pour in greater numbers.

The new shipment had just arrived with the festive discounts.

"Listen, guys. The last stock had a couple of pieces with minor defects, and one of them was pointed out by a customer. I've reported to the corporate office."

"Yes, Ankana ma'am. This is from a different supplier, a tenured one. I don't think we should have such issues with this shipment."

"Hope so," I told my junior as I made my way to my desk.

"Good afternoon, Ankana ma'am."

"Hey, Javed! What's up?" I smiled at one of my temporary staff members.

"Nothing, ma'am. I was just called here for extra help this season. Thought I would drop by to greet you."

"It's always nice to see you. Come to my seat. We can catch up for a bit over *chai*."

"No, ma'am, I believe there is a lot of work. I will see if I can meet you before going, and if you're not too busy by then..."

"Relax, will you? Just come now. Don't be too obedient. You need to learn from other free riders in the showroom," I said aloud as some staff members stopped their work and turned to look at me.

"Guilty conscience," I said, and they immediately got back to their work.

As I went to my seat, Javed said, "I came here last week, ma'am. You weren't here."

"How's that possible, Javed? I've not taken any leave in the past…" I froze, remembering last week's travel to Bangalore. He was still curiously looking at me.

"Yes, sorry. I had to take a couple of days off."

"I was about to ask if all's well, ma'am. But you seem just fine. So I will skip the obvious question." He smiled.

"So then, how's your poetry going? I know it's been a busy period."

"Yeah, ma'am. Work's always there. I ensure I give some dedicated time every week to poetry."

"You always manage to surprise me, man. I envy how you manage to take time out. Whenever I meet you, you always seem to be occupied with work."

He shrugged, "It somehow comes together, I guess. How's your writing going, ma'am? Have you been able to conclude your third book?" I am usually very private about my writing, but Javed was one of the few who earned my confidence to pry into my writing.

"Come on, Javed! I've just started the third book a couple of months back. I'll need a lot of time to bring it to closure. Also, with the busy season, it may take a bit more time."

He nodded as if he understood. He didn't believe I would be so busy as to not make time for my passion, and I confronted him, to which he laughed. "Maybe it is different for different people, ma'am. I feel so many months aren't needed. Won't the flow and continuity disappear if you take that much time?" he asked, without any disrespect.

"Hmm… you have a point. But I don't know. I've never been able to write more than a few hundred words in a day."

"Oh! I have not ventured much into stories. Maybe it isn't easy. I don't know."

"That's okay. We can stick to your poetry. Last month when we met, you'd just started to pen a collection of Urdu poetry, no? How much have you been able to write? I am sure you would need some time to conceptualise each poem, draw a linkage between them to remain within the theme, maybe rewrite a few, edit them, and what not."

"Ahem… I'd come to meet you last week to inform you that I'd completed penning the set of poems I'd planned, and…"

"What!"

"Yes, ma'am."

"Javed, how many poems does the collection have?"

"Around thirty, ma'am."

"You managed to write all of it in a month?"

"It took a bit more than a month."

"Oh! Shut up, Javed… that's awesome. What about editing?"

"It's underway, ma'am. I should complete it soon."

"Congrats, buddy. That's something to be proud of."

"Thanks, ma'am. I just wanted to ask you how I should go about it if I need to get these published."

"Not that I have published anything at all. I'll help you with the list of all the agents and publishers I have. And I can guide you through the process if you need."

His smile was very genuine. "Thanks, ma'am. I will then meet you to speak about it sometime next week."

"Yes, sure. We can do that."

He got up to leave.

"And Javed, I hope you have heard about the inter-departmental competition the corporate HR team has organised for creative writing due to the festive season."

He looked at me, straight-faced. "Yes, ma'am. But why are you telling me that?"

"What do you mean 'why'? You are participating, right? I know it's English only, but I can help translate your Urdu entry into English if need be."

"Eh, no, ma'am. That will not be necessary."

"As in, will you manage to translate it by yourself?" I asked, unsure of his point.

"It applies only to permanent staff, ma'am, not the temporary ones." He smiled briefly and left my desk.

"What shit!" I cursed. I decided to write an email to the HR team about this. How can these people expect such programmes to succeed with such disparities? Idiotic.

Chapter 4

"Mmmm...," I moaned as his fingers were working magic on my shoulders as I lay on my stomach.

"You like it, don't you?" His fingers increased the pressure at the right spot.

"How do you know where my knots are?"

"I can feel them."

"Are knots the only thing you can feel?" I pinched my lower lip.

He brought his face close to my neck and planted a peck. I turned around, holding the towel from loosening up with one hand and bringing my lips closer to his.

Rakesh seemed as hungry as I was as we got into a passionate kiss, and somewhere at the back of my mind, I could feel him pushing away the towel that stood guard between us. "No, Rakesh. Please!" I opened my eyes to find my bedroom quite dark.

"What the hell!" I'd woken myself up from what was a pleasurable dream. Rakesh, of all people? Knowing it was still very early for me to wake up, and considering I was enjoying the dream, I just decided to continue imagining how it could have ended. After all, every dream needs to have a happy ending.

Next, when I woke up from a relieved sleep, there was enough sunlight in the room, and I knew it was later than usual. But I felt quite content and blushed thinking of all the dirty things my mind had imagined before returning to a satisfying sleep. I am such a pervert! But then, if I think of it, I am going to hell anyway. I might as well earn a well-deserved entry.

I looked at my phone to find out the time. Then I noticed there was a text message from an unknown number. I tried adjusting my eyes to the light as I squinted and scrolled through the message. I sat up immediately when I saw Rakesh's name at the end. I hadn't saved his number from his earlier calls. But what a coincidence it was that I got a message from him while thinking of him. This must be a sign, quite unlike what had happened with Dev on the bus. I smiled at my childish thought. I read the message and was very happy to know that Rupa had come out of the coma. It was strange that though I'd never met her, I was relieved she had recovered. I started to type, but then I wasn't sure what to say. So, I postponed replying to his message until I could think clearly.

Some staff members noticed I was in a good mood at work and said so when they met me. I dedicated it to no particular event and said it reflected the great weather outside. They knew I was making up a reason, as the weather was not great. It was typical Mangalore weather. None of us could get to the office without getting drenched.

Once I had settled at my desk, I tried to compose myself to call Rakesh. I felt like a teenager, feeling all blushy. "Dude, he's just some guy who hardly knows you. And it was just a dream. Can you relax and return his call without much thought?" I told myself as another staff member greeted me for the morning, making me conscious of how much she'd heard. Her follow-through seemed quite convincing, and I believed she heard nothing that made her feel scandalised.

I dialled Rakesh's number. "Hi Ankana, good morning."

It sounded too formal to me, but I followed suit. "Hey there, Rakesh. Good morning. Thought I'd call you once I reached my workplace."

"That's no problem at all."

"I saw your message, and I'm… quite happy to hear about Rupa."

"Yes, me too. She recently came out of a week's coma."

"That's incredible."

"Yes, all the family members and friends were too worried. But now it seems better."

"And did you tell her?" I hesitated.

"Sorry?"

"I mean… about Havish." I thought for a moment that I shouldn't have asked. I've been distant, and it didn't seem right to ask.

"She remembered the details of the accident. When she woke from her coma, she seemed to know about Havish. It was difficult for her to… digest the reality, though. The first day since her recovery was really difficult, as she wept uncontrollably and wouldn't eat anything. Doctors were worried that in her present condition, her reaction to the whole thing might put a lot of strain on her body. Thankfully, to put it crudely, the fact seems to have sunk in after a day. She is now showing progress, and the doctor says she'll be fine to be discharged soon. Only since then am I informing people. I missed informing you last evening and messaged you at an odd hour. Sorry if I ended up waking you or something."

"You woke me up in the middle of the night, yes." I had to say that! I tried to make it sound as normal as possible. "But it was very thoughtful of you, Rakesh."

"Hey, no problem at all, Ankana. And let me know if you plan to visit. I can help with staying arrangements accordingly."

"Eh… no Rakesh… I…"

"Listen, Ankana. That's fine. If you want to visit Rupa or some other close relatives, I will get someone to assist you. I am well aware of the equation you shared with Havish. I just wanted to let you know."

"Thanks, Rakesh. I don't think I will be visiting soon. If I plan to do it someday, I will surely contact you. And maybe once Rupa returns to normal, I will call or visit her."

"Hmmm…okay."

"Listen, I know you may have a low opinion of me based on this discussion. I know this is the time Rupa may want support, but…"

"You don't have to explain, Ankana. Just relax for now. All of us are still trying to adjust to the new reality. So, pardon me if I blabbered more than necessary."

"Not at all, Rakesh."

"I got to go now. Do let me know if there is anything."

"Sure, you… have a nice day." I hung up, feeling guilty. I was running away from reality and from the awkwardness of dealing with Havish's friends and family. Was I even gracefully dealing with the death of the closest blood relative I had? I don't think I wanted to know the answer, for I knew I would not like that.

Chapter 5

Weeks passed, and the coming weekend was Deepawali. The showroom was packed with customers, which caused stress for everyone working there, but it was also exciting, as I was confident we'd not just meet but exceed the targets our corporate office had set.

The evening before the festivities would begin, we pulled the shutters down, indicating we'd closed for business, and there were interdepartmental celebrations taking place. There were sweet boxes that I was supposed to distribute to all the staff, and I also had to announce the receipt of the festival bonus, which they all were already aware of, but they made a good enactment of being surprised.

Across all our centres, the HR teams had asked the store managers to plan and run a few games for the staff. Cost pressures, as always, led us to play games that didn't involve spending a single rupee. After forcing my staff to play dumb charades, I got fed up with trying to enforce fun.

"Guys, we can do two things. Either we continue to play these games or call it a day, and you all can go home early and spend time with your loved ones?" I knew the answer I'd get before I could complete the question. Their respect for authority didn't make them say it in so many words, but I asked them to wrap up for the day and leave.

On returning to my desk to pack up, I saw an email from the HR team about the creative writing contest winner. I read the email and ran back to the main area.

"Hey, has Javed left for the day?" I asked one of the staff members. Before she could respond, I saw Javed coming out of the storeroom.

"Javed!"

"Yes, ma'am?" His voice seemed concerned, wondering why I was shouting his name.

"Guys!" I shouted, and the ones present around looked at me with anticipation. "Please congratulate Javed on winning the second prize in the creative writing contest held across the centres in Karnataka."

That was a big deal. And while most of the staff weren't necessarily inclined towards arts, they had enough sense to know that this was not a small thing, and all of us congratulated Javed, who hadn't yet come to terms with what was happening.

Once the crowd scattered and people left one after the other, Javed came to me. "But ma'am, how? I was not even eligible to participate, and I didn't even send an entry."

"You recollect that I'd asked you to pen down something unrelated to your other collection of poems?"

"Yes, you told me to provide some short work that can be used as a reference when we get to some publisher or an agent. You'd said it can help get my main work marketed."

"And we both translated it to English." I smiled.

"Oh god! You sent that as my entry to this competition?"

"Yes!"

"But I thought the temporary staff wasn't allowed to participate."

"I'd just mailed HR expressing my disgust, of course, in a nice way. They said some bullshit about not being able to change the rules but agreed to take your entry as an exception. I managed to frustrate them so much that they had no choice."

"That is so…" He was very happy but unable to express much in words.

"Come now, just bask in the glory, my friend. And I heard that the prize money is decent."

"Thanks, ma'am."

Before the situation could get all sentimental, I asked him to leave and spend time with his family.

I finished packing up and came to the main area to bid goodbye to the remaining staff when a customer entered the showroom.

"Eh... hi sir, sorry, but we are closed for the day and the weekend. Happy Deepawali!"

He looked at me, slightly surprised. "I saw that, but I just..."

"I am sorry, sir. We may not be able to assist you with anything right now. Most of the staff have left for the day. We next open on Tuesday. If you can come then, I will ensure..."

"Ankana..."

"Oh, you know my name?"

He seemed slightly taken aback. "We met at... Havish's funeral."

"Oh!" It was my turn to be surprised, and I stared at him momentarily. "Hmm... yeah, I remember you.... Kaushik, right?" I ventured.

He stared at me.

"Kaushal..."

His gaze never wavered. He stood like a statue.

"Kapish... Krishnan... Kethan... help me out here, Kavy... esh..." I made a face.

He couldn't help but break into a smile. "Kavyesh, really? It's Krishav, Ankana."

"Ah! I'd almost got it... ahem... yes, Krishav."

"I am sorry to just barge in this way. I understand I should have called you. Then I just thought it would be easier to meet up in person."

"But..." What was with this guy? I vaguely remember meeting him in Bangalore when he told me he was Havish's friend. That was for hardly a few seconds.

"Again, I apologise for just arriving unannounced. May I take a few minutes of your time?"

I was too surprised to think straight and didn't want my staff to know more about my linkage to Bangalore by overhearing our conversation. I invited him in.

As we walked towards my desk, I asked him rhetorically, "So you were close to Havish then K… sir?"

"It's Krishav."

"Sorry, I just keep missing your name."

"No problem, Ankana. Yes, you can say that I was somewhat close to Havish."

We sat at my desk. "So, tell me. How can I help?"

"See, I thought about this since Havish's demise and had been completely lost on how I could bring this proposal to you…"

Proposal? I had known this guy for literally less than a minute. What proposal could he have for me? Whatever it is, he better not be a nutcase proposing to have a relationship with me. Wait, if I come to think of it, he's not that bad looking; slightly chubby, yes. But he has a cute smile. However, let me tell you. He cannot hold a candle to Rakesh.

"Ankana?"

"Oh, sorry, I lost you there. Ahem… what were you saying… sir?" Holy crap, I don't know what's with his name and why I cannot remember it!

"So I am Krishav. And, I was saying to you that I am… was… not just a friend of Havish, but I was also his agent."

"Agent? I don't get it, Krishav." Yes! I managed to get his name right this time.

"Literary agent," he paused. "I represented his books to the publishing house."

"What!"

This is where I get to tell you that Havish was a published author. I learned about his ability some years ago when my best friend Sujna, a voracious reader, had informed me that she believed this new author on the block named Havish must be my half-brother. She based her assumption on the rarity of the name and descriptions she'd read about him. I understood from her that he was into books on humour.

Against my wishes, she made me read a couple of chapters from one of his books, which I felt sucked. But then, I didn't express my opinion. I assumed she'd think it was biased. Nevertheless, she too confirmed that the writing was quite sad, and she didn't rate the book any better than two out of five.

I recollect this conversation with Sujna very well, for it was in that very moment she looked at me with her eyes wide open, "Ankana…"

"All okay, Sujna? Is something wrong with my hair, buddy?"

"If you think of it, you used to scribble some good story concepts, and actually, one was used for a play in our college fest, right?"

"Yeah…" I chuckled, "That was some fun. I miss those days. Remember that macho dude from the Commerce section? He was all..."

"Stupid! To hell with that macho guy from the Commerce section, whom you were drooling at throughout the play, and he didn't even notice you."

"Ouch! That hurt, bitch!"

"Ankana, why are you being dumb?"

"Why? What did I do now?"

"That's it! You have not done anything! Why don't you start writing novels?"

"Babe, what are you smoking?"

"Don't be an ass. Think about it. I mean, I know your stories from college. You'd take my opinion on each of the stories and dialogues, no?"

"Well, yes. But…"

"I know your writing is better than your brother's, and your imagination is far better than many contemporary authors. Shit!

Why didn't I think about this earlier? I let you be stuck as a sales girl, and a bad one at that."

"I... how?" I was still not sure if she was making sense. It took a lot of coaxing and explaining from her, and I was bought into the idea of attempting to make writing a part-time hobby. While I haven't seen any success in it, and the probability of future success looks bleak, I still owe Sujna, who pushed me in this direction. Success or no success, I haven't regretted it.

Returning to the present, the store watchman approached my desk and said, "Madam, will you take time?"

"Uh!" I was out of my reverie and had left my mouth open all the time as Krishav sat silently across the desk. "Sorry uncle, you lock the main entrance and leave the small door open. You can leave the keys with me. I will come early tomorrow."

"Tomorrow is Deepawali, madam."

"Tch... I know, uncle. I meant Tuesday. I will come before you on Tuesday. You can leave now, and I wish your family a happy Deepawali."

"Okay, madam."

"Yes, Krishav. See, I remember your name. Ahem... so you were his agent. Right... great... so, what did you want to talk to me about?"

"You may be aware that his writing had served him well. He'd left his desk job a few years ago and was into writing full-time."

Are you freaking serious, dude! What's happened to all the readers? Is their choice that bad?

"Is it? No. Sorry, you may not know, but I didn't keep in touch with him... much."

"Hmmm... I know. I mean that he'd done well for himself, had a good following, and had some good ideas for his books."

"Oh!" That sounded interesting. I honestly didn't know he'd done so well for himself as an author. Last I'd spoken to Sujna about his books, she'd told me that there were two of them, and each was worse than the other. Now, Mr Agent says there were more ideas as well. Wow!

"Sure, but I am still lost. What help can I be of?" I involuntarily looked at my watch as his two minutes had spanned over several minutes, and there seemed no end to this conversation on the horizon.

"Yes, let me cut to the chase. So he had started his latest work and got the story to an appropriate stage before he… was no more. I wanted to ask you if you would consider completing it."

It was as if someone poured, no, splashed, a bucket full of cold water on my face. "You what!?" I almost shrieked.

"It's an unfinished novel. I wanted to check if you want to complete it."

I paused, pretending to think, but I was drawing a blank. "No!" I shouted.

The watchman came running back, "What happened, madam? Are you alright?" His gaze shifted from me to Krishav to see if the latter had misbehaved with me. Krishav gently smiled at the watchman.

"Ahem… nothing, uncle. Sorry, I shouted. You can go home."

"I think I will stay for some more time, Madam," he said. He then slowly walked away, throwing dirty looks at Krishav.

"No, as in?"

"Listen, Krishav, I don't want to be involved in anything Havish was a part of. I don't think I would like to take your offer." I looked away, not knowing how else to make this less difficult.

From the corner of my eye, I could see that he gave a brief nod and got up to leave.

While I said nothing more, I felt compelled to show him out and walked with him to the showroom entrance. It was drizzling outside, and an auto-rickshaw waited for him right there.

Before boarding the auto, he turned around. "I'd still insist you give it a thought. I will call you after a few days."

It came to me all of a sudden. "Wait. How do you have my number?"

He just smiled as if waiting for me to continue.

"How do you know I work here at the showroom?" My heart started to pound a little loudly. I didn't wait for his response and continued, "We met in Bangalore. How do you know I am in Mangalore?"

"Or most importantly, Ankana…"

I waited, wondering what he could probably reveal that would be more important.

"How do I know that you are an aspiring author?"

"Yeah!" It hit me like a ton of bricks. I'd confided only with a few close people about my writing aspirations, and there was no way he was linked to any of them. As I stood stunned, letting the drizzle paint over my face, he smiled innocently for one last time.

"Do give the proposal a thought, Ankana," he said before getting into the auto to leave.

Unable to process things, I returned to my workspace to pack up. I saw he'd conveniently left his visiting card at my desk with his phone number on the back. I crumpled the visiting card and was about to throw it in the dustbin. I couldn't go through with it. Irritated, I put it in my bag before leaving for the day.

Chapter 6

I was super frustrated with this whole episode. I mean, here I was, trying to forget even visiting Bangalore, and then immediately, this Krishav came to mess with my brain. I tried asking myself the reason for my anger, but I couldn't find any. Perhaps, as I'd told Krishav, I didn't want to be associated with Havish in any manner. Hence, I tried to ignore this guy's offer.

The next morning was the beginning of the long festive weekend. As I'd planned, I thoroughly enjoyed watching the final season of *Sense 8* on Netflix on my new Smart TV that I'd bought from the showroom at an employee special discount.

It was night, and I wasn't motivated to start any new series to watch and thought I should get to bed. As I admired the new TV wall-mounted in my bedroom, I started thinking of my showroom and then naturally thought about Krishav again. How did that bugger know so much about me? Especially that I was an aspiring author. I should have taken the pain in my head as a cue to either switch off this thought or, perhaps, go to sleep. But worse sense prevailed, and I spent time thinking of answers to all questions about this Krishav. And I, who prided myself on switching off to sleep within minutes, had never felt this awake recently.

I'd not tossed and turned around on my bed this much in my whole life. My head was aching like hell, with many possibilities and questions bombarding me continuously.

I'd tried calling Sujna, perhaps the only person who'd understand what I was going through, but I knew she kept her cell phone on silent mode when she went to sleep and wasn't receiving my calls. That added to my frustration. "Pick up, Sujna!" I shouted when my fourth attempt to call her failed, and then worried that my conservative neighbour, Uncle Shenoy, might wake up because of my high-pitched voice.

"Fine! She will call back first thing in the morning," I consoled myself. The only other time I'd made so many calls to her was to inform her of losing my virginity. So I was sure she'd know this was very important once she looked at the phone in the morning with four missed calls from me.

I woke up with my phone ringing. It was still dark outside. I answered it, "What's wrong with you, Sujna? Why are you calling me in the middle of the night?"

"It is past six in the morning, Ankana."

"Who on earth calls at such a dreadful hour? This better be something important."

"Hmmm… I guess I will wait."

"What? Is it your birthday? No, is it my birthday? Wait, oh, freak! Oh my god! Oh my god!"

"Good, you remember now."

"Why the hell would you not receive my calls, you fool?"

"You mean, the four calls between one and three at night? Yeah, let's get past the rhetoric and get to the point. What happened?"

"I… can you meet?"

"Hey, you know I've come to Andamans for a vacation, right?"

"Ah, yes! You and your stupid vacations."

"Ankana, what happened?"

"I have to update you on many things that have happened since we last spoke."

"Sure, but please relax first. I am not going anywhere."

I updated her on the events, starting with Havish's death and ending with Krishav's visit.

"Are you freaking insane!"

"What?"

"Did you just tell me that you just blew up a possibility of striking a deal with a literary agent?"

"How? Listen, Sujna, you know I don't want to be involved with Havish or his works in any manner."

"You are being very stubborn; no, actually stupid."

"Why?"

"Whether you like it or not, your brother seemed to have experienced great success in the field."

"So what? Why should it make any difference to me?"

"It may or may not make a difference to you, idiot. But this man, Krishav, has come knocking at your door. It's as if things are coming together for you to unleash your true potential finally."

"But it is not any of my works, right? I am supposed to look at Havish's work and conclude it."

"Wait one sec."

"What?"

"You skipped telling me the part on how Krishav got to know you are a writer."

"Yeah, one of the reasons I couldn't sleep last night. I don't know how."

"What!"

"Anyway, I feel I should drop the proposal."

"Over my dead body!"

"What? Why, Sujna?"

"Don't you see it? This agent has come from Bangalore to meet you in person. That must say something."

"Hmm... you have a point. I should assume some importance for myself."

"Yes, and that's what surprises me."

"Argh... fine. I guess I am just not able to process all this."

"But wait, let's stay with that thought. Yes, I believe you are somehow important in the scheme of things, and you should try to milk this to your best interest."

"How so?"

"Firstly, there are too many open ends here, right? I mean, I seem to have so many questions about this whole thing. I can only imagine your state."

"Tell me about it."

"Agree to meet him."

"Eh… okay, and then what?"

"And tie those loose ends so that you know what's going on in his mind and how he knows so much about you that only people close to you, like me, seem to know."

"Aww… are you jealous?"

"How stupid! And then I think you should test the waters to know how much he will bend."

"Say more."

"During your discussion, why don't you say you will agree if he gets one of your books published?"

"He is not a publisher, just an agent. The best he could do is represent me to the publishing houses."

"You get the drift! If he could get your brother's work sold, why can he not do the same with your work?"

"Hmm… I get what you mean."

"I want to kick your ass. Why the hell did you not call me a day before?"

"Sorry… I didn't think it through, I guess."

"Anyway, now please call him first thing in the morning and get an appointment to speak."

"Yes, ma'am. Will do that."

"And keep me updated."

"Phew… yes, ma'am."

"And Ankana…"

"Oh god, now what?"

"I… I am so sorry."

"Come on, Sujna. You know you are one of the privileged few who has the right to shout at me. Don't be sorry about that, babe."

"That I know already. I won't take your permission to shout any time."

"Then?"

"I am sorry to hear about Havish." She sounded sad.

"Come on, man! You know he meant nothing to me. Let's focus more on this proposal."

She wasn't happy with my indifference but knew me too well to dwell too much on that. "And next time you get into such a situation with an important person, politely say that you need some time to think and that you will get back to them."

"Okay, enough of your wisdom. Get lost." We hung up on each other with no love lost.

Now, I had to think of ways to manipulate this Krishav. He seemed naïve enough when I met him and stupid enough to represent Havish's books. I guess that would be a cakewalk.

Chapter 7

It was a beautiful Deepawali morning.

"Good morning, Ankana, and happy Deepawali."

"Thanks. Wish you the same, Krishav."

"Tell me."

"I guess you didn't expect that I would call you." I wanted to have the upper hand.

"I thought you would reach out next week. I am surprised you reached out so soon." He replied politely, but it hit my ego.

I stayed calm momentarily, composing my thoughts. "I wanted to discuss what you offered the other day. Let me know if we can set up some time to talk about it later in the day."

"Yes, we can do that. I have a free calendar due to the festive season, Ankana. Please let me know when you would like to speak."

"I, too, have a free calendar due to the festive season," I said scornfully.

"That's good, then. In a couple of hours?" he asked.

"Yes, that should be fine."

"So, you want to come down, or should I come to your place?"

"Sorry, what? I can't just take a flight in such short… wait! Are you still in Mangalore?"

"Yes, I am staying here for some time."

"That's… eh… good then."

"So, should I come to your place?"

I looked around the dirty living room, which needed the maid's attention. But she was busy celebrating the festival of lights in her hometown. "No, your place is just fine. You can text me the address."

"Done, see you at noon then." He hung up.

Finding the address he'd given me wasn't difficult, but I was surprised by the locality. I'd expected him to be put up in some posh location. However, this was a moderate establishment. I rang the doorbell upon reaching. I then checked my watch to realise I was a bit early.

"Yes." An old woman with a pleasant face opened the door and looked at me keenly.

"Uhh… ma'am, I… could you please tell me if this is the right address?" I handed my mobile phone to her to show the address I'd received.

"Oh, you are here to meet Krishav?"

"Ah! Yes."

"He just told me a client is coming to meet him. I was expecting some old gentleman and didn't expect a pretty young thing like you. Please come in."

Perhaps this is what they say is love at first sight. I was in love with this grand old lady already. I wanted to hold her tight and kiss her chubby cheeks, but I refrained from doing such inappropriate stuff and just followed her.

She made me sit in the living room and asked, "Will you have tea, coffee, or fruit juice?"

"Ma'am… I don't…"

"What is this, ma'am thing?"

"Sure, Aunty. I don't want anything. I will just wait."

"Tch tch… I gave you three options, child. You must pick one."

All the time, I was looking at her cheeks and wanted to pinch them badly. How could I say 'no' to her?

"Sure, Aunty. Coffee is fine." I smiled.

"Let me see why this Krishav is taking so much time to get ready. It is not right to make pretty girls wait. It will lead to bad karma." She walked inside and popped her head to tell me, "And just so that you know, people whom I like call me 'Gowrakka'," and disappeared behind the curtains before I could say anything.

In a few minutes, Krishav entered the living room. "Hey, I am sorry, Ankana. I hope you didn't have to wait for long?"

"It's okay, Krishav. It was my mistake. I landed up earlier than expected."

Gowrakka came into the room with two cups of coffee and kept them on the table. Krishav took one and was about to sip. But then she stopped him, saying, "That cup is for the pretty lady, Krishav."

Krishav, as I was, threw a confused look at her.

"I am sure you needed coffee with less sugar, no?" She looked at me, and I nodded, my smile becoming a giggle.

"Fine, Gowrakka." He rolled his eyes, handed me the cup, and took the other.

"I will be in the kitchen if you need me for something."

"Sure, Gowrakka," he said and realised she was addressing me, not him. He shook his head as she returned to the kitchen, taking tiny steps.

"Sorry, Ankana. Gowrakka can be quite expressive at times."

"I don't mind at all. She's the most adorable thing."

He smiled gently and said, "So, you wanted to meet."

I realised I had to switch from a casual guest to a demanding client. Deep down, I felt bad, and I didn't know why.

"Yes. Our earlier meeting was quite unexpected, and it caught me off-guard."

"Yes, and I take complete onus on that one."

"Hmmm… so you want to start over. What is all this?"

"Sure, Ankana. See, your brother partnered with me for his last four books, spanning a few years. We had a good working rapport, and in fact, I would go to the extent of saying that it laid the foundation for a good friendship.

"I know you didn't have a good equation with him, so I will skip all the good things I have to say about him. Nevertheless, I presume the reason why I approached you is quite clear. I mentioned already that he'd started with his fifth book, an untitled one. Somehow, he'd gotten into his elements quite early with this one, and he showed all signs of being able to finish this one in a record timeline.

"He'd sent me some chapters, and I could say that half the story was complete. Unfortunately, before he could proceed any further, he and his wife met with an accident, which you are aware of.

"Since Havish passed away so abruptly, I thought I should see if his last work can see the light of day. Thus, I approached you." He paused and looked at me.

"How did you know about me, Krishav?"

"As in?"

"That's a literal question. How did you know who I am or where I live? How did you know where I work? Most importantly, how did you know I write?" I shrugged with the obviousness that he didn't seem to have registered.

"Through your author bio." He grinned.

"What do you mean? I don't think I have interacted with you before."

"Whom all have you sent your manuscripts, along with your author bio?"

"Only three or four renowned agents like Publisher's Pride, Shernahi Kamkarta, KK Literary Agency, and I think… that Pink Stink Agency."

He continued to look at me as if it was understood.

"What?" I was getting irritated.

"My full name is Krishav Karunakara."

"What am I supposed to… oh my god! You are from KK Literary Agency!"

"Well, I am the only person there. So I sort of am KK Literary Agency."

"But that is a big agency, which I know has represented some great authors."

"Why, thank you." He was completely calm.

"And you represented Havish?"

"And was proud of it." He nodded.

"And you say you were a friend of his…" That wasn't a question and was something I was thinking out loud.

He just smiled.

"As per the format, you had attached your author bio, which contained your picture, phone number, and addresses – both home and workplace."

"Oh, okay. But how do you know Havish was related to me?"

"Because he had told me about it."

"Havish, who had not met me since childhood, decides to have a private moment with his literary agent and talks about me?"

"You make it sound quite creepy, but that sums it up."

I had too much to take in. I sat silently for a moment with my hands covering my face.

"Now that Rupa, Havish's wife, is back to normal health, wouldn't she have a say in who gets to continue writing this book?"

"That's a good point. If she wants to, she can push for it. However, the contract with the publisher is a tripartite agreement between the author, the literary agency, and the publisher. The publisher also wanted joint accountability from the agency, so there is enough guarantee that this five-book contract would be honoured. Thus, I have a big say in deciding who will replace Havish."

"So basically, you need me because your ass is on the firing line." I looked straight into his eyes.

Strangely, he didn't seem to change his facial expression at all. "The publishing house has already moved on, knowing the author has died. But let's say even if my ass was on the firing line, what makes you think that you were the only option I had?"

"Then why approach me in the first place?"

"Because..." He paused for a while, and I thought I had him in a corner. However, his following words stunned me. "In one of the conversations with your brother, he mentioned that you could be a good replacement in case he would like to retire someday."

"What! That's bullshit of the highest order!"

"Listen, Ankana. I am trying to be as transparent as possible at this stage. I don't have to explain or justify each sentence I am making. If you don't want to believe me, that is totally up to you. I would like it if you want to take this up. I thought I should give it my best shot because I owed that much to Havish. However, it is your decision. I am no one to insist here. I will be here for a week if you want to speak further. If I don't hear back from you, I will understand that you are uninterested. It was nice meeting you." He got up from the seat, nodded at me, and disappeared into one of the rooms.

In the flow of the conversation, I did seem to forget that I was talking to a very successful literary agent and perhaps should have been cautious about my choice of words. I got up to leave, and Gowrakka appeared from nowhere. She didn't say anything. I guess she'd overheard some parts of the passionate conversation.

She walked me to the door. "Bye, Aunty. Take care."

"Gowrakka will be just fine."

I smiled at her.

"And it was very bad of me not to realise you were Havish's sister. How can I have missed the resemblance?"

"Sorry? You've met Havish?" I was really surprised.

"Not many times, but last year, when I was in Bangalore at Krishav's place for a few weeks, Havish had dropped in a few times. I am sorry about his demise. He was a good boy. Anyway, I think you will be getting late now. You take care." She left me at the gates.

Unwillingly, though, I was learning bits about Havish that I never wanted to. And each time, it was a surprise.

CHAPTER 8

"I know you will want to slap me." I was feeling quite low as I spoke to Sujna over the phone.

"Come on, ya. We can sit and prepare for all such conversations, but I can imagine it isn't easy to deal with reality. What have you thought of as the next steps?"

"I guess I've burnt bridges with Krishav."

"No. I think you are wrong to say that. Otherwise, he would not have left an opening for you. He still said that he would like you to take it up, right?"

"Yes, he did. But I don't know how much of it he meant."

"And were you able to at least table your two books?"

I was silent, and she got the answer.

"Now, I am intrigued by your late brother."

"Me too, ya. Not that I knew him well. Okay, I didn't know him at all. But he seemed to be a different person than I could have imagined."

"Not that you ever wanted to know about him."

"Hmm..."

"Just sleep over this, Ankana."

"And then what?"

"Listen, I can tell you what I think you should do. But this one, I feel you have to decide for yourself, and I am sure you will make the right decision."

"I don't know, Sujna. At one end, I still have that bad image Amma built about my father and Havish. That tells me that I should not go back to Krishav. On the other hand, this can potentially open many doors."

"Just to play the devil's advocate, why is it such a big deal? It is just agreeing to complete a book. Think of it as some random person's story, and go ahead. Why all this emotional trauma?"

"No, Sujna. You've not realised it, perhaps. I believe anyone who creates an art form leaves a deep imprint in that work – one's fears, joys, secrets, fantasies, wishes and many other things very personal to them. It is as if the one who creates it leaves a fragment of their soul in every art form. Hence, when you read a book, you get closer to the creator. You get to know that person better. You get to see what their imagination is all about. That is why I have been uncomfortable with this idea."

"That was… deep. But I get it now. It's okay, Ankana. Trust yourself to make the right decision."

"That's what I am getting worried about. Should I be trusting my decisions on such things right now? While I may write love stories, I am very detached from them. You know that I am a very practical person and hate all the bullshit about sugary love stories."

"Now, now, be careful who you disclose those facts to. If your to-be fans get to hear it, they will not be very happy."

"Very funny."

"Sleep on it, Anku. Whatever you decide, I know you will be fine with it. Because I've known you to own up to your decisions and stick to them, no matter the outcomes."

"Thanks ya. I feel like kissing you right now."

"Oh my! Is this one of your moments?"

"Yeah, sort of. Good you're not around. Else, no one could have saved you."

"Dear God!"

"Here it comes… *ummmmmmma…*"

"Thankfully, you get these bouts only when I am not around in person." She laughed.

"Cheap! Anyway, thank you. I will sleep over it and see what the morning brings in."

Chapter 9

The bell rang loudly as we ran from the class, pushing each other from the narrow path out of the school entrance. It was an unsaid competition to get to the street vendors, who'd wait for the school kids to arrive after the classes.

I had managed to outrun everyone. The rush to get first is also partially because the teachers would wait for us to return for the tuition classes in minutes. The exams are upon us, if you know. I reached the first vendor and asked him to pack a portion of raw mango and the local amla, spiced up with red chilli powder and salt. I insisted he make it extra spicy, and he smiled because he already knew I'd say that.

Then I rushed to the next vendor, disappointed that two classmates had reached him before me. But as they argued with each other, he looked at me, and I asked him for a portion of spiced-up cucumber. My mother had never managed to prepare the same at home that's as tasty. She tried adding green chillies, coriander, and mint leaves but never cracked the recipe. He nodded at me, started to prepare my order, and delivered it in a cone made with a piece of an old Kannada newspaper.

I returned to the first vendor with the spiced cucumber pieces in one hand. He apologised for giving away my order to someone else. My expression changed suddenly, and I frowned, tears about to follow any moment. He laughed aloud, saying he was only joking, and handed me my order. I gobbled up all of it quickly, and the bell rang again, indicating that we were to return to attend the tuition classes.

I was tearing up now because of the spicy snacks, and I badly needed to drink some water. I turned towards the vendors and saw that their water bottles were empty. Without waiting any further, I rushed back to the class to escape being scolded by the teacher. I reached the class and found it empty. I felt like kicking myself, for I could have taken more time to quench my thirst instead of rushing back. I hoped that one of my classmates might have a water bottle when they returned, so I sat on the first bench.

The teacher entered and looked at me, unable to hide her surprise. "You are the only one to reach on time," she said, smiling at me.

I smiled back nervously, with a missing tooth in the front.

"Are you in tears?" she asks curiously.

"Yes, Miss. I ate the spicy snacks outside."

"Then why didn't you have water?"

"I couldn't find time. I didn't want to be late."

"Hmm... so as a reward for being on time, you can choose one chocolate from these." She opened her palm, where I found a variety of chocolates. Perhaps she never ate the ones she got from the students when they distributed chocolates on their birthdays.

"But Ankana, can you please choose quickly? I don't want other students to feel bad that they didn't get any. And I have only so many, so I cannot give one to everyone."

I was spoilt for choice, as I didn't know what to take. I wondered if I could choose the costliest, but I didn't know their prices. I wondered if I should choose the biggest, but then I saw they're all similar in size. I wondered if I should choose the tastiest, but all of them were new to me, and I didn't know their flavours. I heard the footsteps of my classmates from afar, and we both looked at each other, with her raising an eyebrow. "Quick," she said.

I, then, did the only best thing I could think of. Instead of picking one, I opened my palm with an outstretched hand towards the teacher and looked at her. The choice was no longer mine to make. She met my gaze and erupted into laughter. She picked one of the chocolates and placed it in my hand.

My classmates trickled in, and the class filled up within a moment. The chocolate was safe in my grip. I didn't try to see which chocolate the teacher gave me. I just put my hand into my pocket and left the chocolate there, trying to focus on the blackboard, my thirst quenched.

I wasn't worried about which chocolate it was, for I knew the teacher truly wanted to reward me, and thus, she would have handed me what she believed was the best for me.

I woke up from sleep, feeling at peace and smiled. As it happens at times when I'm confronted with a difficult decision, my subconscious weaves symbolic dreams to help me think through. This dream nudged me to agree to Krishav's proposal. This is best for me – it is meant to be.

I got up and, by habit, checked my phone. I saw that there was a text message. It was from Krishav.

"Good morning, Ankana. Please call me whenever you can spare a moment."

I could spare right now. So I called him up. In the middle of the phone ringing, I noted that my voice may still be groggy, but it was too late to back out.

"Hi, Ankana."

"Hello, good morning, Krishav."

"Listen, I… eh…, I don't want to beat around the bush. I am sorry that I ended the conversation quite abruptly yesterday. It wasn't my intent to be rude to you. It's just that…"

"No, Krishav. That's fine. My tone was quite provoking as well. So, don't bother. It's all fine."

"Good, thanks. Last evening, I thought a lot about why you weren't keen on taking this offer up and then decided that reading your brother's work may make you feel uncomfortably close to his thoughts, which I guess you aren't fine with."

"How did you… do you know my friend Sujna?"

"Who?"

"Ahem… nothing. Sorry, I interrupted."

"I am fine with it if you don't want to take this project up."

"I..."

"But I have a request. Please do come down for lunch today."

"Hey, chill, Krishav. It's all good. You don't have to go to that extent."

"Please, Ankana. I insist."

"No, but..."

"And Gowrakka insists as well."

"Krishav..."

"I know it is a festive weekend, and you may have some fun stuff planned for yourself, and..."

"No. There is nothing fun planned."

"Hmmm... then what is the issue?"

"I just don't want to burden you guys."

"Don't be so formal now, please. Will you come by yourself, or should I come to pick you up?"

"No, no, I will come by myself. I... I will be there around noon." And we hung up.

Until now, I was secretly and slightly depressed that I'd not been invited by anyone for a festive lunch. If the stars are aligned to feed me well, I am not the one to complain.

Chapter 10

We were seated on the ground, on a mat, while having a grand meal prepared by Gowrakka. It was only during my childhood that I used to sit on the ground and eat this way, and the homely ambience at the place added a pleasurable nostalgic flavour.

"This type of sambar is something new to me, Gowrakka. Though I usually like it spicy, this is too spicy even for me."

"Eh… I told you to use the red chilli chutney sparingly, Ankana," said Krishav as he saw me sweating and sniffling while gobbling up the delicious food.

"Yes, but did you taste the red chilli chutney? It has a rich, strong flavour that adds to the sambar's taste."

"I add ginger to it, Ankana," said Gowrakka. "It helps with digestion."

"Yes, I surely need help with digestion."

"Should I pass on some sweets to cool you down?" Gowrakka offered.

"No, no, it will spoil the taste of the sambar, Gowrakka. I will eat them later." I sniffled as Krishav passed me a paper tissue for the third time, laughing.

"Why are you laughing at her, Krishav? Please don't be mean. Let her eat in peace."

"I am just…," he said, shrugging.

"And Ankana, I have prepared buttermilk as well. I've added *hing* and *jeera* to it. You can have that once you are done with the main course."

"Gowrakka, I don't think I will have any space left in my tummy to have anything else," I complained, holding my stomach.

"No, no, you should have the buttermilk. Otherwise, you will have trouble in the morning with such spicy food." She had her eyes wide open whilst saying that.

"Gowrakka...," Krishav winced.

It took a moment for me to register what she meant, and I couldn't help laughing. "Sure, Gowrakka. I will have buttermilk later."

***

As we settled on the veranda, Gowrakka brought us betel leaves and areca nuts.

"No, Gowrakka. I don't want this, thanks."

"It is a good habit to end our meal with betel leaves and areca nuts, Ankana. Our ancestors followed excellent food habits, which we completely ignore nowadays."

"It's not like that, Gowrakka. I am sort of allergic to areca nut, I think. I get some chest pain when I have it."

"Oh, that's because you aren't used to having it. Hmm... okay, I won't insist. I will leave it here if either of you wants it." She left us in the open veranda.

There was a good breeze at this hour as we both sat silently for some time, and nothing was awkward about it.

"Is Gowrakka related to you in any way?" I ventured.

"She's not a blood relative if that's what you mean. My grandmother brought her to our Binnypet house in Bangalore during her teenage years as a housekeeper, as Gowrakka's family had expired due to an ailment that had taken a toll on their village."

"Oh, that's bad."

He nodded. "She was very good at her work, and my grandmother had grown fond of her. She gradually became a part of our family. My grandmother ensured we married her to a decent family then."

"Wow, good. You said your grandmother stayed in Binnypet? That's one of the old localities in Bangalore."

"Yes, it is. My grandfather had a high post in Binny Mill and a big house allotted to the family."

"Hmmm… that's some pedigree."

"Nah, it's nothing. You know how things take a turn when you have eleven kids to care for."

"Oh god! Really? Your grandfather had eleven kids?"

"That was hardly above average for that period, no? What about your grandfathers?"

I thought for a moment. "Ah, yes! You are right. One of them had eight kids, and the other had seven. So that's not way off the mark." I giggled.

"Don't mind Gowrakka's frankness. She can get personal at times, without meaning any disrespect."

"Oh, come on, Krishav! She is wonderful."

He giggled like a small girl. "I remember early this year when Prashanthi Menon came home for Ugadi, and Gowrakka got into a small banter with her about why it is not good to consume beef. Prashanthi, being the sweetheart she is, played along, and they debated for about an hour. Only then did she reveal to Gowrakka that she is a vegan, and a new debate started about why we should not even consume milk. Gowrakka's fair face was almost red with embarrassment."

"That should have been fun to witness. Prashanthi is some friend of yours, I presume."

"Eh… yes. Sorry, I assumed you would know Prashanthi. She's the author of…"

"Prashanthi Menon! You mean, the author of *Rangavallika*, the bestselling erotica?"

"Yes, so you do know her?"

"Are you serious? Do you know her? As in, you…"

"Eh... yes, Ankana."

"Wow! And you should know many famous authors personally."

"Hmm... I would not say I know them personally. Some maintain a professional approach with their agents, and I am fine with that. I, too, maintain a professional relationship with them. But there are a few who strike a chord. It's like any other friendship, I guess."

"But whatever little I know about Prashanthi, I never had a good opinion of her. I thought she was quite arrogant and rude to everyone."

"Not at all. She's just a very private person. She'd visited us with her little daughter at the time I refer to. She is very down to earth."

"Had I not heard it from you, I'd surely not have believed that."

"Media can make anyone they like a hero, and anyone a villain." He scoffed and immediately continued as if he remembered something, "You should meet Chowdesh Kiran. He is one such example."

"I assume you are talking about the 'Prahlada' award winner from last year for his exceptional contribution to storytelling?"

"Yeah, him."

"He is so nice, isn't he? The way he holds the audience's attention when he speaks is awesome. Have you watched his TED talk?" I was quite enthusiastic and wondered why Krishav wasn't sharing my enthusiasm.

"Hmmm..."

"What happened?"

"No... let it be." He laughed.

"Now, come on, Krishav."

"I don't want to burst your bubble about him, Ankana."

"You think I will be fine with you not spilling the beans?" I gave him a dirty look.

"He's a frustrating client to represent!"

"What? Really?"

"Yes! He is very rude and often disrespectful. Thankfully, now he deals with the publishers directly. That takes some pressure off the agents."

"This is so cool. I mean, you are like an encyclopaedia of writers. Wait, I have a good one. You are like Karan Johar in the literary industry." I was proud of my reference.

Before he could answer, Gowrakka spoke from the living room. "No! Our Krishav is nothing like Karan Johar in any manner."

I burst out laughing at her intrusion, which I found cute.

"Gowrakka… are you eavesdropping again?"

"No, I am not. I am just cleaning the vegetables I bought this morning before moving them to the fridge. It is not my fault that I have sharper ears compared to people my age." She snorted.

"But I agree with Gowrakka. I am just a small fish in the big ocean." He shrugged modestly.

I nodded, looking at the horizon. "So, how did you get to know Havish? He just approached you with his story, I guess?" I ventured and couldn't miss the pull in my stomach as I spoke.

I think Krishav noticed the change in my tone. "You sure you want to…"

"Well, yeah… I mean… I am just asking a very generic question."

"Hmm… actually no. He didn't approach me with his story. On the contrary, I think he is the only author I have approached directly and expressed interest in representing."

"Come on! You are not making this up to mess around, right?"

"You have Gowrakka to thank about it, though."

"Now, really, you are messing with me." My voice somewhat had changed to squeaky, and I cleared it as I looked at him.

"Why should I, Ankana? I told you about my grandmother bringing in Gowrakka, right?"

"Yes…"

"She also ensured that after Gowrakka mothered her child, Vasu, he would get the same education as the rest of the kids in the family."

"Your grandmother was next-generation stuff, man!"

It was time for Gowrakka to chime in from the living room. "She was the kindest soul I have ever seen. I had wanted to put her photo amongst the gods' photos in my *Pooja* room, but..." Her voice faded away.

"Yes, as we had told you, Gowrakka, *Ajji* would not have liked that," he replied.

He returned to me. "So I studied literature in college. Being a couple of years junior to me, Vasu felt he, too, would like to follow the same path. Today, he works with one of the decent publishing houses. A few years ago, when he'd just joined the firm, he assisted some seniors in selecting manuscripts.

"Vasu was good at his screening, by the way. However, one of his selections was rejected by a senior. That night, Vasu called me and told me that he believed there was a good story. Knowing that his publishing firm wouldn't entertain it, he asked if he could direct the writer to me. He'd never done that before. So I definitely wanted to take a look."

"This sounds like a scene from a movie, Krishav. So it was Vasu who directed Havish to you?"

"Yes, and Vasu was right. I knew the story had potential, and well, here we are today."

I was mesmerised. "This is too much serendipity, Krishav." I chuckled, trying to hide my intense feelings after hearing him out.

Gowrakka came to the veranda with two glasses.

"No, Gowrakka. I've already had your buttermilk. I am full and cannot have anything else now."

"You don't even have room for *paaysa* made of poppy seeds and jaggery?" She smiled, showing all her teeth.

"What! What a coincidence! That's my favourite." I stood up to grab a glass from her.

"Yes, I know."

"You know?"

"Krishav told me...," she stopped mid-sentence, realising something, and looked awkwardly at Krishav, "...not to bring it up. Okay... I have to go inside. There is so much work left." She walked away quickly.

I turned to Krishav, who was busy rubbing his eyes, clearly avoiding looking at me.

"That's... surprising," I told him after a long, awkward silence.

"Sorry?"

"So Havish had..."

"Yes, and I am sorry. I didn't want to bring it up. He'd once told me you liked this sweet."

I was stunned but breathed quietly, looking out of the balcony to regain my composure. "The last time I had spoken to him was when I was hardly seven or eight. How did Havish remember so much about me or my preferences?"

He remained silent.

I thought of leaving soon but remembered my last call with Sujna.

"Can I ask you a question about your proposal, Krishav?"

He was taken aback. He was unable to switch soon. Something told me to proceed with the question.

"If I may ask a selfish question, what's in it for me?" I said.

"Meaning?"

"Hypothetically, if I agree to continue with this book you're talking about, what is my motivation?"

"Ah, like that. Yes, I'd thought about it. See, the author proceeds may still go to Havish's wife unless we loop her into this and discuss splitting the royalty with you. However, I think that's a very complex route, and it is possible that Rupa may want to look at other options like other more accomplished authors, or perhaps may decide not to proceed with the book."

"Oh, that's too much information. I didn't mean..."

"Yes, but you asked, and wait, I'm not done. The option of sharing royalty is complex, and I am not for it. However, I'm supposed to get a portion of the commission. I am happy to..."

"Wait, I didn't mean to get into the money part right now. Stupidly enough, I had not considered that angle."

"Eh... okay. Then what did you mean by motivation?"

"If I agree to your offer, will you help me get any of my works published?"

"Oh! I hadn't thought about that angle now."

"Can you?"

"Oh wait, Ankana. Don't forget that I am just an agent. I don't get to publish books, right? I only represent them to publishers. It is still their choice if they want to proceed or not."

"Okay, so..."

"So?"

"Will you represent my work to the publishers if I accept your offer?"

My question surprised him. He gave it some thought. "See, Ankana, I don't want to lie to you. I recollect your work. Your stories need a lot of rework and I cannot represent them to any publishing house in their current form. I don't mean to be rude. I am just saying..."

"Then you are not thinking about it from my perspective, Krishav."

"I... I know what you are saying. I had always thought that we'd settle on splitting my part of the commission. This part about your manuscripts never came to my mind."

I expected myself to be angry. Yet for some reason, I wasn't. I thought about negotiating but wasn't in that frame of mind. I gave it up for now and thought I should proceed with drinking the *paaysa* that Gowrakka had made.

It tasted delicious indeed, made with perfect ingredients and with that elderly love that showed in the dish.

I finished drinking it and went inside to thank Gowrakka, who wasn't expecting a tight hug from me. "I am happy you liked it, child." She put her hand on my head lovingly.

"I will be taking your leave now."

"Sure, Ankana. I hope to meet you again someday soon."

I smiled and stepped out to the veranda, where Krishav was still seated.

"Can you give me some more time to decide and let you know about your proposal, Krishav?"

He looked up. "And please give me some time too, Ankana. I cannot commit to anything, but let me please come back."

"Sure, that's helpful. Thanks for the lovely lunch."

"Not at all. Thanks for agreeing to come. Should I drop you home?"

"No, don't bother. I'll get a rickshaw or something."

Chapter 11

Sujna and I were on the phone that night.

"When are you coming back from the Andamans ya, Sujna?"

"I am not in the Andamans anymore."

"What? Then why are we talking on the phone? We could have met in person." I was irritated.

"No, babe. I am in Lakshadweep presently."

"Last time we spoke..."

"Yes, I was in the Andamans, and now I have travelled to Lakshadweep."

"You have no better work or what?"

"You need to get out of your showroom occasionally."

"No, I don't need to."

"Haven't you heard Paulo Coelho say, 'Not all those who wander are lost'?"

"That's J.R.R. Tolkien, by the way."

"Fine! Do you want to know where I am travelling next?"

"No, please. Can you focus on the problem I have at hand?"

"Phew, why is it always about you?"

"Sujna..."

"Fine! So he cannot get your books published."

"Technically, even if he wants to, he cannot do it. He is an agent."

"I got that. I meant that he is not keen to represent you either."

"Yes, but he did say he'll think about it and get back."

"Hmm... not very helpful."

"Hey, he also mentioned a portion of his commission. My thoughts were clouded with trying to publish my books, and I had not given much thought to the money."

"Yeah, you were right in doing that."

"What do you mean?"

"Babe, I don't think your brother's books were such a big hit either. Even if Krishav wants to split the commission, I don't know how lucrative it will be."

"Is it? I know writers get paid pathetically, but you think even the agents…"

"I know as little as you do. It is just my sense. Since our last conversation, I again looked at Havish's first two books online. The reviews are quite average. I am not sure he was making much money from his books. I guess he was well set mainly because of the inherited property."

"Hmm… you have done some snooping around."

"That's all I could do out here in Lakshadweep."

"I think I have an idea."

"What?"

"I will read Havish's books."

"You will be okay, right?"

"Yeah, I think I'm somewhat past that phase today. The interaction with Krishav was somewhat liberating."

"Dude, I thought you had a crush on that guy in the bus when you travelled to Bangalore. Then you were having wet dreams about Rakesh, and now it is Krishav. Can you please focus on one guy?"

"Oh, come on! I will be the last person attracted to Krishav. Rakesh, on the other hand…"

"Fine, come back from your La La Land. That's not a bad idea. You read your brother's books and see if you can replicate any of that manure."

"That's rude!"

"Woah! Really?"

"Okay, okay, sorry. I don't know why I said that."

"Right… so you go to the book centre near your showroom tomorrow and…"

"No need, ya. I remember you had got two of Havish's books a few years ago and left them in my collections."

"Ah, okay!"

"I will read those and then see if I need to read any of his recent ones."

"Sure, I will get my hands on his new books and let you know."

"From Lakshadweep?"

"We don't live in the Stone Age, Ankana. Lakshadweep also has the internet."

"Fine, go away."

Chapter 12

As the showroom reopened after a long festive weekend, there was a lot of backlog. Some stock reconciliation had to be done, and there was a minor panic when two television sets and three washing machines were unaccounted for.

I was a bit hassled for a couple of days, and then I heard from our corporate office that they had double-counted the stock at their end incorrectly. Idiots. They didn't even have the courtesy to apologise and blamed it on some random accounts guy. Morons.

By the middle of the week, we began to reach the post-festive lull. This is the stage where the customers realise that they should have bought the new TVs and washing machines during the Deepawali sale, and a few of them try to bargain, hoping we will be able to sell to them at a cheaper rate. They leave when we explain to them that it unfortunately doesn't work that way.

That evening, I searched my old cupboard of books, where I had stashed all my stuff. You would find my tenth-grade slam book and all the Khans' postcard pictures that I used to buy during my high school days at a rupee per copy. I have no clue why I used to buy them, for they had no use whatsoever. I wondered if, considering all of these Khans still played the protagonist roles, these postcards would have some vintage value in the eyes of collectors.

Then I saw some books neatly bound away. I was surprised that I was so good at maintaining my college books, though I couldn't remember ever binding them. I took out one of them, and as I opened the initial few pages, I realised they were erotic fiction. It took a moment for me to understand that these were my mother's copies, which she'd chosen to bind and hide away from curious and judgemental eyes.

I knew that if I began looking into every row in the cupboard, I might not find time to sleep tonight. I then went to the top-most row, where I had put some classic fiction and other books that I'd thought of reading sometime, perhaps in this life. I could vaguely recollect that a couple of years ago, when I was moving into this house, I had disposed of many of my belongings. Then I saw Havish's books, which I had almost thrown away. Hoping to understand his literary abilities, I had left them somewhere here.

"Hmm… yes, there you are!" I said aloud as I got my hand on the first book. I honestly didn't recollect the title, and it was a bit unsettling that it read – *Who was the Party Pooper?*

I mean, seriously? Would I be biased against Havish if I thought this was a pathetic title, and even a first-grader could have come up with something more sensible and creative? Are such titles even allowed to be put out there?

While searching for the other book wasn't as difficult because I knew it would be somewhere closer to the first one, it was more difficult to digest the book's title. It read – *Rocket in My Pocket.* "How god, how?!" I shouted out loud and realised it was pretty late at night. Mr Shenoy from the neighbourhood doesn't like loud noises at night. I went to my bedroom, covered my face with the pillow, and shouted, "How god, how?!"

Some of the frustration was vented out due to my repeated shouting, and I felt neutral as realistically as possible in such a situation.

I struggled to choose which of the two disasters I should start with first. I wasted time by delaying the obvious but then had a brilliant idea to check their ratings on a popular book review website.

I was almost sure these books would have poor ratings when I opened the website. I was surprised when I saw that the ratings were around three out of five, which may not be very good, but certainly better than what I'd assumed. A few more minutes on the website revealed that a few hundred readers had submitted their ratings. "That is not bad at all, man!" I said to myself.

Maybe I had judged the books by their covers and titles. However, I vaguely remembered that Sujna had made me read a few pages of one of these books years ago. I only remembered feeling miserable, though I didn't remember anything about the story or the content. I decided to give it a fresh go. "You need to be open-minded, Ankana," I told myself, though I felt I was trying to imitate Sujna.

I decided to go in chronological order and picked up *Who was the Party Pooper?* to read first.

I had promised myself that I would read for an hour like a neutral party without judging anything about the content or the writing style. Trust me when I say I have a low attention span, which could give a goldfish a run for its money. But still, I didn't get distracted by all the pings I kept getting on my phone and by the latest Netflix release, *Polar*, which had quite average reviews (like Havish's books), but I still wanted to watch it.

My face was a façade, like that of a Russian spy. You could not have known what I was thinking while reading the book. You would be surprised to know that I jumped when the timer went off, indicating I'd completed one hour of reading. I slowly nodded to myself, perhaps imitating a Buddhist monk who'd seen divinity, said hello, and returned to the world to lead a peaceful life.

I reached out for my phone and called Sujna.

"Hey, Ankana."

"I need a few minutes of your undivided attention."

"What happened?"

"To discuss Havish's books with you. I have not read all of it, but I read one of them for an hour just now and wanted to share something with you."

"Hmm… okay. Which one did you read?"

"*Who was the Party Pooper?*"

"The party on the island? It's been quite fun, but you know I am an early sleeper, so I decided to hit the bed so that…"

"Tch tch, Sujna!"

"What?"

"I am not talking about your party. I'm speaking of Havish's book – *Who was the Party Pooper?*"

"Oh… oh, okay, sorry, I'd completely forgotten the title. Yes, what about it?"

"I was shocked earlier when I saw the title, and the book cover had a cartoon with a double entendre."

"Ah, yes! I vaguely recollect the picture. It had a guy, and the thing in his trousers…"

"No, Sujna! That's *Rocket in My Pocket*. Will you please stop interrupting me?"

"Sorry, go on, please."

"They say that we should not judge the book by its cover, and they are so right."

"Really? I thought you wouldn't like it much. I won't interrupt you. You go on."

"When I saw the titles yesterday, I felt they were so cheap. But now, after reading a good portion of this book, I realised that my initial judgement was wrong."

"Wow, you seemed to have liked it."

"After reading the book for an hour just now, I didn't feel it was cheap. *I felt disgusted*!" I screamed.

"Woah, what happened, Ankana? Why are you shouting at the top of your voice?"

"Unbelievable, man! It was just trash, Sujna. Havish had written trash, and a few hundred people rated it above average on the review site. How is that possible?"

"Listen, you just relax for now."

"This is soft porn, man! I thought it would be a slap-stick comedy, but this is a slap-ass pathetic attempt at porn comedy. He might have just written porn, but no! He wanted to make it hilarious! There are only chauvinistic sex jokes here and there, which I didn't even find funny. The last portion I just finished was so bad that I wouldn't have chicken tikka, chicken lollipops, and sizzlers for life! At least, not for some time now."

"Calm down, Ankana. Some people do like such stuff. You don't have to judge them. Many other writers follow a similar approach and have been successful. It is a mass market, I guess, and as they say, 'sex sells'. All said and done, tell me, why should you be so hassled now?"

"What do you mean? Why should I be hassled? How can Krishav think I will agree to write such trash?"

"Ah, yes. I know what you mean."

"No. You don't know what I mean. Let me read the latest piece I finished."

"No need, buddy, I trust you."

"Of course not. You have to experience at least a part of what I'm going through since you're not here to lend me your shoulder to cry on or bang my head against."

"Fine, fine. Read it now. I am all ears."

***

Pranav received the call, and even before he could speak, the voice on the other side began, "Hi there, sweetie pie. Whatcha doing?"

"Hello, sorry. Who's this?"

"Come, come now, cutie. Don't you remember me? Let me give you a hint. You tried calling me last night."

"Last night?" Pranav looked at the caller's

number again and realised it was Natasha when he saw a few 69s in them. "Oh, hi Natasha."

"Finally, you recognised my voice, baby."

"What's with your language and reference? You sound so kiddish!" he asserted himself.

"Ha-ha, do you want me to talk like an adult? What sort of adult stuff do you want me to talk about?"

"Wait, how do you know this is my number?" Though Pranav saw her at the recent party where a certain notorious activity had taken place that he was investigating, they'd not spoken in years.

"Of course, I had your number with me. I've been waiting for your call. What took you so long?"

He did not know what to say.

She continued, "What are you doing?"

"I was sleeping when you returned my call."

"Ah, sleeping. All alone?"

"Yes, why?"

"You want company?"

"No, I am fine being alone." He felt it almost difficult to converse with her.

"So tell me, baby, why did you call? Finally!"

"Nothing in particular. I just wanted to catch up, you know? For a cup of coffee or something?" He intended to understand if she had anything to do with the notoriety at the party.

"Coffee or something? I have been waiting for this!"

"Huh? No-no! Only coffee. The one with 20% chicory mix."

"Sure. Should I come to your place then?"

"Nope. We shall meet somewhere else."

"No problem, sweetie. My place, then. There's no one at my place."

"No! I meant a café or restaurant."

"Oh, that's sad. Anyway, text me where you want to meet me and have a cup of coffee and something while I get ready. I need to take a bath, and right now, I am..."

"Okay, see you later today then." He ended the call without letting her complete the sentence. What's with this girl? he thought.

He did not want to meet her near his house, so he chose a small restaurant near her place and messaged her the address. Surprisingly, she was there within minutes.

"Hello, hottie!"

Pranav, who was lost in thought, returned to reality instantly. "Hi, Natasha. You can call me by my name, please."

"Oh my-my! You are feeling shy, I see."

"Not shy, but embarrassed," he retorted.

"Sure, Pranav, we will get to call each other nicknames later, I presume." She winked at him, which he tried to ignore.

"What do you want to order for lunch?"

"You!" She was witty.

"Something that's on the menu here."

"Lollipop, Pranav."

"Huh... lollipop?"

"I love to lick it when it is warm and sticky, and then suck on it well before I bite into it, such that only a thin stick is left behind, Pranav. Can you please order that for me?"

"Excuse me, Natasha. What are you talking about?"

"I was talking about the dish chicken

lollipop that is famous here. Why? What were you imagining?"

"Never mind." He turned to the waiter and ordered one serving of chicken lollipop.

The waiter politely stated, "But, sir, just one serving of lollipops will not suffice for two people."

Natasha intervened. "Don't worry about that. You can get one serving. I am sure I will suck on my friend's lollipop and take a bite or two while he is eating."

"Sorry ma'am?" The waiter was stunned by what she said, but he calmed his nerves when he realised it was an intended pun and smiled coyly.

"Natasha, can you please stop that?" Pranav whispered.

"Stop what? I have not even started to eat."

The waiter continued, "Anything else, sir?"

Again, Natasha spoke, "You know, my friend here loves breasts."

Pranav burst into a small coughing fit, and the waiter had to stifle his laughter by holding the notepad and the pen tightly and biting his lips.

After regaining control, the waiter smartly answered, "Yes, ma'am. One portion of chicken breasts sizzler for sir," and started to make a note, giving him a chance to smile while he did not have to look at them.

Natasha, with a straight face, continued, "Please ensure that the breasts are big, firm, juicy, and dipped in the right amount of oil to ensure that they are shining."

Pranav tried hiding his face in his hands, assuming the others around might overhear the conversation.

"Sure, ma'am. Anything else?" the waiter asked.

Before Natasha could open her mouth, Pranav said to the waiter, "Please cancel the chicken breasts sizzler and replace it with tandoori chicken tikka. That should be it, thank you."

But Natasha could not be stopped. "Yes, my friend here loves warm flesh with a hole in the middle!" The waiter could not control his laughter anymore and acted as if he was coughing. He left the table, excusing himself.

"Do you mind cutting out the adult humour in the restaurant, Natasha?"

"What adult humour? It is all in your dirty mind. I only meant what I said."

Pranav excused himself to go to the washroom to regain his composure. It was always easy to make an impression with the clients he met for the first time and establish credibility. However, dealing with old acquaintances like her, who have known him for years, was difficult. He took several deep breaths in the washroom, stood in front of the mirror, said encouraging words to himself, and walked out in a few minutes to join Natasha.

"So I was saying, Natasha..."

"We have said enough. Can we do it now?"

"What?"

"The appetisers are served, and we can eat now."

"Ah, sure."

He looked at the ordered dish and was looking around for the waiter.

"What happened?" asked Natasha, biting into a piece of chicken lollipop.

"There is no fork to eat my chicken tandoori tikka."

"It's okay, Pranav. You can insert your finger into the hole and put it in your mouth."

Without further argument, Pranav just continued to eat it with his hands.

The waiter returned to their table, almost as if hoping to hear Natasha talk more, and she did not disappoint him.

"Hope you are liking your dishes, sir and ma'am?"

Natasha replied, "Yes, but you forgot to get a fork for my friend here. Poor thing, he has been trying to stuff his thing into hot holes before he can put it into his mouth to relish the taste."

"Oh! My apologies, sir!" The waiter saw that Pranav's face had turned red with anger and embarrassment.

Natasha was almost done with her chicken lollipop, and the waiter said, "I see you are done with your dish, ma'am. May I..."

Pranav intervened now and said, "Yes, ma'am is good at swallowing things quickly."

Natasha was impressed and raised her eyebrows, smiling. "Of course." She then asked the waiter, "You have Chicken 65?"

Again, before the waiter could respond, Pranav spoke, "Though ma'am would have preferred 69, she may settle for 65 this time."

"Score!" she laughed now, and the waiter joined in with a big smile. She dismissed the waiter for the moment.

"Not bad, Pranav. I didn't know you had developed a spine over the years."

"It was always developed, Natasha; I just don't go around showing it as you do." He was referring to the backless garment she wore.

"Impressive! This is like my Yorkers are being scored for boundaries," she said metaphorically.

"Well, I always had a thing for fine legs," he replied, returning her question with double-edged humour.

"I am so loving this conversation, Pranav. I never knew this side of yours."

He smiled. "Amongst many other sides, I guess."

***

"Can you believe this? How did this make him a bestselling author?"

There was complete silence from Sujna's end. I just remembered that throughout my monologue of reading the excerpt, Sujna did not react.

"Oh shit! You have fallen asleep, haven't you? You made me read the entire stuff, and you were sleeping all the while? I will come to Lakshadweep right now and…"

That was when Sujna put her phone off mute, and Ankana could hear roaring laughter from the other end.

"Come on, Anku. Some parts were really funny." Sujna continued to laugh, to my surprise.

"Are you freaking kidding me?!"

"It is just some harmless fun. Yes, the quality of the story seems quite poor, but you have to admit that some of it was witty. I quite liked the pun intended during the chicken sizzler order from Natasha, and of course, that Pranav guy's comeback with the 65-69 line."

"One of the most voracious readers I admire is saying this is not trash. What has the world come to?"

"Okay, now shut up and listen. Think about movies as well. There are some great ones and some trashy ones. The great ones with some stretch win some awards that no one has heard of, and some trashy movies win the mass appeal and make money. Yes, you and I may not like the latter, but why must you judge others' views?"

I was still fuming, but somewhat understood her point.

"I haven't seen your recent novels. You have been very secretive about them. So I have no recent reference to say whether you can write such stuff, though I believe you aren't the person for the job."

"You know why I haven't let you read any of my work."

"*Arre*, I am your friend. I could help you, right?"

"I know. But you have read a lot of books, and I… I would be worried about your critique. I know you love me enough to not want to hurt me if you find it bad, and I also know that you are a lousy liar. So I will catch you when you are trying to say things to make me feel good."

"Anku! Don't be sad, please."

"I cannot write this, Sujna. I think I will just call Krishav right away and tell him."

"Don't be an idiot."

"Eh… what do you mean?"

"You will do no such thing right now. As I always say…"

"Sleep over it?"

"Yes!"

"What will change between now and morning in this case?"

"Nothing will change. So why the hurry of calling Krishav in the middle of the night and saying something he's not keen to hear?"

"Fine! You have a point, as always."

"And listen, I have been held up with folks and haven't been able to look into your brother's latest books that you wanted me to. What if his writing style had improved? I will try to do it tomorrow and let you know, okay?"

"Sure, but let me know tomorrow, please, huh? I don't know what could have changed from the first book to the latest, but I don't want to leave any stone unturned. I have taken time from Krishav. So it is not about meeting up with a timeline or something."

"Then good, and you eyeball his second book about some rocket in the pocket tomorrow."

"Do I have to?"

"Eh… yes. We just spoke about not leaving any stone unturned."

"Okay, sure. Bye now."

"That's it?"

"What do you mean?"

"Aren't you going to kiss me?"

"Come now. If your folks hear you, they'll mistake you for a lesbian."

"Oh, come on! I am going to kiss you today. Ummmmmmmma!"

"You are so stupid, Sujna." I giggled like a kid.

"Of course I am! That's why we are friends. Now, go and sleep over things. Bye for today!"

The next day was no better. The second book – *Rocket in My Pocket*, was simply a bore, with raunchy and double-meaning jokes inserted for the sake of it. As I had promised myself, I did give it one complete hour and read without any distractions. By the end of it, I wondered if I should take breaks to distract myself from the self-induced tragedy of reading Havish's books on humour. Trust me when I say I've never had a headache from reading a book since my school days. Here I was, holding my head with both my hands and trying to massage it by gently banging it from all angles.

I reached for my cell phone to check the time, which was way past Sujna's sleeping time. I decided not to make her party to the same headache. I also saw that Krishav had messaged earlier: "Something urgent has come up, and I must leave for Bangalore tomorrow. Can you please meet me in the morning? I know it's a workday for you, but I can come to your place earlier if you are okay with it."

It seemed to me that something was wrong, so I tried calling him. There was no answer—weird guy.

I messaged him, "Sure, the earlier, the better, please."

Then I took a paracetamol tablet and went to sleep.

The phone rang, and I woke up abruptly. I could almost feel my headache increase multi-fold. I held my head tightly again and didn't immediately reach for the phone. Thankfully, the ringing stopped when I went for the water bottle.

The ringing started again, surprising me. For a moment, I thought it must have been Krishav trying to return my call, or I assumed he must have had some emergency and was trying to reach me. I reached for the phone and saw it was Sujna.

I felt relieved that it was my best friend who was calling, and I needn't be too worried. But then I saw the time was two at night, and it suddenly hit me that Sujna had never been awake until such time. I received the call and said, "What happened, Sujna?" I assumed she would bark at me for not receiving her call earlier.

"Ankana, am I on speaker?"

"What? No!"

"Are you alone or with someone else?" She sounded scared.

"Dude, what happened? Why are you scaring me this way? Of course, I am alone. Is all well with you?"

"Yes, I was just worried about you. Good to hear you are in no danger."

"What do you mean, Sujna? Why will I be in danger?"

"No, listen carefully. I got held up at a party with my folks, and couldn't research your brother's recent books."

"So what? You can do it tomorrow. Why did you have to..."

"Shut up and listen!" her voice turned serious.

"Once I reached my room, around my usual sleeping time, I felt guilty for not helping you out as promised." She paused. I knew better than to interrupt right now.

She continued. "So I searched the internet for Havish's latest books."

"Okay…"

"And you know what I found?"

"What?"

"Nothing!"

"What are you saying, Sujna?"

"There are no recent books that he had written."

"What do you mean?"

"Precisely what I just said. The two books you have are the only ones he's ever written. I thought I was missing something obvious. So I went on a hunt to search for anything on the internet, but no. There is no trace of him at all in the past years."

"But Krishav told me that for the last few years…"

"Exactly why I panicked and called to check on you."

"Then you mean he was lying?"

"Lying? Dude, I was almost shitting in my pants when you were not receiving my call. I imagined the worst possible things he might be doing with you. I would have called the police if you'd not received this call."

"Sujna, don't scare me like this, ya." It was my turn to be shitting in my pants, almost.

"And you'd told me his full name is Krishav Karunakara, right?"

"Yeah."

"I couldn't trace a single picture with that name and description on any social media app."

"What shit?!"

"I am not kidding. Open your laptop and check if you want. And anything that exists about the literary agent Krishav is in the form of texts, be it interviews, articles, or blogs from the authors. No freaking photo of your Krishav from KK Literary Agency exists on the internet! He seems to be a ghost."

"What do you mean?"

"I mean, the one you met up with maybe an imposter. I don't know his plans, but I don't want to think about that."

"My stomach is churning now, Sujna. I've never been this scared in my life."

"No, no, you seem okay now. So that is good."

"Hmmm..."

"Don't meet him at all, okay? Call him on the phone tomorrow, act casually, and tell him you are not interested in..."

"He is coming to meet me in the morning."

"What the hell!?"

"He'd messaged me at night saying something had come up and he must leave for Bangalore urgently. He wanted to meet me before leaving in the morning, and I agreed to meet."

"How stupid can you be?"

"Arrey, how could I have imagined he is some maniac?"

"That's true. Sorry, I shouted at you. Okay, you message him saying something has come up and you cannot meet."

"Yeah, I will do that right away. You continue to wait on the call."

"No no wait. Hello! Ankana!"

"Yes, I am right here. What happened?"

"Don't do that. What if he learns that you've figured it out and makes a move right now?"

"Oh shit, yeah!"

"I think you just leave the house right now on your scooter, and I will give you an address to go to. I have a colleague whom I can trust to…"

"My scooter has issues. It's not working."

"What? What do you mean? I thought you had a problem with it a month ago and got it repaired."

"No, Sujna. It's been lying in a corner for the last month. I've not got it serviced yet."

"Dear god! You are unbelievable! How lazy can you be?"

"Now, don't keep insulting me, no. I am already scared."

"In your locality, you won't even get autos or cabs easily now. What do we do…?"

"Can that friend of yours pick me up from here?"

"That's a long shot, ya. And her husband works in some other city, and as far as I know, she comes to the office in an auto."

"Oh god, what do I do? He seemed so nice, and even Gowrakka seemed so genuine. All his stories were so convincing. I am such a fool."

"Okay, listen. Let's do this. You try to sleep until early in the morning. When you wake up, lock your house and get an auto. I am sure you will find one at that time. I will send this colleague's address to you after I speak to her. You go to her place, and we will see what's to be done next."

"How will I stay here now?"

"Don't be nervous, Anku. You have locked your main door, right?"

"Of course!"

"And if I recollect, it is a strong teak wood. It won't give way so easily. And you are not in some forest. There are adjacent houses. So, people cannot just break into your house without creating chaos. So you are safe there. But in the morning, moving away from there is better."

"Sure. Can you stay talking to me?"

"Of course."

"One moment, I will ensure the door is properly locked." I left the phone on the bed and went to the main door. Instead of the standard two latches, I locked all five latches that were never used. The rust didn't help make my job easy, but it was a question of life and death here. I didn't care if this woke up Shenoy Uncle. I would have welcomed something like that.

After ensuring all locks were in place, I returned to the bedroom and picked up the phone.

"Why do you have to take so much time, Anku?"

"Sorry, I couldn't lock one of the latches as it had slightly rusted."

We spoke for a long time into the night. I calmed down gradually, which usually happens when I talk with Sujna.

"I am feeling sleepy now, Sujna."

"Good, you have to leave early in the morning. So you better take some rest now."

"Bye, Sujna. Thank you so much."

"Chill now, Anku. I know you would do the same for me. Now relax and try to get some sleep."

The possibility of Krishav attacking me seemed too distant, and sleep welcomed me sooner than expected.

I opened my eyes and knew I'd overslept because of the sunlight coming through the window. My conversation with Sujna was still raw in my mind. I just got up, and without brushing my teeth, I just went to pick up some clothes when my phone buzzed.

Assuming it would be Sujna, I picked up the phone, only to see it was Krishav's call. In my panic, I dropped the phone to the floor. "Relax, don't panic now, Ankana. Don't receive his call. Just get out of here right now," I told myself. I got my purse, picked some clothes, and got to the door. It wasn't easy to unlock all the latches, but I did so quickly and opened the door. I found Krishav standing there with a sinister smile on his face.

Chapter 13

"Hey, Ankana. Good morning," he said.

"Hi… good morning, Karan… I mean, Krishav."

He shook his head, smiling. "Really? You still don't recollect my name?" He turned his attention to the suitcase he'd got along with him.

I shut the door and put two latches in record time, without wasting a moment.

"Ankana, is everything okay? What happened?" His voice mocked concern.

"Leave right now, Krishav or Karan or whoever you are. Else, I am calling the police." I typed 911 on my phone, remembered that we were in India, and changed it to 100, ready to call the police immediately.

"Is this some bad joke? Are you feeling okay?" His voice genuinely seemed surprised.

"I figured out the truth about you. You are some imposter, perhaps a serial killer. One move from you, and you will be in prison." I was growing increasingly nervous with the suddenness of it all. I cursed myself for oversleeping.

"Listen, are you out of your mind? What is happening?"

I went to the window next to the main door so that I could see his face and also keep an eye on him in case he reached out to his suitcase to get any murder weapon out of it.

"I know you've faked everything, Krishav. My friend and I figured it out. You should leave right now. I am serious. I will call the police."

"Dear god! What is wrong with you, Ankana? I thought you were playing some pathetic prank that I didn't follow. But you look quite serious. What did I do? What did you figure out? Please tell me so I can explain if there's some misunderstanding." He seemed too genuine to me. Perhaps he's a practised serial killer who's an expert in human emotions.

"We figured out that Havish had not written any books in the last few years, the period you claim to have helped him publish some four books," I told him, scrutinising his face through the window grill, hoping to call his bluff.

"That's so stupid of you. I thought you'd figured that out long ago. One look at the internet, and you would know you won't find his name in any recent books."

"What do you mean?"

"I mean, I assumed you figured he was using a pseudonym, a pen name. Hence, you had not asked me about it."

"That's rubbish. You just made it up."

"No, I didn't. Why do you think I wanted to meet you in person before leaving for Bangalore?"

"How should I know? You are the serial killer."

"Oh, come on, Ankana!"

"And well, we also figured that there is no picture of you on any of the KK Literary Agency websites or articles. How do you explain that?"

"One second, who is 'we' here? Is there someone with you inside?"

"What if there is?"

"This is so stupid." He was looking away from me. "At least will you let me in so that we can speak in private and I can explain it to you?"

"And let you murder me in cold blood?"

"No! I don't even hate your manuscripts that much to want to kill you."

"So why don't you explain why there is no picture of yours on the internet?"

"It is simple, you stupid girl. Last year, when Prashanthi Menon's erotica was released, she got trolled very badly by many self-proclaimed culture leaders. I tried to support her by putting some strong points against those people in my blogs, and both she and I received life-threatening messages from an extremist group.

"The cyber police had to intervene to do damage control, and they strongly suggested Prashanthi and I remove our pictures from all websites to reduce the risk of recognition or attack.

"Prashanthi didn't want to follow the instructions, as all books published by her already had her photos, and she was adamant about not shying away from such troll threats. However, the police were particular that I remove my details, as I had been quite offensive in my responses to the trolls. That was when I had to delete all my social media accounts and remove my pictures from the websites."

"This is a nicely cooked-up story," I said, but somewhere, I was now not as threatened as before.

He reached into his pocket, and I shouted, "Don't try to move. I know you might have a weapon with you."

"Please, just shut up now." He seemed irritated as he took out his phone and searched for something. He then came to the window, and I stepped back a few paces.

"What is that?"

"These are some pictures of Prashanthi when she visited me last year in Bangalore. You can see four of us together at my place – Prashanthi, her daughter, Gowrakka, and me."

"Oh, okay." I knew Prashanthi by face, and I was now beginning to believe there was surely some mistake that Sujna had made.

"And let me recollect your stories, which I'm sure you've sent only to the agents or publishers. At least, I know the latest one that you sent. I think that's the third story that you have yet to complete.

I remember that you had not even given a title to it. It was about some widow falling in love again with some young guy..."

"Okay, okay, that's enough." I was convinced. He was right. I hadn't named the book yet, and he was right about the gist of the story.

If I say I was embarrassed, I am sure you would tell me it was an understatement. If I say I was ashamed beyond comprehension, you may agree that is somewhat the correct summary.

I opened the latches and gestured for him to enter without being able to look at his face. He shook his head as he stepped into the house. When he saw the bag of clothes I had packed, he remarked, "So you were about to run away from your own house?"

"It was a misunderstanding, clearly."

He sat on the plastic chair in my small veranda and laughed his wits off. There were tears in his eyes, and he was holding his stomach while laughing, which I would say was uncalled for.

Unable to contain my own embarrassment, I joined him in his laughter.

"Okay, enough now. Mistakes happen. Please stop, Krishav."

"Okay, fine." He wiped away his tears, but then I started laughing again.

We had laughed off all we could in some more time and looked at each other without saying anything.

"So? Serial killer?"

"I said that I am sorry."

"And I surely would like to meet your friend, who seemed to be your partner in crime. Was it Sujna?"

"Woah, how do you know?"

"You had once used her name when we chatted over the phone."

"My goodness! How did you remember that so well? I don't even think I spent much time on her."

"I have a razor-sharp memory."

"Now that you say it, it must be right. You remembered from Havish's conversation about the sweet dish I like." I was nodding to myself.

I thought of something. "But Krishav, why didn't you just ring the bell when you came to my door? Instead, you were standing there with a sinister smile."

"Ah, that's why you associated me with a serial killer, with a sinister smile."

"Yeah, well."

"By the way, I rang the doorbell twice."

"What?"

"Yeah, and when you didn't answer, I waited a few minutes and called on your cell phone, which you didn't receive again."

"Oh, okay. Now I get it. I must have woken up when you rang the bell. I didn't realise it."

"Anyway, I hope your nerves are settled. It's a coincidence that I came to talk about the very topic... in a much different way."

"What do you mean?"

"About your brother's recent books."

"Mind if I go first? I want to tell you what I think before your words influence me."

"Go on."

"See, Krishav. You were right when you assessed earlier that I was worried about continuing with Havish's story mainly because when you read someone's story, there is a slight possibility of feeling close to the author's thoughts, which I was uncomfortable with."

"Okay."

"After our initial conversation, I thought about it practically, and the idea didn't seem as threatening. I got convinced to read two of Havish's works between the last two days, and I don't believe I can do justice in replacing him in..."

"Havish's works? You mean, you read the rocket in the pocket and the party pooper one?"

"Yes, and I don't think I will be..."

"Those two books are terrible! Why did you waste your time?"

"Exactly what I am trying to… wait, what?"

"Those books are slap-stick humour, which often doesn't even make you laugh. I could not even finish half of each."

"Really!?"

"Yes. I know that it got some portion of the audience interested. However, they are bad. Period."

"This is rubbish! Then why did you even represent them to the publishing houses?"

"Please! I had nothing to do with getting those two published. Havish partnered with me only after those disasters were behind him."

"Oh… okay." This was not something I had thought about. Now, I remembered that this guy had insisted several times that he'd partnered with Havish only over the last few years, and these two novels had come out much earlier.

"But still, Krishav. I honestly don't think I can write like Havish. I am convinced I will fail miserably, and it would be too late by the time you realise I wasn't the right fit."

His response was a calm smile. Something told me more was to come, so I waited patiently. He said, "You will be surprised by the similarities between your writing style and your brother's."

I shook my head, looking away from him. "I think you vaguely remember my stories, yes. But I don't think you have revisited my writing style, or you are too drunk right now not to see it."

"I don't mean to boast about myself, but there must be at least some talent in me that I have represented some good books and authors, Ankana."

"Of course, Krishav, you don't even have to begin to explain. But this is quite black and white here, and I don't know how you cannot see what I am seeing. Even Sujna..."

"So in your first story, Ankana...," he began.

"Sorry?"

"I was talking about the first story you submitted nearly two years ago. Was it not about a story between a married couple, where the husband suspects the wife of adultery and employs a private investigator to prove it? In the end, when the husband feels miserable for doubting his faithful wife, is when you reveal that she indeed had an affair, but she was clever in misleading the investigator throughout?"

I was too impressed by his summary to reply immediately. I nodded briefly and then said, "Yes, in that love story, I wanted to show how..."

"Please don't call it a love story. And your second book, wasn't it about some guy falling in love with a girl at first sight, but then he knows nothing about her, and..."

"...and he goes about finding her whereabouts through some information and clues until he meets her in the end. I tried to bring about the desperation in a lover's heart to try and do whatever it takes to find out about his loved one, yes." I shrugged.

"Are you even hearing your own words?"

"Of course, Krishav. Listen, I am extremely impressed with you remembering the details of my love stories, but how's that even connected to..."

"No, Ankana. These weren't love stories."

"Sorry?"

"Looks like you have assumed that you were writing love stories. You are so convinced about them and keep raving about love throughout your stories, but if you dig deep into your stories, there is hardly anything about true love. You are good at writing mysteries, which might have a weak layer of a love story at the outset. I had decided not to represent your books because your stories lacked that identity; I couldn't categorise them as a decent love story or a good mystery."

"What are you saying, Krishav? I still am unable to comprehend what you just said. They are love stories, and not…" I was busy trying to introspect to say anything.

"It's okay, Ankana. That is a façade that impacts every writer. Why just a writer? It impacts everyone in all streams of work."

"But then… why would you not highlight such things to aspiring authors? Had you even hinted anything about it, I could have given it a thought, and maybe…"

"Look, I am sorry, okay? Maybe I am a jerk, like all other agents and publishers out there, who do not respond to the struggling writers with anything, let alone give proper feedback for them to improve. I had tried to do it a couple of times earlier in my career but realised that people want to pretend that they know better, and all my counsel was a waste of time for them. So I just let it be. Once my agency started doing well, I started to outsource the manuscripts to other reliable editors to screen, and I lost all the personal touch I used to have with the writers. Over some time..."

All he was saying was going over my head. How can this guy talk such shit? How can he say I don't know how to write a love story? Wait, that's what he just said. When he tried to give feedback to some writers, this is exactly how they reacted.

"Ankana…"

"Huh… yes, I was just…"

"I said, I am sorry. I had only read your first story. The other emails you'd written were sent to the contracted editors to review."

"And now you have come to me, expecting me to do a favour to you?"

"Listen, I know it looks unfair to you. I have tried to be as honest as I could. And also, yes, you may call it a favour that I am asking of you, but it is more for Havish than me."

"Ha! I believe you."

He was about to say something, but let it be. I covered my face to process all that was happening. Too many scattered thoughts and words were bombarding my mind. I heard Krishav get up and walk towards the door.

Something struck me earlier when he talked, and I wanted to interrupt and understand him correctly. But my ego had stopped me from saying anything at all. That was something important. Krishav is leaving now. Wasn't that something I had to ask him immediately? Shit! Why do I forget things, assuming they are so obvious that I will remember them later? It was something about my book, not my style of writing... yes, he said I write good mysteries.

"Krishav!" I realised I had said it louder than I wanted to. But it served me well, for this guy was about to get his suitcase and leave.

"Yes, Ankana." He came back to the door without coming into the house.

"You said that I am good at writing mysteries?"

"Yes, you have a natural flair for it. If you consciously focus more on..."

"Wait, Krishav." I was irritated with his preaching. "I thought I used to write good love stories, but you tell me I mixed that up with mystery?"

"Hmm... yes, something like that." He nodded.

"Then how on earth is my writing similar to Havish's? He used to write lousy humour. Where is the connection?"

"Your brother, after his first two books, realised he wanted to diversify. You know, sort of experiment with another genre. He experimented with mystery."

"Oh!"

"Yes. However, his earlier-earned fan-following had branded him in a certain way. He realised it once he got rejections from more than a few agencies and publishing houses when he sent them his mystery story. As I'd told you earlier at my place, it was then that Gowrakka's son Vasu directed your brother's manuscript to me, for he saw that the mystery plot was worth considering.

"You obviously can imagine that I liked what Havish's story had to offer and agreed to represent it. But when we were about to sign the deal with a new publishing house on his first mystery book, he came to me with an idea. He said it would be difficult to get new fans to follow him that easily, as his brand of humour had earned a certain reputation, which was a double-edged sword. I hadn't given it much thought, but he was right. He proposed to get his mystery novels published under a pseudonym. The publisher, too, liked the idea, and we went ahead with that."

"So Havish's recent books were all mysteries?"

"Yes, and what has been left incomplete isn't any unfinished love story or humour. It is an unfinished mystery."

I had goosebumps all over my body hearing that sentence. Wow, Havish was, after all, not a loser who wrote senseless books he thought were humorous.

"But why hadn't you told me earlier?"

"I am a literary agent. I cannot disclose the real names of authors who use pseudonyms. If I do that, I'd be doing injustice to the author and the publishers. Hence, apart from his close family, the publisher and me, no one else knows the connection between him and his new books."

"And you couldn't trust me immediately to disclose about him…" I ended that for him.

"Yes… I knew you never liked him. So, I wanted to reach a stage where I could be comfortable sharing this much. In our first conversation, you cornered me when you were trying to know more, and I had specifically said that I was trying to be as transparent as possible?"

I nodded while looking out of the window.

"Listen, it was not to..."

"No, you don't have to explain. I understand, and what you did was ethically right. Perhaps I would have done the same as well."

"Only when we caught up recently did I feel that I could take that one further step and tell you more."

"Ideally, I'd have to sign some non-disclosure agreement or some shit like that if you were to reveal so much to me," I said, and he nodded. He had said all these to me because he trusted me. He didn't say it with words but with actions.

He looked at his watch. "So, that was the last information I had for you before you could decide. I have some work in Bangalore. One of the authors has delayed his submission timeline to a great extent, and the publishing house is furious about..."

"If it is okay to..." I interrupted him.

"Yes?"

"I would like to read some of his work. I mean, the other two weren't quite impressive." I tried to smile.

"Of course, let me message you some of his work, and you can get them from any bookstore."

"Sure, I will wait," I said.

"Hope to meet you again."

I realised that there was a possibility that we wouldn't meet in case I turned down his offer. Somehow, that didn't make me feel good. No, I don't develop a crush on every guy I meet. I thought I had formed a decent bond with this individual, which wasn't easy for me.

"Hmm... what was the name he went by? What was Havish's pen name?"

"Rāghavānka."

CHAPTER 14

"Ankana!"

"Huh?" I seemed to have gone into a trance.

"What happened? Why did you stand up like a jolt of electricity passed through you?"

I was still coming to terms with it. "Havish was Rāghavānka? The famous mystery writer? Wow! Havish was Rāghavānka!" I was talking to myself out loud.

"Why don't you take a seat, please?" Krishav held my hand and made me sit. I let him help me.

I sat thinking, and Krishav didn't say anything. He waited for me to gather my thoughts.

My thoughts soon went to the first time I'd heard of this name, on the bus on my way to Bangalore. The passion with which the co-passenger Dev had spoken about Rāghavānka was enviable. Now knowing that he was talking about Havish was difficult to digest.

"So his books did well?" I randomly asked.

"Quite well. They were all best-sellers. It wasn't as easy-going initially. But his second book struck a chord with the readers. His last book – *Two and a Quarter Murders* – was out hardly a month before his demise."

"Oh!"

"So you'd heard of his books?"

"Huh?"

"You knew about Rāghavānka?"

"No, not actually. It's just that I heard from someone about his books, and quite passionately at that." I tried a difficult smile.

"I have a flight to catch, Ankana. But I can stay in case you need me around."

"That's okay, Krishav."

"No, I am serious. I can postpone this if required. It's a weekday. Not many would be starting their travel back to Bangalore. I will be able to get the next flight without any hassle." He insisted.

"That's nice of you, but I will be fine. I just need some time alone."

"Okay, sure. I understand. I will get going then." He stood up.

"Sure, I will call you. Just give me some time."

"Of course. Feel free to reach out to me for anything."

"I will."

I messaged folks at the showroom that I would be on sick leave today. I wasn't entirely lying, for I felt feverish after last night's drama and the conversation with Krishav. The last twelve hours had been too intense for me.

I returned to my bed, pulled my knees closer to my chest and held myself tightly. I didn't know what to think.

My phone started to ring, and I saw it was Sujna. I didn't want to speak with anyone, but at the same time, I knew she would panic if there was no response from me. I received the call and told her briefly that it was all a small misunderstanding with Krishav and that I would connect with her for a detailed conversation later. She let me go when she was convinced.

I then remembered that I hadn't eaten anything, and it was past my breakfast time. My cook hadn't returned from her festival vacation yet, and I surely was in no situation to cook anything. I stepped out of the house to the nearest hotel to eat.

After ordering a portion of *sheera* and *dosa*, I tried finding Rāghavānka on book review websites. That guy Dev wasn't exaggerating. It was not just about the quality of the reviews, but I also saw that the count of people giving ratings to his books was aplenty. Surely, he was a big name in the making, if not already, in the literary space.

After I reached home, I called Sujna up.

"Holy shit! Are you bloody messing with me?" she said as soon as I divulged Havish's pseudonym.

"So you know that name."

"What do you mean? I've read all his books. I cannot believe this. You are Rāghavānka's half-sister? Wow!"

"Yeah, well. Get used to it."

There was a long pause at her end. She was trying to follow my suggestion to get used to it.

"Okay, Sujna. Are you done?"

"Yes, I guess I am… but the freaking fact remains that Havish was Rāghavānka!"

"Sujna!"

"So you agreed to Krishav's proposal?"

"No, not yet. I don't know if…"

"Don't you dare reject it!"

"Oh, ho! Sujna, I don't know how to write a mystery novel. I don't know why Krishav believes I can."

"If he is saying you can, there must be some truth in it, Ankana."

"I don't know. He was saying something like that. But you know me. I've not even read a single murder mystery in my whole life."

"Yes, and to know that you've not read even a single novel by Agatha Christie makes me feel ashamed to say that you are my friend."

"Shut up. I don't even watch such movies. What motivates people to read or watch stories of people being killed and then try to find out who did it? It is so stupid. You might as well do a crossword puzzle, where you may exercise your brain better."

"Listen, babe. There are worse things you will hear about love stories as well. Don't get into that mode."

"I don't know, man."

"Ankana, Rāghavānka is a big name, a valuable brand. Not everyone gets to complete his novels. Don't even think about letting this opportunity go because of some preconceived notions."

"Then you just want me to accept it."

"That's what I want, of course. You should think about it and make yourself want to do that."

"How do you propose I go about wanting to do it?"

"Read one of his books, or at least read a couple of Agatha Christie's novels that I recollect gifting you years ago. Surely you've not opened a single page of that."

"Hmm…"

"Come on! You seemed keener when you had to read Havish's lousy humour books. What is the big deal in reading his mysteries?"

"Fine! I will do that." We hung up.

I downloaded one of Rāghavānka's e-books on my phone immediately. Though I'd have preferred the paperback, I didn't have the time or patience to order it online or to go to a bookstore to purchase it.

I sat down to read and boringly waited for the first murder to happen in the book - *Two and a Quarter Murders.* Strangely enough, it seemed to get interesting after the first murder. I was caught off guard when the second murder took place. I'd been placing my bet on this second murdered person being the murderer of the first person. By the end of the book, I realised one thing about myself. I had more appetite to read about saucy murder mysteries than I'd hitherto believed.

I felt hungry and wondered why this should be the case, considering I'd had a heavy breakfast not long ago. When I looked at the clock, it was well past lunchtime. I couldn't believe I'd gotten so hooked on the book that I'd lost track of time and hunger. My eyes started to hurt as I read the story from my phone, as this was not something I was used to.

I ordered something to eat from a nearby restaurant. I then searched for the books that Sujna had gifted me, written by the famous author Agatha Christie. I was glad to have a paperback, and I started to read *The Murder of Roger Ackroyd* while having my mid-day meal.

This was the longest I'd taken to have lunch and the fastest I'd finished a book.

"Shit! I'd been missing out on a whole meaty genre of books all my life!" I said to myself.

I knew that I'd tasted blood, and I wanted more. I impatiently searched for the other book from the same author that Sujna had gifted me years ago. I threw around books while the search was on, which wasn't my usual way. Finally, I found the other book – *The Unexpected Guest,* by Agatha Christie. Just as the sun went down, I also finished reading this book. It was a record for me to finish reading three books in a single day!

It was a strange feeling I was going through. Though I was tired, and my eyes were sore, all my senses were alarmingly awake and excited. I tried Sujna's number, and she wasn't receiving it. I guess she was busy travelling between her current place of vacation and the next one.

I couldn't resist and called up Krishav.

"Hi, Ankana. Serial killer here. Please tell me." He laughed again.

That joke will not get old very soon, I presumed. But what the hell? I felt it was funny now that I looked back.

"Hey…"

"It's Krishav," he added.

"Tch… of course, I know."

"One can't be sure with you calling me different names every other time."

"You told me about that thing in the morning with some author and the publishing house. Is that sorted?"

"Not actually. This one author says he's having writer's block and unable to write even a page of the novel, whereas we are well past the deadline with the publishing house."

"Oh shoot! Hope it will be sorted soon."

"Yeah, these publishing houses can sometimes be difficult to deal with. Anyway, what's up? I wasn't expecting your call so soon."

"I read a book by Havish and a couple more murder mystery novels by Agatha Christie," I said, naming the two books of the great author.

"Nice! Sujna has good taste in books."

I was getting used to this. He could see a few things clearly without me telling him.

"Yes, that's correct. Sujna had gifted those books to me long ago."

"And then, let me guess, you hadn't touched them until today?"

"Yes, wow! Anyway, I think they were good."

"Right. They are."

"Even Havish's book was not that bad."

"True."

"So I was thinking about your proposal."

"Right."

"I am in."

"Phew, great. We will complete some formalities in our next..."

"Wait, wait, Krishav."

"Yes, what?"

"I am still not sure how I will be able to write a mystery. After reading a few from that genre today, I am excited about writing one."

"I understand."

"I am worried that I may fail."

"That is not your problem, Ankana. I am taking the bet on you. You don't have to worry about it."

"That's what concerns me. Why are you blindly trusting someone like me to deliver this work? Havish's four books under the name of Rāghavānka have been best-sellers. I am a no one. On what basis are you betting on me?"

"You recollect that I told you I had read only your first manuscript submission and had outsourced the second to someone else to review it for me?"

"Yes."

"Havish was the one who had reviewed yours."

"Oh!"

"I had gotten quite close to him, and once, when he and I were chatting about me getting many manuscripts to review, he offered to help. I let him review the list of all the manuscripts he could choose from. He recognised yours without effort and was excited that you had started to write. He then offered that he'd want to review all your work."

"Okay..."

"If he'd not directed me to that detail, maybe I would never have registered that you had a flair for mysteries. He funnily boasted about you both sharing your father's genes so you could have that investigative mindset. I am not entirely sure what he meant. He then requested me to represent your novels or give you detailed feedback. I didn't do it as it would be unfair to the rest of those who write to me with their manuscripts.

"And once, he told me you should be his backup if he doesn't want to continue writing as Rāghavānka someday. I thought it was a joke back then, but now I am unsure. I don't know why he said that, but it is clear in my memory. Thus, you are right in that way. I am relying on his judgement more than mine."

"Krishav, you are not thinking with your brain, but with your heart."

"I know." He was quite blunt about it.

"It's too much of a risk."

"I know."

"Krishav, speak in sentences, please."

"It is quite clear to me, Ankana. I don't make emotional decisions. However, Havish and I shared a different rapport. If he believed you could replace him, I must respect his judgement and at least give you a chance."

"I am more nervous now than when I had called you."

"Good."

"What?"

"You should be nervous. You are being asked to fill a big pair of shoes."

"Wow, that's encouraging."

"Don't get too hassled, Ankana. Think of it practically. You have a chance to reach out to thousands, even lakhs of readers. Not everyone gets this opportunity. I am sure Sujna will say the same."

"What nonsense? Are you both together in this?"

"Well, I just assumed this is something she would say."

"But after all, my name won't even come out, right? It will be under the pseudonym of Rāghavānka."

"Yes, correct."

I was silent for a bit.

"See Ankana, if you aim only to obtain fame, money, respect, and validation from others, as well as all other externally focused stuff from writing or any form of art, you are already setting yourself up for failure."

"Say more."

"Do it for yourself, and do it so well that you should be proud of what you have written. Don't try to write for others. That is a sure-shot recipe for failure."

"Hmm… okay. Thanks for that."

"Actually, Havish told me that."

"Oh, this guy keeps popping up every now and then."

"It is a very clear example. He wrote his first two humour books, keeping a certain audience in mind. They did somewhat well, but we know they weren't great. Then, he wanted to write for himself without even sharing his true identity with the readers. We both know how that went."

"Is it necessary to bring Havish's example into every conversation?"

"Okay, fine. I will try to refrain from doing so."

"Good."

"You are still in, right?"

"Yes."

"Great. See Ankana, it will take time and effort to formalise. So, I will send you Havish's unfinished script anyway. You read it and start your work on it while I work on the formalities in parallel, okay?"

"Fine."

"And for now, please don't send this incomplete manuscript to anyone, not even Sujna."

"Sure. But I already told her that Havish was Rāghavānka." I was sort of embarrassed that I couldn't keep the secret.

"That's fine. I am sure Sujna won't tell others about it."

"How do you know?"

"I trust her. Expect the manuscript from me by tonight. Bye."

"Trust her? You hardly even know her. Hello!" He'd disconnected by then.

I saw that Sujna had tried returning my call during Krishav's conversation. I dialled her number.

"Yes, babe."

"I accepted his offer."

"Yes! I am so proud of you right now."

"What? You weren't proud of me earlier?"

"Shut up! You know what I mean."

"Okay, listen. You cannot share about Havish being Rāghavānka with anyone." I was unconsciously sounding strict.

"Duh! Why would I do anything like that? It will die with me."

"Wow, okay."

"So, when are you getting started?"

"Krishav will send me the script tonight. I will see."

"That's so exciting, man—Rāghavānka's incomplete manuscript. Only a few in the world had access to it, and now you."

"Aren't you interested in reading the script?"

"Mad or what? How's that right? Don't even try to send that to anyone. It will be very unethical."

"Hey, listen, are you and Krishav seeing each other behind my back?"

"Eh?"

"Okay, I guess not."

"Why did you say that?"

"He seems to know you quite well."

"Ha! That's mutual."

"How's that mutual when you had branded him a serial killer just last night?"

"Ah! Correct. I missed that minor detail. Anyway, you excited?"

"More scared than excited."

"Take it like any other challenge, Anku. Don't let the reputation overwhelm you."

"I'll see. Will keep you posted."

I kept myself busy with some household work and refrained from downloading more books on mystery on my phone. I knew I would exhaust myself if I tried to do that. Soon, it was time for me to sleep. As I made my bed and was about to get into it, I got a text from Krishav that he'd sent me the unfinished manuscript on my email address.

"No, I am not going to look at that tonight. Its time will come, and that will be on my weekly off," I told myself and switched the lights off to sleep.

Well, yeah, you guessed it. I could hardly contain myself for five minutes. I was up and switched on my laptop to look at the manuscript. Sujna's words echoed in my mind – "Only a few in the world had access to it, and now you." Only then did the weight of this episode seem to sink in, and I momentarily felt that weight on my shoulders. Trust me, it felt very heavy. I blamed the few teardrops that formed in my eyes for the strain I'd put on my eyes the whole day.

I opened the document to see that Havish had not named it yet. I named the working title 'The Unfinished Mystery' without thinking twice.

I took a deep breath and started reading it.

Chapter 15

******The Unfinished Mystery******

Situated in the Palm Beach suburb, Florida, Grayson Villa was very spacious. While it was Nathan's grandfather, Ned Grayson, who'd bought this part of the land decades ago when it was a farm, with cultivation in his mind, it never kicked off due to several reasons.

However, Ned had a sharp brain and was not averse to taking the required risks. In addition, his rich father-in-law trusted Ned's decision-making. Thus, he'd managed to diversify and do well in many businesses. The vineyard they owned was perhaps one of the biggest in the region, and many renowned wine connoisseurs adored the quality.

Since Ned's passing, his two sons, Matthew and Titus, took over the reins and continued from where their father had left off. Titus was to look after their vineyard, and Matthew took charge of the rest of the businesses.

Matthew knew his father had a soft spot for this big piece of land, and hence got a rather large resort built as memorabilia, with a big portion of it dedicated as a guest house for the family's private use, and named it Grayson Villa. With eighteen rooms, a party hall, a dining room with an attached bar, a swimming pool, a dedicated mega kitchen connected to the sitting area, a half basketball court, a tennis court, an indoor games room that included a squash court and two billiards tables, a gym, and a dedicated set of staff, Grayson Villa was synonymous with luxury even by Grayson family standards.

However, Nathan's parents decided to visit New York this Christmas season to celebrate the festival with some important names in their industry. It was supposed to be a formal gathering.

Nathan had decided to skip the visit to New York against his father's wishes, hoping to spend quality time with his fiancé's family. Surprisingly, many last-minute changes resulted in him spending time away from his fiancé. He wasn't very happy about it. He was now put up at Grayson Villa to celebrate with some of his old friends whom he'd invited on short notice.

****

Grayson Villa

"And when were you planning to tell me?" Claire's voice didn't hide her surprise, almost bordering on astonishment.

Nathan didn't respond immediately. He was contemplating.

"I asked you a question, Nathan, and it is a simple one. What is taking so much time?" Claire was angry now.

"Do not raise your voice, Claire. Yes, I didn't inform you earlier about Gwen being here. So what?" Nathan, too, was losing his cool.

"Now you've begun to hide things from me?"

"That's rubbish. I don't need to hide anything from anyone."

"I am not anyone. I am your fiancé, remember?"

Again, Nathan chose not to respond to the rhetorical question.

"I told you I'm meeting up with my old friends over the long Christmas weekend, didn't I?"

"And you missed highlighting a little detail that one of the friends you are meeting just happens to be your ex-girlfriend of six years!"

"It's no big deal, Claire! You know there's nothing between us anymore."

"I used to think that."

"I cannot fathom why you are being unreasonable."

"I bet you can't, or perhaps you won't."

"You are the one who made changes to our plans and are spending the Christmas week away from me to be with the love of your life!" Nathan was fuming.

"Really, Nathan!?" She was hurt, and her tone couldn't hide it. "When I disclosed that at the beginning of our relationship, I never thought you would use it against me. No one except you knows how I felt for Henry in my younger years."

"That applies to Gwen as well."

"You mean there is no difference between the two situations? I have come to Highlands to attend Henry's wedding, for crying out loud!"

"And you wouldn't let me come there!"

"How often do I tell you that my family has not yet accepted you?"

"Let's not go there. Who doesn't let their family know that she's gotten engaged? They know me as some new boyfriend of yours. Every important person in my family was present to attend the engagement. It's been almost a month, and not even one person from your family knows we're engaged. You were supposed to disclose it immediately, and I was to be a part of the Christmas celebrations along with them."

"We've been through that already, and many times at that. Yes, it was more difficult to let them know than I'd anticipated earlier. Hence, when Henry's marriage was announced, I wanted to spend this week with the whole family during this wedding and get them to warm up to our engagement."

"Wanted to?"

"Yes, now I am unsure about the whole thing." There was a difference in her tone when she said this. It was cold and distant.

"Are you freaking kidding me?" he shouted.

"I have to go now." She was calm as if she hadn't heard him.

"Don't you dare hang up on me!" Nathan's voice quivered with fury.

"Go and spend time with your Gwen." She hung up.

"Gwen's just...hello! Claire!" Nathan held his phone tightly, as if trying to squeeze the life out of it, and turned around to smash it on the wall when he saw Gwen standing at the door that was ajar.

Nathan's anger turned to concern, for he got worried about how much of his side of the conversation Gwen had heard. "When did you..."

Gwen avoided his gaze, looked down momentarily, and tried to meet his eyes again, embarrassed. "I am sorry. I didn't mean to intrude. I heard your loud voice and came to see if you were okay. But I realised that I...I shouldn't have come to the Villa in the first place."

"No, it's not like that, Gwen. Claire is just.." Gwen didn't wait for Nathan to complete the sentence and walked away.

"Shit!" he muttered under his breath and ran his hand through his hair out of frustration.

He unlocked his phone to dial Claire's number again but thought better. He needed time to calm down and think. He put the phone on the table and left his room to join the others.

****

Highlands, Florida

It wasn't just Nathan who was loud on the phone. When Claire hung up after her heated exchange of words with Nathan, she thought she heard something outside the room, making her panic. She stepped out to find the corridor empty.

She got back to the bed after closing the door. Her mind flooded with a barrage of emotions and questions.

"Does Nathan still have feelings for Gwen, like I secretly have some feelings for Henry even now?" she whispered to herself.

Claire had tried to reason with herself earlier that she was right in delaying to share her engagement news with her family. It had happened all of a sudden, to be fair to her.

****

It was just the last month when Nathan had invited her to his house for the second time. Earlier, she'd met only his parents; on this day, he'd said he wanted to introduce his larger family to her. When he saw they were getting along fine, he proposed to her in front of the whole family.

Since the beginning of their relationship, Claire had a feeling that Nathan was the one, and in many ways already conveyed it to him. However, this sudden gesture made her nervous. She had decided to go with the flow and accepted his proposal, as all his family members cheered.

Yes, all his family members were happy, or were they? She now thought about an expression of disgust she registered for a fleeting moment when she looked around at everyone after accepting the proposal, or maybe it was nothing. She wasn't sure.

Her eyes then settled on Nathan's father, Matthew. He seemed to remain expressionless as always. Her instincts told her that he wasn't very happy about the engagement.

She was then positively distracted by Nathan's mother, Cassandra, and his Uncle Titus' daughter, Amelia. Cassandra took Claire's hand and said, "Welcome to the family, dear." And she lovingly touched Claire's cheeks.

Then Amelia surprisingly embraced her and quickly whispered in Claire's ear, "Relax, it is okay. You will be fine." When they broke their hug, Claire registered perhaps the only heartfelt smile in Amelia's eyes amongst everyone present.

That night, when all the family members had dispersed, Nathan had insisted on Claire staying overnight. He was over the moon and made love to her passionately, calling her 'wifey' many times.

Claire wasn't sure why she wasn't as happy as she thought she'd be. Each time he called her 'wifey', there was a pull in her guts, which she assumed to be a nervous reaction of her mind to this new reality, as she laid her head on his chest and slept.

Some tickling in her ears woke her up, which irritated her more than pleased her. She opened her eyes rather abruptly and gasped for breath to comprehend the change her life had undergone overnight.

Nathan was still trying to tickle her ears with his tongue. He was successful in his objective to wake her up, but it wasn't something Claire was used to or liked. Seeing that she'd woken up, he whispered, "Good morning, wifey. It's time for my morning jog. I wanted to check if you want to join me."

"Oh! I almost forgot what a health freak you are. It looks like I will have to change my sleeping time to marry you."

While it was intended to be funny, she realised mid-sentence that there was more truth in it than she'd wanted to admit.

"Hell no! I will never force you into anything, Claire. You can wake up anytime you like when we are married."

"I was just...kidding," she smiled. "And wait, I think I will leave for home immediately with you."

"No, wifey. Wait for breakfast, and then go."

She'd already gotten up and started to get dressed. "Next time, Nathan. You know this wasn't planned." She tried to smile.

"On the contrary, it went exactly as I had planned." He smiled. She could see how happy he was.

"And listen, Nathan, I have a request."

"Of course, wifey!"

"Can you please not call me wifey?"

"Eh...what?"

"It is a bit sudden for me, right? I hope you understand. Give me some time to get used to all this. I am..."

"No, wait. I am sorry, you are right," he reflected. "Yes, I agree. I might have thought through this a hundred times, but you wouldn't have...I am sorry, Claire."

"It's okay. Relax now. Please thank your family members on my behalf for their hospitality."

"Come on! It is now your family as well. There are no obligations. Now, will you please cover your derriere quickly, lest I pull you to the bed and proceed with whatnot?"

They were at the gate when they met Amelia returning from her jog.

"Hey there! Good morning, love birds," she greeted.

"Good morning, early bird," Claire smiled.

"You look tired, Amy. Did you overdo it?" Nathan said.

"Please don't say that. I am hardly doing my regular three miles," she panted and continued, "I should not have taken a fortnight's break from my jog." She referred to something only she and Nathan knew, and Claire nodded.

"Okay, I will take your leave then, guys."

"Sure, wi... ahem... sure, Claire," Nathan corrected himself mid-sentence.

"Hey, wait. Claire, how do you think you will travel out of here? There is no public transport for almost a mile." Amelia asked.

"Oh!" Claire was surprised and stared at Nathan for not letting her know.

"Shoot! Is it?" he asked in general, being ignorant.

"Let me drop you to the nearest station," Amelia suggested.

"Huh... no, I think I will walk. That should be fine." Claire's voice was not convincing, as she expected Nathan to offer what his cousin was offering. However, he didn't seem to get the hint.

"Right then. That's settled. Thanks, Amy. Bye, Claire." Nathan left the gates, looking at his watch.

"Listen, Amelia. It's really okay. I can..."

"Claire, relax, will you? It is not that I am compelled to. I want to give you a ride. Will you please allow me?" she asked, without any false expression about her.

Claire nodded and smiled.

Once they'd started, Amelia probed, "So, you overwhelmed?"

"Hmmm..?" Claire had heard it clearly, but she wanted time to frame her response.

"Sorry, that was a wrong question. Of course, you are."

Claire was having difficulty hiding much from this girl. "How do you know?"

"Come on, Claire! You don't have to be a psychologist for that. Nathan pulled a big surprise on you, and you were completely caught off-guard."

Claire knew better than to reply. She continued to look at Amelia while the latter kept her eyes on the road.

"I am really happy." She was smiling at the road.

"Why is that?" Claire was genuinely surprised.

"Because I like you." There were no two ways about Amelia.

"But you don't know anything about me."

"Listen, Claire. I am sure Nathan hasn't said a word about me till now. Yet, he pretty much shares everything with me. I say pretty much because I had no idea about his actions yesterday. Anyway, so I have been in the know about you since you guys started dating."

"Hmmm... now that makes me nervous." Claire, indeed, was nervous.

"Nothing to be nervous about. I approve of you." Amelia laughed at her own remark, making Claire laugh as well.

"Thank you." Claire felt she had to acknowledge.

There was an awkward silence momentarily. "Nathan treats me like a little sister, and the thing about him is that he goes all out in any relationship. I know he loves me, and I love him like a brother I never had. He is really happy about you. And whatever little I have seen and a lot that I've heard about you, I look forward to having a good equation with you."

Claire felt good hearing this and said, "It's so nice of you to say that."

"Wait, now you are sounding like the rest of my relatives. Too much of a socially acceptable answer."

"Oh! That's being mean to your relatives."

"Come on! Tell me honestly. Haven't you seen Nathan behave that way sometimes, at least? Sounding all formal and sophisticated?"

"Well...in the beginning, yes."

"See!"

"You will get me abandoned from the family way before I become a part of it."

"Do I guess right that your family doesn't know about this?"

"Are you a detective, Amelia?" Claire was surprised.

"What? It's just common sense. My idiot brother, sorry, I mean your respectful fiancé, had told everyone at home that he'll invite you to introduce you to them. And then he goes 'pop' and proposes to you, leaving you hardly any time to socialise with all the people you didn't know or care about. Then my brother takes you to the room, and well, let's leave that part out. Then he gets you out early in the morning. It's common sense, as I said." Amelia shrugged, and they reached their destination.

Claire wanted to ask something but was hesitant. She decided against it and was about to get out of the car when Amelia's hand held hers.

"What is it that you want to ask me?"

Claire smiled, thinking there was no sense in dodging this girl with words.

"It's fine, go on now. Is it something you want to know about me, Nathan, or our rich and mad family?"

"Well, actually, yes. It is about the latter."

"What about my mad family?"

"No! I mean... the rich part."

"Okay, what about it?"

"I guess by now you know that I come from a..."

"You come from a family that is not wealthy." Amelia was blunt, but Claire didn't find her words harsh. She quoted reality without sounding disrespectful.

"I don't know if the rest of your family is fine with..."

"They are not," said Amelia, and Claire was taken aback by her promptness.

"Care to say more?"

"Listen, most of the family is old school and believe we should have ties only with people with similar social, cultural, and financial status. To them, marriage is more of convenience, a sort of compromise. That's something our grandfather Ned believed. It's not about Nathan or you but applies to everyone in the family, including me."

"Hmmm... okay."

"And sorry to break the news, but I feel even Uncle Matthew is unhappy with the whole thing."

"You... know..?"

"He can be all expressionless, but his eyes never betray him. He and Gwen's father, Mr Jeffery, are business partners. They started a joint venture, to which Uncle Matthew diverted much of his wealth. I hear Mr Jeffery has the upper hand in that business because of his influence with some key people in higher places. I believe you know about the history between Nathan and Gwen."

"I...am aware."

"So when Nathan broke up with her, I believe it didn't go well with Mr Jeffery. Gwen was devastated. I did feel bad for her, but I think she's moved on now. However, I feel that Uncle Matthew thought Nathan's separation from his six-year relationship with Gwen was only temporary and that it would be a matter of time before they reconciled. Then, all would be fine with his joint venture with Mr Jeffery. But well..."

"Nathan proposed to me, and Mr Matthew knows that nothing can undo the damage with Mr Jeffery now."

"Yes, but that is frankly their problem, Claire. I don't think it is right to build a business on the basis of a personal relationship. They shouldn't mix the two, if you ask me."

"Not everyone thinks that way, Amelia, and maybe they are right. That's how empires used to run in the past, and now business empires replicate the same."

"I think you are wonderful, and my brother has hit the jackpot by finding you. Returning to the family, if you try to fit in too much, they will never accept it. Hence, there is no point in trying to be one of them. Just be who you are; some good family members also recognise a worthy relationship when they see one. They will uphold the sanity if need be," Amelia concluded.

"Why do you say 'them'? Aren't you a part of the family?"

"Ha! I am an in-betweener. My father brought me up differently that way. Sometimes, the family tries to treat me as an outsider, but I push through. That part of my grandpa's genes has come to me in abundance."

"I must be proud to have you on my side, then?" Claire said with a twinkle in her eyes.

"I was on your side even before you knew me."

Claire, surprisingly, felt close to Amelia. After a long hug, she kissed Amelia's forehead before they parted.

****

Claire came back to the present. She knew she'd spent too much time in the room, and people would start missing her if she didn't return soon. She got changed and went out to join the others.

While a good twenty people had assembled at the dinner, there was still room for more. Other relatives were to join, while the close ones had already arrived. While Henry was Claire's third cousin and not necessarily a close relative by blood, they had been friends since childhood.

Claire had always gone to Henry, who was a couple of years older than her, with all of her problems. More often than not, he would help her find good solutions. There was just one problem that she'd never told him about, that she'd been infatuated with him since she could remember.

Thus, it was ironic that she sometimes went to him, even with her relationship problems in her wild teenage years. To test the waters, she'd sometimes gotten extremely descriptive of her physical relationships with her partners, trying to see jealousy in his eyes or to know if he had any feelings for her. But he never said anything that could make her believe so. In fact, after giving his advice, he would politely tell her that she should not be sharing such personal details with anyone.

She'd grown to believe that it wasn't meant to be, and after those teenage years, she had been involved in a couple of serious relationships. By then, in her mind, she had gradually labelled Henry as her teenage crush.

Only when she recently heard about Henry's marriage, which came to her immediately after her engagement, did she somehow not feel too happy about it. She couldn't pinpoint the reason. She then thought the lady he would marry may not be good enough for him. Perhaps that lady was not as good as herself, Claire's conscience mocked.

This was one of the main reasons she hadn't disclosed anything about Nathan to her family yet. On the one hand, she wasn't sure if she'd made a hurried decision about Nathan, considering the angle of his rich and orthodox family, and on the other hand, she wanted to introspect about her feelings towards Henry. She illogically and secretly wanted to believe that she would get over Henry completely only when she witnessed his marriage. This was an out-of-sort behaviour for someone quite mature and wise like her. However, these trying times were revealing her hidden side. She accepted this flaw in her for now and decided to move on.

"You okay?"

"Huh!" Claire came out of her daze. "Yes, Henry. Of course. Why do you ask?"

"Oh, nothing. Just that I've called your name twice, and you didn't even register."

"Sorry, I've just been thinking about... something back home."

"Or someone?" Henry smiled.

She shook her head and mocked a frustrated expression.

"Must be someone special," he said, turning away from her to face the rest of the family at the table.

She wanted to respond but kept looking at him sideways without saying anything.

She then thought about it. She lost her cool with Nathan today because she thought he was doing what she was doing. He was trying to test the waters with Gwen. He perhaps wanted to see if he still loved her or if she still loved him. Then maybe he would get married to Gwen.

She thought she did right by expressing her willingness to break the engagement. Then again, she knew Nathan would get stuck to her like a leech. "I will kill him." This crude and primal thought surfaced in her mind unexpectedly, yet very clearly.

If Nathan dies, then her engagement is off. Maybe she will sneak into Grayson Villa that night, which was a couple of hours' journey, and end Nathan's life. Then, she will return in time to express her love to Henry, and Henry will be more than willing to accept her. They do it in the movies, and it seems so easy. The act of killing may be difficult, but then she'd heard that poisoning someone was the easiest way. "Wait, what the hell? Am I thinking all this?" Claire was shocked with herself. She had no idea why she'd gone all the way to kill her beloved fiancé in her thoughts. All that was happening around her for a long moment was a blur. She was scared of herself. She wasn't aware that she could have such murderous instincts. "Who am I? Are these thoughts even mine?" She began sweating, though the hall was air-conditioned.

Claire didn't wait any further, left the dinner table to get the bottle of vodka from the refrigerator, and went up to the terrace. Amidst all the chatter, no one missed Claire's exit, except for Henry.

****

Grayson Villa

Nathan came to the decorated balcony of the vast guest house to smoke. He wasn't a frequent smoker but resorted to it when he was faced with extreme emotions. He wanted to spend time alone and reflect on what was happening to him, and there was nothing like a good puff to get you thinking right.

He had sensed Claire's irritation since the engagement. He was no fool in picking up emotions, though many believed otherwise due to his brawnier outlook. "Maybe I should have waited and not jumped the gun," he thought to himself.

For some reason, she had turned all the plans for their time together this Christmas weekend upside down once she'd heard about Henry's wedding. He was clever enough to figure something about Henry lurking beneath her exterior mask. However, he felt it should be up to her to approach him if anything needed to be communicated.

The conversation earlier in the evening was going reasonably well. However, the topic of Gwen upset Claire more than he could have imagined. He didn't even feel there was any reason he should have given any importance to Gwen's presence. Thus, he'd made a casual reference about Gwen on the call, but the outburst caught him off-guard. "Did I do something wrong?" he thought to himself.

Nathan was furious because he always thought Claire to be more mature than him, which was one of the reasons he held her in high stead. In the initial days of their relationship, she highlighted the importance of communication. He'd liked how she could decipher the most complex emotions and make things easy between them. Only with Claire he'd opened up so much about Gwen. It was not that he had stories to share about her, but that a lot of pent-up misgivings had led to the fallout with Gwen that he'd not been able to share with anyone, leaving a void in him. He thought Claire could sort him out well, and she had.

Her reference of ending the engagement hit him where it hurt. He wanted to drive down to Henry's wedding right now and confront her. But he knew that it would only complicate things even further. Moreover, she mentioned that she would talk about her engagement with close family members at that gathering.

He realised something during this time spent alone on the balcony. He wouldn't be able to live without Claire. As he looked down at the ground beneath the balcony, it was filled with sharp artistic structures made from hard rock. He had the urge to jump and kill himself in case Claire happened to be serious about ending the relationship.

He felt a hand land on his shoulder, which calmed him. His suicidal tendency wore away. He didn't have to turn around to confirm that it was Gwen's hand.

"Sorry about... earlier," she said.

"No, don't be. It wasn't your fault I was screaming at the top of my voice."

"Yes, really. I tell you, your father didn't build the walls quite thick."

He just chuckled, more to ease the tension in his mind.

"Add to that the echo you get in these big rooms," he said.

"Listen, I am sure whatever it is, it will be fine," she said, her hand not leaving his shoulder.

He turned to look at her. "I hope so, Gwen."

A car's headlights beamed up to them from the main gates.

"Good. We have company," she said as the two looked at a car getting in.

"Hmmm...that's a big car." Nathan was curious and began to walk down the stairs to greet the guests.

"Hello there, Nate!" said the lady as she got out of the car.

"Hey, Martha! Didn't realise it was you guys."

"Why, of course, it's us. You said it will be the four of us, and I was sure that we would be bored to death before others joined us," she exaggerated, which was a part of her nature.

"Come on! I am not such a bore after all. And it is a matter of time before others join in, and we will have at least a dozen of us soon," Nathan said, trying to redeem himself.

"I am just kidding, pothead." She gave him a cursory hug.

"I didn't know you guys had a new car. So I wondered who entered the gates."

"Oh yes! Isn't it lovely? Albert bought it to celebrate our fifth anniversary last month." She almost jumped in the air.

"Oh, I am so sorry I missed wishing you that day! How come you guys didn't call for a party?"

"We wanted to keep it somewhat private," said Albert, who'd parked the car and approached the two.

"Hmmm...mysterious there, Albert." Martha held her husband's arm.

"Fair enough."

Albert caught Nathan's smile, but for some reason found it suspicious.

"It's been a long time!" Kory came out of the house to join them.

"Kory's already here?" Albert said.

"Yes. Kory and Gwen reached together this afternoon," Nathan addressed the couple.

"Oh! That's awesome!" Martha seemed more excited than necessary.

Once they entered, Nathan showed them their room.

"We have the whole guest house to ourselves for two days?" Albert observed.

"Yes, sir," Nathan smiled.

Albert looked around, a little concerned. "I don't see any staff around."

Martha shouted, "Exactly what I was about to ask!"

"Considering it will only be a few of us, I've given the staff leave to spend time with their loved ones. If we need domestic help, you know the other portion of the Villa still has our commercial resort, right? I've told the caretaker we may reach out if necessary."

"Hmmm..," said Albert.

"Ah, and won't they be kind enough to serve the proprietor's son when needed," jibed Martha.

Nathan just shook his head, smiling. "You both freshen up and join us for dinner. The Chef has promised me some great dinner for the next few days."

"Chef Harrison, right?" clarified Albert.

"Yup."

"That's great! I am starved and was worried that you would ask us to make do only with liquor for a few days," said Albert. A shade of Martha's exaggeration could be seen in him, similar to how many couples subconsciously imbibe some of their spouse's qualities over time.

Nathan was content to see Albert speak heartily for the first time since his arrival. He'd missed his friend's banter and hoped to make amends with him during this visit.

****

New York

"Your brother just called," Cassandra said, as Matthew entered the executive suite.

"What does he want?" Matthew said, grumpy.

"Nothing in particular, dear. He just wanted to speak to you, as it has been long since he'd caught up with you. He wanted to ask about your health and your joint venture. I told him all's well and that you'd call him whenever possible."

"Such a bastard!"

"Matthew, please!"

"I am sure he wanted to witness my downfall with joy."

"Please don't say that. He is your brother."

"One hell of a brother he is. Took away the vineyard from Father. He knew that the liquor business would never see a downtime and then shoved the remainder of filth to me!" He was quite enraged for someone who usually kept his emotions to himself. Only his wife had the privilege of being an audience to this side of him.

"Wasn't it a fair allocation of businesses, as you'd said earlier?" she tried to reason.

"Are you his wife or mine?!" he shouted, making her gasp with surprise.

While Cassandra knew that Matthew didn't necessarily like his brother, and she'd witnessed their growing rift over the years, she had never seen her husband so angry with his younger sibling. "I am sorry. You know I care for you and would do anything to help you return to your normal self." It was all she could manage in a meek voice.

"My son may have made it difficult for me, but I will get back."

"Yes, dear. Nathan should have thought about you before..."

"There are thousands of women out there, and Nathan had to pick Gwen to mess our lives up! Earlier, Jeffery used to eat out of my hands, but ever since Nathan dumped Gwen, he treats me like shit. I wish I never had a son like him."

"You've been saying that many times lately," she said, shaking her head.

"You will see. I will get my credibility back. I will bounce back strongly. We don't have to beg Titus for alms."

"I am sure you would come back strongly. Even otherwise, there's always my father's business that you could join. He's old and has repeatedly expressed needing help managing the hospital chain."

After a brief pause, he spoke. "Sorry, I shouted." He ignored her reference of joining her father. He was too proud to join his father-in-law, unlike his father Ned.

She simply nodded.

"Did Titus say anything else?"

"Oh, nothing. He just wanted the address of the place we are staying in. He wanted to send you and Nathan the best wine bottles as usual."

"Ha!" he snorted.

"I am sure Jeffery will see sense, honey. I feel he has already started to. Remember he'd not even come to our silver jubilee anniversary celebration after Nathan and Gwen split? Now, he has come all the way from Florida to join us, no?"

He looked at his optimistic wife and nodded. "That is true."

****

Highlands, Florida

"That's too much vodka for one person." Henry came up the terrace and saw Claire gulp one more swig.

"Who told you I was here?"

"It is hard to miss when you walk out right in front of everyone."

"Only you noticed, though."

"You cannot blame if others were too involved in their conversations to notice."

"Or just plain drunk."

"Don't tell me you are high. I thought you had a good capacity. And I see you haven't even got through one-fourth of the bottle."

"How does it matter to you, Henry? Should you not be with the others in the gathering? It's different that they didn't miss me, but you are the groom-to-be."

"That's okay. There are four more days to go."

The two stood in silence for some time.

"Give me a cigarette," she said, extending her hand.

"Sorry?"

"Will you give me a bloody stick to smoke?"

"Woah, where do you hide this aggressive creature when you are with others?"

It brought a faint smile on Claire's lips, despite herself.

"I keep the creature deep in the dungeons and lock it up within gates made of thick iron bars."

"Does he know about the creature?"

"Who do you mean?" she said, now alert.

"I saw the ring on your finger when you arrived two days ago. I guess you must have forgotten to remove it, and when one of our aunts asked about it, you lied to her that it was a fake stone."

"Were you stalking me or what?"

"It was right there before everyone's eyes to see."

"What if I say it was just a gift, and you are reading too much into it?"

"Then I would say that you are a good liar, but you don't lie to me very well, and then I would say that I had a small glimpse at the stone on the ring. It seems too expensive to be a gift from a good friend."

"Piss off." Claire was nervous.

"Claire, you don't have to hide things from me. Of course, I will never ask you anything you don't want to share."

"Yes, I am engaged, okay? And he's quite well-off."

He chuckled and shook his head. "Isn't that something to be very happy about? Shouldn't you be excited to share that with the family? Why all the secrecy?"

"Says the one who kept his relationship hidden till he announced his wedding last month," Claire tried to get back at him.

"I never hid anything from anyone about Bianca."

"Then, how come all of a sudden?"

"Claire, we've been seeing each other for over a year. You know my nature. I don't go about telling others about my personal life that easily. But yes, we had no engagement as such. She comes from a moderate family, and I didn't want to burden them in any manner."

"Ha! Always Mr Nice Guy, aren't you?"

"Hmmm... something is indeed bothering you. You are trying to be more spiteful to me than usual."

"I asked you to piss off a while ago."

"Fine." He started to walk back.

"Wait!" Claire wanted him to stay.

"What is it?" he asked.

"I asked you to give me a cigarette."

"I've stopped smoking, Claire."

"What the hell! Seriously?"

"Yes, why?"

"You were almost a chain smoker. Perhaps that was the only cool thing about you. How did you let that go?"

"Ouch! That hurt."

"Good!"

"I sort of gave up that habit once Bianca and I got serious about our relationship."

"What! You must really love her. Hadn't you once told me that it is the one thing that you will not give up for anyone?"

"Yeah, I vaguely recollect saying something like that."

"Phew... she surely has chains around your neck." Claire wanted it to pinch him.

He looked at her sideways, knowing she could see him from the corner of her eyes. He said, "You know what? I guess she does have chains around my neck."

Claire turned to look at him, and her expression softened. "I...I am sorry. I am being too mean." She turned away to ensure he didn't see that a tear escaped her eyes.

"That's okay, Claire."

He came to her and put an arm on her shoulder. She mocked, trying to escape his grip, and he held her tighter.

They stayed that way for a long time. Claire wanted to rest her head on his shoulders but held back that temptation with solidity.

"You remember Claire, when you came to me often during your teenage years asking for my advice on guys?"

"Of course I do."

"And you used to talk about every issue you had?"

"What's the point, Henry?"

"You may be double that age now, but you know you can still do that, right?"

She paused before responding, "Things change, Henry."

"Which is fine as long as we want them to."

"Oh, enough of your Mr Mature show!"

"See, if I am trying to be Mr Nice Guy, won't Mr Mature tag along anyway?"

"How is it that I always lose the argument with you? I usually get my way with others," she complained, further softening up.

"So, you want to talk about it? I am fine if you don't want to."

"It's not that simple."

"Let me make it a bit simple, for starters. A little birdie told me you felt differently about me in our teenage years."

"What the hell! How did you..." She looked at him keenly.

"Should that matter?"

"Of course! I haven't said anything to anyone about it, and it doesn't mean I am confessing anything right now." She was visibly trembling.

She tried to pull out of his grip. "Let me go."

He released her and watched as she fiddled about nervously. "It is not a big deal. When you spoke in the room on your phone with your fiancé, I guess you were quite loud and..."

"Are you crazy? Were you snooping around my room?"

"Ahem... there are only three rooms in this house, Claire. Even the groom doesn't have a dedicated one. Don't act like there was some invasion of your privacy with ill intention. And secondly, no. I didn't hear anything. Bianca had wanted to go to the room to change for dinner. She saw it was locked, and before she could knock, she heard your voice. You mentioned how you felt about me during your younger years to someone. She just thought she should leave the place instead of intruding."

"And come to complain to you? Bitch!" Claire was unsettled.

"It's my fiancé you're speaking of. And come on, Claire. She didn't create any scene or confront you or any stupid thing like that, right? She came to me and let me know so that I could speak with you and sort things out."

Again, there was a long pause. "You're right. I mean, she was right in doing that. I am sorry. Just that... that was not something..."

"Not something that should have reached my ears?"

Claire gave him a sideways glance and looked up at the star-lit sky. She shook her head visibly. "It's surely not one of my best days."

"Hey, come on. We've all been there. It is no big deal," he reasoned.

"This is embarrassing, Henry. I was so close to you in our teenage years, and I had strong feelings for you, which I hadn't disclosed all my life. All of a sudden, amidst all this confusion that I am already going through, you come up and tell me you know about that secret of mine. It is quite unsettling, okay?" Claire's voice had given her away. She could no longer hide her emotions, and tears were flowing down.

He pulled her closer to hug her sideways, and she had no intent to resist. "It is fine, trust me."

"How is it fine, Henry? I had a huge fight with Nathan over this. I referred to ending our engagement and stuff."

"But why? Listen, I've always known you to make the right decision. Yes, you are surely confused initially, but in the end, you ensure everything adds up."

"I mean, the context under which the engagement took place was not under my control. It is hard to explain."

"Hmmm..."

"And then, once I heard about your marriage...I don't know why, but something has been bothering me since then. I am a bad person, Henry."

"No, you are not bad, Claire. You are just confused. Perhaps confused to a greater proportion at this phase."

For the first time, she let her head lean on his shoulders. It felt nice.

"I always had a hunch that you had a crush on me back then, but it was just a hunch."

She chuckled for a second.

"Not sure if I am helping you here, but I hope you will be relieved to know it wasn't one way. I, too, had feelings for you."

"What!" She straightened up to look him in the face.

"I did. Bianca knows, and that's why she thought she should let me know when she overheard you this evening."

"Why did you never tell me, Henry?"

"Maybe for the same reason you never told me. I was never sure. Moreover, I don't think we would make the right match. We are very different people. We can surely be best friends, but not a couple."

"How do you know that without giving it a try?"

"I just..," he shrugged and looked at her.

It was perhaps a moment of weakness, but it only felt natural for Claire to pull his face towards her and kiss him. When she saw no resistance from him, she kissed him more passionately, the way she had always dreamt about.

She pushed him onto a stone slab on the terrace and climbed onto him, removing his shirt. "Claire, I think it's not..," he wanted to say something, but she moved her lips back to his, and she could feel him beginning to relent. She could feel him kissing back with the same passion as hers.

Claire removed her blouse, leaving her topless. Her beautiful features were visible to Henry under the only night lamp on the terrace. Looking at the lust in his eyes, she got down to kiss him again, and they embraced with their skins touching each other.

Claire, in a hurry, opened his zipper and moved her hand inside.

That seemed to bring him back to reality, and he stopped her hand. "Claire, no."

"Something in my hand tells me it is a yes."

"No, I... we both are engaged to be married to different people. We cannot do this. I am sorry." He got up with some difficulty, and before dressing himself up, he tried to cover her bare chest.

"But Henry, I want this. I know you want this too."

"I would be lying if I deny that, yes. But neither of us can change what is right. You love someone else, and you are to get married soon. I love Bianca, and I cannot ever cheat on her."

"What if I am not engaged anymore? And it's not that you are married yet. You have a few more days to go," Claire pleaded desperately.

"It is the alcohol talking, Claire. You know too well the right thing for both of us."

"The right thing is for us to make love right now under the stars."

"Claire, please wake up. I am sorry that I, too, got carried away."

Claire was heartbroken. She sobbed without caring to cover her bosom. Henry tried to hold her, but she slapped his hands away.

"Get the fuck out of my life!" she shouted, and he retreated without saying anything further.

****

New York

"Jeff, will you please stop being difficult?" insisted Matthew when others had left the table.

"How do you mean?" Jeffery had a straight face.

"You have been quite annoyed since Gwen and Nathan broke up, and..."

"Correction, Matthew, you mean since Nathan broke up with Gwen."

"Argh..." Matthew tried to compose himself. "Yes, that is correct. However, why should that disturb our relationship as partners and friends?"

"I am not like you, Matthew. I cannot distinguish between my personal life and my business. They are the same to me." Jeffery was very stern, and his jawline showed when he was angry.

"I know what happened made it difficult for you. But..."

"For me? Do you know what Gwen went through? I have never seen her like that. And to know that it is all because of your son..." Jeffery was now fuming with all the pent-up frustration.

While Matthew wasn't necessarily happy with the outburst, he was glad that Jeffery was at least venting rather than bottling everything up. "I can imagine it must have been difficult for you and Gwen, but would it be right to force them to be together in the long term? Will your daughter be happy if it is a relationship of compromise? Isn't it better that it ended when it did than for it to have become something bigger and then ended? That would have been devastating."

Jeffery wasn't one bit convinced about what Nathan had done. Nevertheless, being wise, he saw meaning in what Matthew referred to. It would have been a catastrophe if the relationship were to have gone on to the next leg, as marriage, and then ended.

Seeing the opening, Matthew continued, "You have to let me contribute to our business. We've not been faring well for the past couple of quarters."

"How do you mean? I have done nothing."

"Come now, Jeff! My inputs and decisions have been overruled without an exception for the past couple of quarters."

"I don't know what you are talking about." Jeffery was not very good at masking his emotions.

"Since I don't have the majority holding in our venture, I am overruled every time. It does not take me a magical crystal to figure out that you are voting against my decisions, and you can see that it is not helping our business survive, let alone thrive."

"You are accusing me of..."

"Please, Jeffery. Why can't we move on when our children have chosen to move on and remain good friends?"

"Ha! Like hell, they have!"

"Why, they are at the Grayson Villa with some close friends, getting together to celebrate the festive season."

"Utter rubbish. Gwen told me she's..," he tried to remember. "Hmmm..."

"Yes, Cassandra called up the Grayson Villa to check on them."

"Okay..."

"Will you please give it some thought then?"

Jeffery looked Matthew in the eyes for the first time during the conversation and gave a faint nod that many would've missed had they not known the man as well as Matthew did.

****

Grayson Villa

It was a sumptuous dinner served at the Villa.

"Mmmm... the mango soufflé is heavenly," said Kory, her eyes closed, trying to enjoy the taste on her tongue.

"Will you please stop making such sex noises, Kory?" Gwen complained.

"Why would I? It tastes better than having sex. Ummmmm.." Kory continued.

"Tastes?" Martha probed.

Kory had her mouth full to reply and chose to wink at Martha, and all of them giggled like school girls.

"What are these doofuses doing sitting at the other end?" Gwen asked in general.

"Men! I am sure they wanted to get to the drinks before they finished the desserts," Martha said, attempting to sound carefree.

"I don't understand why they must have serious conversations in such a lovely ambience," Kory observed once she finished her soufflé.

Martha looked at them and spoke distantly, "Yeah, I suppose they shouldn't be discussing something serious there." There was a bit of nervousness about her manner that the other two missed.

****

"We drove across four states," said Albert.

"You'd not done that before, had you?" Nathan was curious.

"Nope. I am telling you this new car is a freaking beast."

"I like the burgundy colour. The finishing touch is excellent."

"It is a beauty and a beast." Albert was quite happy with how he framed the sentence, and Nathan gave him a high-five.

"Good, buddy... good to catch up. You've been difficult to get hold of for the past several months. What's happened to you? You were not even receiving or returning my calls. It got me a bit hassled. It was so unlike you."

Albert shrugged and took another swig from his beer bottle, preparing himself for the difficult topic ahead.

"Is it because of the money, Albert?"

Albert's grip on the glass stiffened. He said in a practised tone, "I told you that I will return it in a year, Nathan. And you know that I keep my promises."

"Come on, man. I know you too well to doubt your intentions. Hence, I wonder why you've been so distant since then."

"Just that a lot of things are going on." Albert shrugged again.

Nathan wasn't convinced, but he didn't want to push it. He just said, "Listen, they say that when you lend money to a friend, you lose the money and the friendship. I don't want our age-old friendship to..."

"I just told you, Nathan!" Albert was furious. "You will not lose your money. I will pay it back. Is that why you called us here? In the guise of celebrations, you wanted to check on the money you lent me?" he said, raising his voice slightly. Though the women were in the same hall, they were seated at a distance too far to hear the exact words and with music in the background. However, the tone made Kory look at them to see if all was well.

"That's not fair, Albert. Of course, I know you will return the money. And please...keep your voice down."

"I noticed the look on your face when you saw the new car. I am sure you wondered if I used some of your money to buy that one."

"This is ridiculous! What is with you? I don't recognise you anymore." Nathan looked at his friend intently. "I couldn't care less about where you put the money. All I'm concerned about is that you are fine and you've not gotten yourself into some shithole."

"Don't bother about it. I am fine," Albert answered, without looking at Nathan.

"Then good. That's the end of that conversation. Can we please relax and enjoy the time here?" Nathan requested, putting up a funny expression that you bring out only with a few close ones, without worrying about being judged.

"Fine."

"Come, let's join the rest."

"You carry on. I will be there in a moment." Albert nodded to Nathan, and the latter walked away to join the ladies.

Albert looked at Nathan intently as he was walking away. What he had hoped for hadn't materialised, making him more angry than disappointed.

"Son of a bitch!" he muttered under his breath, still staring at Nathan.

Albert had always been ambitious. He'd always wanted all the luxuries in life that money could buy. Most of his friends came from well-to-do families. That's because he consciously chose such friends.

Albert's job as an investment banker gave him some respite. He was good at it, and the incentives in his job were high. Somehow, once he was thirty years old, he felt he had underachieved against the steep targets he'd set for himself.

Six months ago, an opportunity presented itself. Albert came across a lucrative scheme that seemed genuine. There were examples of how people trebled their investments and quit their regular jobs. It, however, required a substantial initial investment. He approached Nathan, asking for that money urgently and promising to return it within a year.

While Nathan insisted on knowing the reason, Albert refrained from disclosing anything, worried he'd be caught if he lied.

Greed blinding his judgement, Albert hadn't realised that if something seems too good to be true, it is usually that - too good to be true. It was indeed a scam, and he lost all the money. All those who flaunted sky-rocketing growths hitherto weren't to be found. Along with the others who lost money, Albert had approached the cops. The search continued to find those who had fled with the money.

Albert's confidence had taken a beating since that incident. He'd grown weak and paranoid, growing suspicious even of Martha cheating on him, which had made their relationship brittle. A couple of times he had spied on her, only to know that she was always on the right. Tired of this, she had taken him to a relationship counsellor. With effort, their relationship was getting back on track. At the same time,

Albert's concern about returning money to his friend worried him. He'd not trusted his wife enough to let her know about this loss of his, so it was a secret that was killing him from within.

He avoided all gatherings in which he knew Nathan would be present. He was too scared of taking Nathan's calls, assuming he would ask about the money. When Nathan called him last week, Albert knew he could not keep missing his calls anymore and that it was only a matter of time before Nathan would grow suspicious.

Albert then gave it some detailed thought. He knew that Nathan was blessed with wealth. What if he approached Nathan in a weak moment? Nathan might forgo that money he'd lent and tell Albert he needn't worry about it. That was the sole reason he'd returned Nathan's call, and he was presented with the chance to meet his old friend at the Villa. Albert jumped at it and suggested meeting up a day earlier before others started trickling in to make such a discussion possible.

Unfortunately for him, Nathan had no plans to let go of the money. He expected Albert to return it, which would surely not happen. Albert was now desperate. He wanted to explore ways to escape this mess, even if those methods were questionable.

****

While Nathan was walking back to the ladies, Gwen excused herself to use the washroom, and Kory got a phone call and stepped out of the hall to receive it.

Nathan joined Martha. "Two of them just left when they saw me coming."

"The effect you have on women," Martha quipped.

"Shut up, Martha." He smiled, which was not returned.

She looked at her husband, still sitting at the other end, sipping his beer. "Looks like you and Albert were catching up on a lot of serious stuff."

"Hmmm...nothing out of the ordinary."

"He is lost in deep thought."

"Maybe he has some stuff from work on his mind."

Martha's voice grew anxious by the second. "He wasn't happy as his annual bonus was way below his expectations. He had promised me the car and loaned the remainder against my suggestion."

"Oh, that's.."

She was now whispering. "He already has a lot on his mind, Nathan."

"What do you mean?"

"I hope you didn't say anything that will put him under more stress." Martha's voice trembled, and she looked at Kory standing outside the hall. She glanced once towards the washroom to confirm that Gwen hadn't returned.

"Oh god! You are talking about your.."

"Yes! Please don't pretend."

"No! You listen, Martha. We haven't spoken about it since that incident. I have not forgiven you. Yet, I promised you that I'll keep it a secret. So, I will stick to it, no matter what happens. But that is contingent on you sticking to your side of the promise. Else, the deal is off."

"Okay..." She seemed slightly relieved.

"You have no idea how difficult it is to hide something like this from..."

"You have to, Nathan!" Martha insisted. Kory was almost done with her call and was walking back.

Nathan just looked at Martha and nodded.

"Why is everyone pairing up and talking secretly?" Kory complained loudly.

That made both Martha and Albert tense, and though they were seated at a distance, their eyes met, and both looked away immediately, worried if Nathan had betrayed their secret.

****

Grayson Villa, last February

"Chef Harrison!"

"How is Master Nathan doing?" the chef replied. Nathan could almost sense the elderly chef's smile at the other end of the phone.

"Good! Can do better with your stuffed crab, though."

"I would love to prepare it and send it across. It may take at least a few hours to reach you, even if I request the best chauffeurs to deliver it to your place."

"But Chef, the whole taste is in..."

"..having it fresh and hot, just out of the oven," Chef Harrison concluded it for him, and both men laughed at that.

"Let me make it easy for you then, Chef."

"Pray tell me how. Do you think I should

relocate to Mr Matthew's residence for a few days so that I can prepare all your favourites till your appetite is satiated?" Chef Harrison was employed since the resort was constructed and had been loyal to the Grayson family. He loved pleasing the little kid, Nathan, with his culinary abilities, for he was quite fond of him. Even after years, Harrison didn't mind going out of his way to please Nathan's palate.

"You know what? That's one excellent idea. But yes, Father would say things considering it is the holiday season and the resort is fully occupied. That is surely an idea to explore some other day."

"Right, but how do we address your crab-craving presently?"

"How much time to prepare it, Chef?"

"Why, it would take me hardly half an hour."

"Then I shall be there by then."

"As in? Are you travelling to this place?"

"Yes, I am on my way. Will be there in half an hour."

"That is great to hear. I will look forward to improving the dish than the last time."

"You know you don't have to do that. You manage to make it perfect every damn time!"

The coy chef always had trouble receiving praise. "Well, let me get started then." He hung up.

Nathan's meeting with one of his father's clients at Palm Beach had ended sooner than he'd expected, giving him some time to visit their resort attached to Grayson Villa on his way back home, with a slight detour.

On reaching the resort, he entered the kitchen and hugged Chef Harrison from behind, as he had done since his younger years. As usual, it raised many eyebrows in the kitchen and drew the usual timid expression from the Chef.

"This is a pleasant surprise, though, Master Nathan. It's been some time since you visited." He looked at the oven. "Give me fifteen more minutes, and I will be done."

"I am in no hurry, Chef. Take your time."

"Let me ask the helpers to set up a table for you in the Grayson Villa."

"What's the point in opening up the Villa just for me? I will have it here at the restaurant."

Harrison was genuinely confused. "I thought you would join your friends for lunch, wouldn't you?"

"Sorry?"

"Mr and Mrs Tait are staying at the guest house. I thought you wanted to join them for lunch."

"Albert and Martha are here? I...no, I wasn't aware."

"Eh...I am sure you must have forgotten amidst all your business travels. I distinctly remember Mrs Tait telling me she'd informed you of their arrival. They've been regulars for a couple of months, no?" Chef Harrison was still smiling, whereas Nathan seemed a bit distant.

"I will beat the bugger up," said Nathan and dialled Albert's number. It was disconnected the first time. He tried again.

Albert received it and quickly muttered, "I am at a client lunch, Nathan. I will have to call you back." He cut the call before Nathan could utter a word.

"What the hell!" Nathan said to himself.

Chef Harrison looked concerned. "Is all well, Master Nathan?"

"Hmmm...Chef, you mean Albert and Martha come to the restaurant for their meals?"

"Eh, no. I suggested that in one of their earlier visits. However, Mrs Tait requested to be served in the guest house. I've nominated one of the waiters to take care of that." He smiled.

"You met both of them, then?"

"Hmm...not actually. Mrs Tait comes down once in a while. I asked her if she and her husband would like to join a bonfire set up by a group arriving on their first day. She politely declined and mentioned that her husband had a mild fever. I checked if I should ask the doctor assigned to the resort to take a look, but she said it was something minor and she had given him the basic medicine. Oh yes, yesterday she confirmed that he was doing well." By the end of the sentence, Chef Harrison figured that something was amiss.

He looked at Nathan. "Did I do something wrong? Should I have checked with you about their visit?"

"Not at all, Chef. You did the right thing. Let me come back in a moment after meeting them, okay? I am sure the lunch would be ready by then?"

"Oh yes, yes. Do you want me or...someone to accompany you?"

"What for?"

"Ahem...nothing. Let me get back to the crab then." He smiled, wearing his professional mask, and left Nathan alone.

There was a small gate connecting the resort and the Grayson Villa. Nathan took that, trying not to make a lot of noise. He came to the play area and found no one. It was the same with the bar, the pool, and the gym. He cursed himself for not asking anyone which one of the eighteen rooms Albert and Martha were occupying, but then decided that they might not be aware.

He needn't have bothered as he saw someone almost jump out of a room quickly. It was a man only in his briefs sporting a visible boner. As Nathan had suspected, he didn't know who this man was. The latter didn't look in Nathan's direction and went to the door opposite the room he'd emerged from, laughing his heart out.

He was quickly followed by Martha, equally joyous, covering her bust with a pillow, and the only garment she wore was a pair of panties. "Come back, you bastard!" she shouted, and sensed someone's presence before she could enter through the opposite door. She turned to find Nathan standing in the corridor, looking livid.

"Oh... Nathan... I was..." Martha was shocked at finding him there.

The other man came out of the room to look at Nathan. Unaware of who the latter was, he said, "Some privacy, please?" and shrugged at Nathan.

"Quiet, Shawn," Martha muttered.

"What? Should I pass on some tip so he gets out of here?" Shawn whispered to Martha, but Nathan could hear it quite well.

"Shut up, Shawn!" Martha looked at Shawn with purpose. She then turned timidly to Nathan and said, "Nathan, I...can explain."

"Explain," Nathan managed to say.

"Bro...what's the problem?" Shawn attempted, disclosing that he was dumber than he looked.

"Shut the fuck up!" Nathan's voice echoed throughout the corridor. This made Martha stand at attention, and the gravity of the situation crept up her spine.

"Shawn, go to the room. Now," Martha said it loud and clear, and he obeyed.

"I...am sorry." She wasn't able to look Nathan in the eyes.

"Get dressed and meet me at the bar," he said and went away.

Martha took some time to join Nathan at the bar, and he, too, had enough time to cool his nerves.

Martha entered, much more presentable than earlier. "Nathan...I.."

"What is wrong with you!?"

"I am sorry."

"No! You are not. Albert works his ass off to keep the family together. This is what you do behind his back?"

"It was a one-time thing, I swear."

"Don't lie!" His tone was harsh. "Should I call Albert and check if you two have visited Grayson Villa frequently for the past few months?"

She knew she was caught. Taking some time, she faintly shook her head.

"How could you use my father's guest house for all this?" he said, hurt.

"I...you'd once told the Chef in our presence that we could use it anytime. I just... thought it was a safe place."

"This is unbelievable! I don't know how Albert would react if he learned about..."

"No... no! Please. Nathan, don't do anything like that."

"What do you mean? You are openly having an affair, cheating on my best friend. You expect me to forget this and let you..."

"No, I promise. I will end it immediately. Please don't say anything about this to Albert. He will break. He will be devastated. I love him, I really do," she pleaded.

Nathan knew Albert too well. He had built his life around Martha, and she was right that it would kill him.

"Whatever it is, just end this right now and get out of here." He left her abruptly.

****

Returning to the present, Martha moved her drink to the other hand, as it was getting slippery with sweat.

Little did Nathan know that Martha had continued her infidelity. Shawn, an intern at her office, was too much of a temptation to let go without indulging. She grew more demanding with Shawn as Albert lost interest in her.

She grew more audacious with the affair, to an extent that drew suspicion from Albert. It was then that she took him to a counsellor, and the harsh reality was revealed to her that her husband was looking down the barrel emotionally. Something snapped in her, and she immediately called it quits with Shawn. She dedicated herself to making her husband get back to his normal self. However, the guilt of cheating on him had stayed with her, gawking at her now and then.

For some reason, Martha had observed that Albert was avoiding Nathan, which worked well for her. While she'd earlier doubted so, she knew Nathan hadn't revealed anything to her husband. She was scared that if Nathan decided to talk someday, it would be the end of the road with Albert. Taking care of Albert in these past months had given her a purpose in life and this relationship. She loved her husband too dearly to let anyone interfere and spoil it - no matter the cost.

****

It was an hour past dinner. They were spending time by the poolside.

Nathan loved spending time in the water and was the first to enter the pool. It was cold in the night, and it was a heated pool. Closing his eyes, he was trying to wash away all the intense emotions of the day. It was indeed helping him.

Kory was next to jump into the pool in her two-piece bikini, splashing water over Nathan and breaking his tranquillity.

"Kory!" he screamed, mocking anger.

"Oops, did I do it again?" she mimicked in a lusty voice, blinking her eyelids.

"I will kill you!" Nathan chased her in the water, but Kory was a more expert swimmer and escaped from him quickly.

"Old duck," she teased him when she was far away.

Martha joined them by the pool and said, "Gee! I thought he was hardly a year older than you."

"I am in my twenties, and he's entered his thirties. That's a hell of a lot of a difference."

"Ouch!" Martha laughed, looking at Nathan and jumped into the pool in her one-piece swimsuit. Unlike the other two, she was elegant in her strokes and hardly fluttered the water as she swam by.

Nathan said appreciatively, "Always the swan."

Martha started with butterfly strokes and shouted, "This is the best pool I know of!"

"True that," shouted Albert, sitting on the side with his bottle half-finished.

"Says the one who never gets into the water," mocked Kory.

"Say whatever you want to; water is surely not my element," he said, looking at Gwen.

"Why aren't you joining us, Gwen?" Martha gestured for her to come into the pool.

"No. Not today." She had to say it aloud, as there was a lot of noise because of all the splashing.

"Why's that?" inquired Nathan.

"She forgot her thingies at home!" shouted Kory, teasing.

"Bitch!" Gwen shouted back.

"Big deal! Why don't you jump in any way in your inner-wear? It's just us." Nathan shrugged.

Gwen was shaking her head, almost embarrassed.

"Woah! Unless you aren't wearing any!" Martha and Kory laughed out loud.

Albert looked at Gwen. "Don't listen to them, Gwen. Just strip and get in. I am sure neither of the boys here would mind. What is nudity, after all, but natural?" he said, trying to sound philosophical.

Gwen poked him with the pointed end of the umbrella next to her, inviting more laughter from those in the pool.

Nathan thought of something. "Listen, Gwen. I think you still have some of your clothes in the room you used to occupy."

"Woah!" the other two girls shouted and hooted as Albert avoided looking at Gwen and Nathan.

"Come on, morons! He's engaged to be married," Gwen argued.

"So what?" Kory shouted back, showing her tongue and trying to look lusty, which was surely not working out.

"Shut up, you guys!" Nathan, too, was blushing.

"I searched earlier. The wardrobe must've been emptied." Gwen made a sheepish face so that he didn't register any disappointment that may have lingered in her.

"Ah! The staff must have moved it to the other rooms. Some of your stuff is still lying in my spare wardrobe. You know my room, right?"

"Of course, she knows your room!" Martha chimed in as she and Kory high-fived.

"Horny bitches," Gwen said and walked away.

"Hey, I heard that. It's my wife you speak of," Albert mocked anger.

"Then take her to a room and do something about it!" Gwen shot back, and she'd got him. He laughed heartily, saying that he would do that in some time.

Kory wasn't one to be left behind. "What about me, sweetie?"

"I am not worried about you. You don't travel anywhere without your vibrator," Gwen silenced her, too.

"Touché," said Nathan.

Within minutes, Albert, too, didn't want to be left behind, and got a few swimming pool balls to throw at Nathan and jumped into the pool fully dressed.

"You are nuts, Albert!" Nathan said, continuing to float in the water.

"Let's play ball!" Albert shouted.

"Fine! Kory and I will take on you both!" Nathan challenged.

"Whatever." Kory didn't seem least bit interested.

Once Martha began with her provocative comments, Kory got into her competitive mode, and played wild to win.

At the end of fifteen minutes, all of them were tired. Kory wasn't. She was all energised and gave back Martha her comments. After getting bored of targeting Martha, she also took her turn to strip Albert, though not literally. They couldn't get back at her, for she never gave them a chance to win back in the game.

"Where is Gwen?" Nathan asked once they started missing her.

"And here I thought she would need less time to return wearing fewer clothes," Kory complained, and Albert giggled.

Kory eyed Martha, lifting her eyebrows. Martha was too oblivious to Albert's current behaviour. She was just happy that he was enjoying himself and shrugged at Kory.

Amidst all this, Gwen entered without making any noise. Kory was the first one to notice her. "Hot! Wow, babe, you must thank your stars that I am not bisexual."

Gwen let the thin layer of cloth fall from her perfectly toned body to reveal a very sensual two-piece bikini that did very little to hide her modesty.

"You won't know unless you try," Gwen winked at Kory, again managing to shut her up.

"We were missing you, Gwen. Kory was going with all guns blazing at us." Martha pouted her full lips.

Gwen stood at the edge of the pool at its deepest point and dove into it like a professional.

"That bikini looks new," Nathan tried to have a neutral conversation.

She smiled and swam by him.

The married couple was no longer interested in the remaining three. They had gotten touchy-feely and were panting heavily.

"Want to get out of here?" Martha asked him, feeling him up under the water.

"Yes, let's do that, dear." He planted a quick kiss on her lips.

Martha was the first one to get out of the water. She offered him her hand as support to come out, but he hesitated.

"Can you get me a towel, dear?"

"Look who's shy!" Kory teased him.

Albert had wanted to sneak out without getting their attention but was now caught. "What does a poor guy do in such a state?" he shrugged.

"You're scared that we will know something we shouldn't?" Gwen, too, pitched in.

"Leave them alone," Nathan tried to intervene.

"You don't have to keep playing the referee always, Nathan," Gwen tweaked her nose, looked at him, and then returned to Albert.

"Darling, I am getting cold. Will you please?" Martha nudged.

Albert saw she had no towel with her and looked at her naughty eyes as she held his hand and helped him out of the water in his current state.

"Woah! Nice, Albert," Gwen shouted.

Kory lustfully said, "There's nothing to be ashamed about at all."

"You guys are disgusting," Nathan addressed all of them as Albert looked at him, put both his hands up as if surrendering to his wife, and shrugged while leaving the pool.

Kory then said, "I, too, am tired. I will retire for the night."

Nathan wanted to continue for some more time but felt that it would be awkward and announced, "I am leaving as well."

"Gwen, you?"

Gwen said, "I will stay for some time. I just came to the pool."

"Ah, yes!" acknowledged Kory. "I will hang around for some more time, then."

"Goodnight, folks. See you in the morning," Nathan said, and left the pool in a slight hurry.

****

Once he reached his room, he remembered the conversation with Claire over the phone. It seemed like a distant memory. That's what a good swim usually did to him. He glanced at his phone in the room to see if there were any messages or calls from Claire. There weren't any. He wasn't completely disappointed. He knew Claire well and was sure she would be reflecting on the same. He hoped tomorrow might be a better day for a chat with her.

He heard some music from the window. He could see the swimming pool from up there as he approached it. He saw Kory stepping out of the pool, playing music and dancing without a care in the world. He smiled at her light-heartedness; somewhere, he envied that as well. He could remember that's exactly how he was a few years before. Time had changed him, or he had let time change him.

In his deep thought, he tried to find Gwen in the pool. He saw that she was looking right at him. Due to the dull light and the distance, he couldn't be sure though. His first thought was to duck as if he was doing something creepy. But then he stood his ground and casually moved away from the window.

He changed into his nightclothes and got to the huge round bed. It surprised him that though he was mentally and physically tired, he felt wide awake. This happened to him a few times a month. His family doctor had advised him to try a few pills to put him to sleep. Nathan had always refrained from consuming them, but now he thought he should try it.

He put his tired back on the bed and felt the pain and the relief.

****

A gentle knock at the door woke up Nathan. He hated being disturbed in the middle of his sleep, which usually resulted in a headache. He saw the wall clock; it was the middle of the night. He always slept with lights on. It was a habit since childhood that he'd never been able to get rid of.

He dreaded whether Martha or Albert wanted to have one more conversation about their secrets. He sincerely wished that wasn't the case.

He got up and went to the door. On opening it, he saw there was no one outside. He stepped out to see that the well-lit corridor was empty as well. He wondered momentarily if he had just dreamt the whole knocking episode. Then again, he heard the knock and his name being called out.

"Oh, okay." It was a knock on the other door, the internal one connecting the next room, and he could hear Gwen's faint voice.

They had all occupied three rooms in the guest house. Kory and Gwen had occupied the one adjacent to Nathan's room, and the married couple occupied the opposite room.

Nathan opened the door. "Hey Gwen, you are up late." He rubbed his eyes.

"I am so sorry to bother you in the middle of the night. Can I have the spare keys to the fourth room?"

"What happened? All okay?"

"Yes. Just that Kory is.." She looked at her friend in her deep sleep, and Nathan followed the gaze. Kory was snoring pretty loudly.

He couldn't keep himself from laughing.

"That's mean of you!" Gwen slapped his arm.

"Says the lady who wants to escape to another room because of the snoring."

"It's actually my fault. I should have remembered that she snores more when very tired."

"I thought she needed your company."

"Yes. She's scared of sleeping alone. But once she is asleep, she wakes up only in the morning. That's not an issue."

"Okay, you...hmm...come on in then." He moved aside, letting her in.

"Again, I am so...so...sorry to disturb you."

"Hey, come on. Don't bother."

"I see you still sleep with the lights on. I could see the faint light from the other side of the door."

"Yes. You know that I cannot sleep otherwise."

"Wait! Please tell me that you don't have a headache!"

"Well..," he smiled and shrugged.

"Oh..," she cringed.

"It's fine, Gwen. Really." He was searching amongst the keys, shaking his head. "Argh! They all look the same!"

"Hmm... they aren't labelled. We can try a couple of them." She opined without much conviction.

"Well..." He was not sure.

"I will get my luggage bags along so that..."

"What? No! Just...forget it, Gwen. You sleep in my room."

Gwen felt awkward, and it was visible on her face. "Or it's okay. I mean, I can try to get used to Kory's..."

"Relax, Gwen. You can sleep in my bed. I will take the couch."

"No, I cannot take your bed away from you now."

"It's no big deal."

"No. I am calling for the couch first."

"Gwen, please. It's already quite late in the night."

"Yes, and we should get to sleep," she said, moving towards the couch. Seeing this, he dashed to the couch and they fell on it together.

"I claim the couch. I reached first," said Gwen.

"Says who? There's no one tracking that race. It is your word against mine."

"Please, Nathan. You don't have to be a gentleman always."

"Oh! Come on! I cannot give the couch to my guest."

She opened her mouth to say something but visibly shook her head.

"What?" asked Nathan.

"Nothing." She looked away.

"Tell me what it is, Gwen."

"It's odd when you address me as your guest." She tried a quick smile with some difficulty.

"Not fair. You know I didn't mean to hurt you by saying that."

"I know...okay...I know you too well to assume you would say that to hurt me, Nathan. But it's just..."

"I understand, and I am sorry. Fine, hereby I declare that the couch is yours."

"Yay!" She raised both her hands in triumph.

"Good, now let's get to sleep."

"Yes, I will just be back in a moment." She rushed to Kory's room from the connecting door as Nathan's gaze followed her keenly. "Don't bother. You go to sleep," she said.

Gwen returned with a small box.

"Are you serious?" said Nathan, lifting his arms in the air.

"What? A girl's got to eat. Swimming makes me hungry." She didn't understand his hatred towards a box full of biscuits.

"Do you still carry your box of biscuits every place you travel?"

"Why, of course! What if I feel hungry in the middle of the night? I cannot expect your Chef Harrison to wake up from his slumber and present to me a mouth-watering dish." She said as a matter of fact.

Even after years of knowing Gwen, this fact about her tickled his funny bones. He looked at her absently while she finished a biscuit and smiled at him.

She seemed to consider for a moment and said, "Nate, Kory's snoring was just one reason. We didn't talk about me overhearing a part of your conversation with Claire. I thought of speaking about it without anyone around."

Nathan laid back on the pillow for support. "There's nothing to talk about, Gwen."

Gwen shook her head. "Is she upset that I came? I think I shouldn't have."

"That's not fair. It is not your fault, and please don't blame yourself for her unreasonable outburst."

"You two are engaged. Of course, it is fair for her to think about what's best for you."

"That doesn't give her the right to assume wrong things, draw incorrect conclusions and insult people close to me."

"Ah! Looks like you stood up for me," Gwen smiled.

"Please!"

"I have never met her. You didn't invite me to the engagement."

"It would have been.."

"Very awkward, indeed. I hope to meet her someday when things settle."

"Only if things go well."

"Hey, cheer up. It'll all be forgotten in a couple of days." Gwen took another bite from the biscuit.

"Okay, fine, give me some," he said.

"Hmm..?"

"The biscuits, Gwen. Pass some to me."

"Look at you! You laughed at me hysterically just a while ago. You hypocrite!" She threw a biscuit at him, which he missed, and it fell on his bed. He quickly put it in his mouth.

"Who am I to deny when a biscuit finds a hungry mouth?" he said, trying to laugh with the biscuit in his mouth.

"Thank god I didn't throw pistachios at you," she said, sounding relieved.

"What? Are you saying..."

"Of course, Nathan!" She was irritated that he hadn't understood that much about her. "What's the fun with only having sweet biscuits when healthy salted pistachios can also be carried? I've told you before that when I get bored of..."

"..biscuits, you dig up your reserve of salted pistachios," he completed it for her.

"Attaboy! There you go. You still remember it," she said, throwing a couple of nuts in her mouth.

He was staring at her.

"What?"

"What? Aren't you going to pass them to me?"

"Of course not! I have only half the usual reserve and..." Before she could complete her sentence, he'd jumped in a flash and landed on the couch, lunging at the small box she'd kept hidden from him earlier.

"No, Nathan!" she tried to defend her small box.

"Yes, Gwen!" He held one of her hands in his vicious grip and attacked the box with the other. After a minor struggle, he got hold of it.

"This is not fair. You used brute force on a damsel," she complained and punched his arm.

"Ouch! That hurt."

"Good, it was meant to."

He ate a couple of pistachios. "Hmm... they're always so fresh and crunchy. Where do you get these from?"

"Get lost!" she mocked anger and looked away.

"Why, thank you. Keep looking away, and I will finish off the entire..."

"No!" she got back at him, and they laughed like they used to before. While it felt all normal when they were in the middle of the harmless fight, he felt awkward that he'd almost pulled her onto his lap.

She'd taken hold of the box of pistachios and looked at him. "What?"

"Nothing." She was dangerously close to him, but seeing that she didn't make a big deal out of it, he didn't point it out to make her feel conscious.

"How's your headache now?"

"Actually, somewhat better considering my focus was shifted onto other things," he chuckled.

"Here, let me massage it for you." She moved her hands to his forehead.

"Hey, that's fine." He moved his head away in reflex.

"Nathan! Relax." She shook her head and looked at him to indicate that he needn't make a fuss.

He didn't resist any further as she began to massage his forehead. While it was indeed helping him feel relaxed, he could tell that his body was reacting to her physical touch.

"Is the pressure okay?" she asked.

"Huh?"

She raised her eyebrows without repeating her question.

"Yes. The pressure is just fine." He closed his eyes.

"It is a point in your neck from where this pain stems," she observed.

"Wow, looks like someone has done her research," Nathan tried to lighten the mood.

"You are right. I took an acupressure treatment lately, and that lady explained it to me. She was quite good. Let me try this." She moved her hands to his neck.

She moved on his lap to adjust her grip, and he could not control his bodily reactions. She too could feel it, but smiled, ignoring it, and continued massaging his neck.

"Yes, there Gwen! I can feel it in my head when you are massaging that point in my neck."

"See, I told you," she whispered in his ears, which added to his unease.

"Ah..," he moaned out of relief.

"Better?" She adjusted her hands to cup his face.

He opened his eyes and nodded, looking deep into her eyes. He was slightly breathless by now, and his eyes travelled between her lips and eyes.

"What happened, Nathan?" She ran her tongue over her lips.

He pulled her face to his and began to kiss her. She responded to him without a second invitation, and they used their tongues to pleasure each other.

In a moment, he had undressed her, and she had done the same to him as they made passionate love on the couch. However, Nathan seemed to be the more desperate and wild of the two.

"Easy, Nathan. Ah!" She didn't care if Kory could hear them.

He hardly spoke a word as he continued feeding his primal instincts.

"Nathan, relax. I am not going anywhere. You... ah!"

She realised the only way from here was to meet his tempo; hence, she reciprocated the same hunger he displayed.

Nathan knew he wouldn't last long. All the same, he didn't seem to care about that anyway.

Nathan felt at peace in his post-coital bliss, leaving behind all the tension of the past day. He felt drowsy; he continued to lay naked on Gwen and drifted to sleep, with her patting his head gently.

****

Highlands, Florida

Claire had escaped to her father's car to find some privacy and locked herself inside. She cried for a good part of the night. She was in terrible shape. Her hair was dishevelled due to her pulling it at times. Her eyes were tired, moist, and red and seemed to be lodged deep into their sockets.

Though it was now the middle of the night, she could not think of sleeping. She felt she was very close to making Henry's mind change, and it all slipped out of her hands. Her thoughts returned to unearth ways of getting back Henry in her life from this point. Of course, it meant something out of the ordinary had to transpire.

"What's happening to me?" She felt frightened and continued to cry, but her tears had dried up. She took a huge gulp from whatever was left in the bottle of vodka, finishing it.

The sane part of her mind was still shouting at her, asking her to sleep, and it would all be fine in the morning. Henry was never hers and never will be. Meanwhile, Nathan would wait for her. Throughout their relationship, no matter what little banter they had, Nathan would call up in the morning, irrespective of whose fault it was, and by the end of the conversation, all would be sorted.

That thought and her drunken state gave her some solace. She rested her head on the seat, hoping that morning would bring relief.

****

Grayson Villa

There was a loud bang at the door. Nathan was irritated as to who that was. As he came to his senses, something soft moved beneath his body, and in the next moment, he remembered all that happened last night.

"Look at you two lusty dogs!" It was Kory standing at the interconnecting door.

"Oh god! Oh god!" Nathan said, not caring about his nudity in front of Kory.

Gwen was awake by now and moved her hand into his hair. He softly pushed it away.

Then she looked at Kory. "Some privacy, please?"

"Exactly! Some privacy, please! Do it behind closed doors! God!" She pulled the door shut on them.

Nathan sat with his face covered in his hands, mumbling things. Gwen crawled to him, rubbed his shoulder and said, "Relax, it's fine."

"No. It's not fine, Gwen," he spoke, his fingers still covering his face.

She said nothing, rubbed his shoulders with both hands and rested her head on them.

"I am engaged to Claire. I cannot be cheating on her. I am such an evil person."

Gwen took the situation under control and moved to face him. "Listen, Nathan. You have not committed anything evil, okay? You have to get yourself together."

He was cringing his face with some emotional pain that she could not comprehend.

"This should not have happened, Gwen." He looked at her in the eyes. "I am sorry. I feel like I took advantage of you and..."

"Nathan, it was mutual, and no, you didn't take advantage of me, okay?" She tried to reason, but he was not looking at her.

"Look at me, Nathan." She pulled his face in her hands and made him look into her eyes. "It is your decision, Nathan. We either continue from where we left or...or think if this really should not have happened."

"Gwen."

"Yes, Nathan. We have to decide if what happened last night was our beautiful relationship flowering again or if it was just a mistake."

"It was a mistake, Gwen. Please." He was in pain.

"Okay, okay." She tried to calm him down again. "Then so be it, Nathan. We have to move on from here instead of writhing in pain, no? What good has guilt done anyone? We had a great time last night. Let's move on from here towards different paths. It doesn't have to be so tragic, right? We are consenting adults, and at that moment, we needed a release from all the pent-up frustration, and we enabled that for each other. Moreover, we'd not had break-up sex the last time," she said, trying to lighten the situation.

"I am sorry. I..."

"No! This is where it ends. We are not going to talk about it again. I don't want us to be awkward like our fathers, with cold war between them all these months. It had ended badly the last time, and I will not let it end the same way. You hear me?"

He nodded, trying to contain his emotions. He pulled her for a hug, and they held each other tight for some time.

"Ahem... Nathan."

"Hmm?"

"You do realise that we are completely naked, and your tool is now sort of poking my privates."

He released her immediately and backed away. "Sorry, sorry!"

"Gotcha!" She fell on the bed and laughed her heart out. Embarrassed, he, too, joined her laughter with a relieved smile.

Nathan spent much time in the shower, splashing the shower water on his face. To him, it was a sort of metaphoric cleansing of his sins. It also was to wake all parts of his brain up truly. After that, he spent time in front of the bathroom mirror, shaking his head continuously and slapping himself more than just playfully. "Okay, all will be fine. I've got this under control. Today is when it all ends."

****

Highlands, Florida

Due to the unsophisticated sleeping conditions in the car, Claire woke up within a few hours of her sleep. Her head still throbbed, and glimpses of her dream flashed before her eyes. She stared at her face in the mirror in a dark room, which she recognised as Grayson Villa, with an evil smirk occupying it. The next flash showed Nathan's dead body at her feet and a sense of satisfaction in her chest. She snapped out of her thoughts, cringing. She exited the car to freshen up and think clearly and made herself presentable so she wouldn't invite uncomfortable questions. Then, she went into the house where everyone was present.

She didn't want to think about Henry for the time being or about Nathan. She decided to eat something hot, which always helps an exhausted mind. She spoke to a few relatives who had just arrived and tried to be normal.

While she wasn't sure what she would say to Nathan after yesterday's unwarranted debate, she thought it was only right to call him and say a few words so he wouldn't get too hassled. She tried his number, but there was no response. She thought maybe it was a tad early for him, though she was somewhat relieved that she could postpone talking to him. Her inner voice mocked her, "Of course it's early for him. Won't he be exhausted after screwing Gwen all night?" Another thought popped in her mind, "Don't you remember relieving him from this world?" She ignored these strange thoughts and decided to take a small walk in the suburbs.

****

Grayson Villa

"Way to go, partner!" Albert welcomed Nathan with a high-five at the breakfast table. It was almost brunch time.

"Albert!" Gwen stared at him as if he'd betrayed a commitment.

"What? I didn't say anything about it in particular."

Kory and Martha giggled, not wanting to push it any further.

Nathan did not reply and got busy serving himself for a big breakfast. He observed that things were very quiet at the table, with people only talking in stolen glances.

"Fine, guys! Gwen and I slept together last night, okay? And it's not going to happen again. Can we all please be mature about it and move on?"

"Oh! Not going to happen again?" Kory seemed disappointed.

"No!" Nathan looked her in the eye and responded.

"Any other questions on this? No? Good. Can we please eat in peace? Thanks!" Nathan was louder than usual, obviously trying to make a point.

"So, Nate..," Albert began.

"No, Albert. Throw out your bad jokes on the matter," Nathan warned.

"What the hell, man! I just wanted to say that your father had called to check on you. It seems he tried your number and there was no response. So, he just felt worried and wanted to check if all was well."

"What? My father had called?" Nathan was genuinely surprised. "As in? Mom called and said something on Dad's behalf?" he inquired again.

"No. Your father, Matthew Grayson, had called. They passed on the call from the resort to the guest house extension. He didn't say anything important. He just said he wanted to talk to you. When I said you must still be sleeping, he wanted you to return his call whenever possible," said Martha.

"Thanks, Martha." Nathan felt odd. His father never called this way. It was his mother who'd call in case there was some message that had to be passed on.

Post brunch, he returned to his room and looked at his cell phone. He saw that he'd missed two calls - one from Claire and one from his father.

He returned Claire's call first.

"Hey," she replied.

"Hey. You... okay?" he asked. With the background noise, he knew she was amidst others.

"Yes... I think so," she said non-committedly.

"Okay, good," he said, tongue-tied for the first time while speaking with her.

"We will talk when we meet."

That pricked Nathan, as he was expecting some form of apology because of her reaction the previous evening. Had this conversation happened without him sleeping with Gwen last night, his response might have differed. However, he was going soft on her presently.

"Sure," he replied. Claire was surprised with his lenient response. She'd thought he would argue with her, probably making her disconnect the call. However, Nathan's mind had moved on to his father. He wanted to end this fruitless conversation so that he could speak to his father and understand if there was some problem.

Someone asked Claire to pass on a bag in the background. "You seem busy," he said.

"Yes, sort of."

"Okay. Call me when you can speak then."

"Hmm..," she said and disconnected the call. She was surprised that Nathan seemed detached. She was expecting him to push for a compromise. Nevertheless, she was in the midst of relatives demanding her attention. Her mind moved away from Nathan for the time being.

Nathan immediately dialled his father's number.

"Hello." His father had received his call before the second ring, which again was unusual.

"Hi, Dad. You called?"

"Yes, I generally just...you are okay?" asked Matthew Grayson.

"Of course, Dad. I am doing fine. Is all well with you?" Nathan probed.

His father's conversations with Nathan were always crisp and concise. That's one of the reasons why Nathan never felt as close to his father, while he shared a very different chemistry with his Uncle Titus. The latter had inherited the gift of the gab from old Ned, and it was easy to talk to his uncle about any topic under the sun.

"Yes, all good. See you after New Year's then." His father was about to disconnect.

"Dad, wait. You usually don't call to check on me. It's difficult to decipher through your limited expressions, and a conversation over the phone makes it impossible for me to understand anything. Can you tell me what is with you properly, please?"

"Eh... nothing... I..." Matthew was trying to search for words.

"Should I come down to New York?"

Matthew was tempted to say 'yes' but resisted the urge. "It's just stupid, Nathan." He tried to chuckle.

"That's okay. You are my father. You are allowed to talk stupid stuff with me."

"I...well...I had a bad dream...about you."

"Oh, okay. That explains it."

"Hence, just wanted to check if you are alright."

"That's very..," Nathan was tempted to say 'sweet' or 'cute' but refrained, saying instead,

"..nice of you, Dad. Don't worry so much about me."

"Hmmm..."

"How are things at your end, Dad? You said it was a formal vacation, though I will never understand how the words 'formal' and 'vacation' go hand in hand."

His father laughed, which Nathan wasn't prepared for.

"It seems better. Looks like there is a possibility that Jeffery may finally decide not to make my life hell."

It was a topic that Nathan had seen his father dodge over the past months. He was glad that he was now speaking about it.

"I...am sorry, Dad. It's all because of me."

His father did not reply immediately. "Initially, Nathan, I blamed you for all this."

That hurt Nathan, but he knew his father wasn't done.

"When things are looking down, it is easy to blame someone else. However, we cannot build a business empire solely on personal relationships. Somehow, I understood that over time, and I hope Jeffery also sees it that way. He needs to understand that I am not the only one to face a loss in business because of his indiscretions. I tried to tell him that yesterday. I think this time, he was more receptive. Else, let's see. We have to look at growing other businesses as well."

"Wow..." Nathan hadn't heard so many words from his father at once. This was new to him.

"What?"

"Nothing, Dad. Can we not look to partner with Uncle Titus on the vineyard piece? You know, maybe expand it in some manner?"

"Eh... I don't think Titus is worried much about my loss. His is an evergreen business. Doesn't matter if the world is going to hell, people will still buy wine."

Though Nathan wanted to disagree about Titus, he joined his father in hearty laughter about people buying wine even during a catastrophe.

"That reminds me. I hear Titus' grand collection of wine bottles is dispatched to all family members. We received ours this morning. I hope you got yours."

"Oh! I need to check, Dad."

"And Cassandra has sent across the cake to you. I guess it must be delivered today."

"Really? Mom kept her tradition of baking plum cake for me?"

"Eh... I have no idea what cake. She'd made people's lives difficult here to get the ingredients. She wasn't as worried about taking me to the health check-up at her father's hospital on time. So, I am sure she did bake them," Matthew snorted.

"What do the health check-up results suggest?"

"They have nothing new to say. Not sure why we pay for that."

"Last I knew, we don't pay a penny. Mom's name is good enough, at least in the Palm Beach branch."

"Yeah, yeah, I just meant that the results seem the same every time - Sugar and blood pressure are on the borderline. They made me wait a long time due to some additional tests, as they thought I was growing old. I repeatedly told Cassandra that this could wait until we returned to Palm Beach. But she wasn't one to listen. Kept insisting that the New York branch has more advanced technology and such bullshit."

"Hmmm. Hope there's nothing to be concerned about."

"Nothing. There are some medicines and health supplements that I am supposed to start taking to remain in sound health. I was unsettled when one of them was a sizeable container, and I tried to understand what that was from your mother. Soon, I realised the names meant nothing to me. They sounded like the names of Greek gods. We've shipped those along with the cake so you can take them back home."

"Yes. Sure, Dad. Makes sense."

"And...how's Claire?" Matthew asked hesitantly. He was not excited when his son announced their engagement the second time Matthew met her. Hence, he'd been a bit distant about her the whole time.

"She's doing okay, Dad."

"Hmm...enough for now. I need to get back."

Strangely, for a moment, Nathan felt like a little child again. He felt the need to hug his father like never before. He remembered hugging him often in his childhood. When Matthew came home from work, he would throw his tie on the table and lift Nathan to hug him tightly. Nathan used to wriggle and laugh while held in the air, carefree. He couldn't remember when and why they stopped doing that.

"Love you, Dad," Nathan said, perhaps for the first time in several years. He didn't expect his father to reply.

"Love you too, son," he said, to his son's surprise, and they bid goodbye.

****

Nathan wanted to stay alone for the rest of the day and declined his friends' invitation to join them for a game of squash. Albert was glad when Nathan declined, for he said it was easier for the four of them to play the game instead of wondering what the fifth one would do.

As the afternoon progressed to evening, he called up Amelia.

"Hey, bro! What's up?"

"Hey Amy, you busy?"

"Of course! But go on."

"Nothing. I just wanted to talk. I can speak later if you're in the middle of something."

"Hold on for a sec." There was loud background music. Clearly, she was at a gathering or a party.

Nathan could hear the noise reduce significantly, guessing that she'd moved to a quieter place.

"Phew! Tell me now. I've come to my room."

"Hey, sorry. Did I make you.."

"Save your niceties for others. What's up?"

"The usual."

"I know my brother well enough that he will call me when he feels sad."

"What? No!"

"Leave your ego aside while speaking to me."

"I just...felt like speaking to someone close."

"Awww.."

"..who will not make it awkward talking to me."

"Fine, fine. So, you and Claire fought."

"How the hell...she spoke to you?"

"Woah! Relax. No one spoke. It is just obvious."

"Shit! Am I that predictable?"

"To me? Yes."

"Hmmm...I don't know, Amy. Things are falling apart all of a sudden."

"What triggered the fight?"

"When I was speaking with her yesterday, she got pissed that Gwen's here as well."

"Huh...Gwen's at Grayson Villa?"

"Yes. Claire briefly referred to ending the engagement."

"That doesn't sound right. Claire seems too mature to say something like that."

"Exactly what I thought as well."

"Strange. Did you try speaking to her today?"

"Yes, I did. She was in the middle of many people and couldn't speak properly. So we decided to talk later."

"Hello! I was in the middle of people as well when you called. If you want to talk, you don't give such excuses."

"Now, don't make me feel more miserable, please."

"Okay, listen, bro. You chill for today. Let me think. If need be, I will speak to her."

"No. Don't do that. It will only make matters more complicated."

"I understand. I won't do anything before agreeing with you."

"Yes, please."

"For now, though, stay away from Gwen. Don't start something you will regret later."

"Hmm..," Nathan cringed, hiding it in his voice.

"Cheer up now. It's not your last day on Earth. Shit happens. You will deal with it. We will deal with it. Go swim or play something with the others."

"I will do that."

"You need me to come over?"

"Mad or what? No, I will manage. I just needed to chat. I am good now."

"Sure?"

"Yes, Amy."

"Okay, good. Catch you later then."

****

"Nathan!" Kory shouted, knocking on the door.

"Come in, Kory."

"You sure? Are you completely dressed this time?" she asked playfully and laughed.

"Get lost!"

"Okay, okay, relax. I am coming in," she said.

Kory wasn't done yet as she entered with her eyes closed.

"Should I open my eyes now, Nathan?"

He threw a pillow at her that caught her right on the nose, sending her back a step in shock.

"Haha!" Nathan sat laughing on his bed.

"You imbecile! I would have hit my head on the door now!" she said, fuming.

"Because the cotton pillow pushed you away? Right."

"Idiot! Anyway, your mother has couriered a lot of stuff from New York. Gwen tells me these are medical supplies for your father. Should I leave them here?"

"Sure. I will take them to the storeroom."

"If you want to get ready to join us, I can take this to the storeroom," Kory offered.

"That will really help. Are you guys done with the game?"

"Yes. Martha and I beat Gwen and Albert, playing the best of five. We were so tired that we freshened up at the bath right there."

"Right. I will see you in a bit. Thanks, Kory."

"No problem."

****

Nathan freshened up and joined the rest in the party hall.

"Even the cold bath isn't helping with the warm weather," Martha complained.

Albert looked at Nathan enter and mocked, "Finally, the princess arrives!" standing and applauding.

"Not fair, Nathan. You promise us a good time, call us early, and disappear into your room," complained Martha.

"Sorry, guys. I am here now."

"I've been waiting to ask you this since afternoon. Why the hell does this bottle of wine cost ten times more than the regular one?" Albert was curious.

"Ah! Uncle Titus' goods have arrived then?"

Albert was edgy. "I was asking something! Do they put some gold dust in it, eh?"

"It's vintage, Albert." Nathan took it in his hands. "Strange. I thought Uncle Titus was supposed to send two."

Gwen and Martha snickered and looked at Albert. He said, "I thought you wouldn't miss one of them, you know?" and seemed naturally stupid.

"Are you hiding one with you?" Nathan asked.

"Gwen wouldn't let me open it. She kept saying it was a family thing and I had to wait for you to do the honours. Utter rubbish that was," he complained.

"Thank you, Gwen."

He turned to Albert and said, "It is a weird family thing. My grandpa, Ned, used to send a bottle each to all close family members and ask them to open it up on Christmas Eve. It gave him a sense that all of us were together. The tradition has continued through Uncle Titus."

"Oh, man! So we don't get to open it till tomorrow?" Albert was disappointed.

"But then, Albert, you must note that I am Uncle Titus' favourite nephew."

"Hello! There aren't any other nephews!" Gwen interjected his melodrama, adjusting the cuff of her full-sleeved top, and Martha and Kory laughed at it. Albert was too absorbed in Nathan's monologue.

Nathan continued, ignoring Gwen. "As I was saying, I am his favourite nephew, and I requested him to make an exception for me, to which he obliged."

"Hence, he's sent you two bottles? One that we can open today?" Albert's eyes glimmered with childlike excitement.

"That is correct!"

"Can we do it now?" Albert was curious.

"Can you not wait, Albert? It's just wine," Martha retorted, giving him a subtle, stern stare.

"Hey! I was just checking."

"Of course, we can do it now," said Nathan.

"Can I open?"

"No way! Being born into the Grayson family allows certain privileges."

"Fine!" Albert said in a resigned manner.

"Really? We are using these glasses?" Gwen complained, referring to the ones lying around in the hall.

Kory and the couple looked at the two, unable to follow.

"Ah, of course!" Nathan acknowledged.

"Kory, mind helping me out with the storeroom keys?"

"Ah! The Grayson pedigree needs help from a mere mortal," she bowed to him as they laughed at her silly gesture.

Nathan entered the storeroom and tripped on the medicines that Kory had left right in the way before switching on the lights. He complained to her about it and moved it to a safe corner. Recollecting the conversation with his father, he looked closer at the big container to learn it was Thiopental. He smiled, thinking his father had alluded this to some Greek god's name.

Nathan carried an antique wooden box out of the storeroom, and Kory locked it on their way back.

Nathan then opened the box's lid, which contained four chalices.

"Wow! These look precious!" Martha shouted out.

"Yes, they are. They have a history. These are chalices from Rome," Nathan explained as the others marvelled at the intricate work on the silver chalices.

"Your grandfather indeed had great taste." Albert, too, was impressed.

"This wasn't his thing. Uncle Titus got these from Rome."

Nathan then popped open the bottle. It received a spontaneous cheer from the others, which seemed to be a very special moment.

Each one took a chalice except for Kory, who was a teetotaller.

"Can I get a chalice for myself from the storeroom? I can have some fruit juice as well, you know?" She felt left out.

"Since they arrived at Grayson Villa, these glasses have seen only wine and nothing else, Kory," Nathan said, changing his voice to sound like a historian, which didn't help her.

"I am sure your staff even washes these chalices in wine." She made a face, pulling another chair to sit at the table.

"You can hold mine if you want for some time," Martha offered.

"Tch tch! Don't spoil the mood now, Kory." Nathan finished filling all four chalices set on the tea table.

"Cheers, everyone!"

"Wait, I will get orange juice in a normal glass!" Kory stepped away and got a glass for herself.

The four chalices and a glass clinked, as the group said, "Cheers!"

After a sip, Martha closed her eyes and said, "Ummm...this is some fine wine. The taste lingers in my mouth and nostrils."

Albert was done in one swig. "Is it? I don't understand these intricacies."

"Albert! Where is your finesse?" Martha reprimanded in a whisper, and Albert was apologetic.

Soon, they were done with one serving, and Gwen served everyone across the tea table for the second time. While serving Martha, who was seated at the other end of the table, Gwen missed the chalice and spilt wine.

It made people's hearts skip a beat as they gasped. "Holy shit! What waste of precious elixir!" Albert shouted.

"Sorry!" Gwen looked at Nathan.

"Hey, relax. It's fine," he said, joining them in cleaning the part of the table.

"Can I lick it off the table instead?" asked Albert, quite keen.

"Albert!" Martha was disgusted.

"Ahem... of course, I am kidding, folks." He tried to make a bad comeback that didn't work, as everyone continued to laugh.

Kory added indifferently, "Albert is right. Don't understand all of your false pride."

Albert looked at her, and they exchanged a heartfelt nod.

"You are saying that because you don't even drink," Martha said.

Kory readily poured a sip of orange juice on her side of the table. In the same breath, she knelt to give it a lick. She winked at Martha and high-fived Albert. Immediately after, he cowered under his wife's glance.

Nathan looked at the clock. "Hey, Gwen. How come you've not made a hue and cry about dinner yet? It's well past your dinner time."

"Oh my! True. Can we get something from the resort kitchen?" she made a face, pleading.

Nathan went to the intercom and asked Chef Harrison's men to leave food at their dinner table.

Gwen announced, "Folks, I think we have just enough wine left for one last round." Looking at Nathan, she said, "Unless you want to leave some for others when they arrive?"

"We can finish. We will use the other bottle on Christmas Eve."

"Anyone wants to serve?" Gwen offered.

"I will!" Kory took the elegant-looking bottle from Gwen. "When will others start trickling in? I am bored with all of you already," she complained.

"Same here, Kory!" Martha repeated after her. Somewhere, it seemed less of a tease and more of a fact, which only Kory, who was completely sober, registered and chose to laugh off.

Albert finished his third serving of the drink quickly as well. He was careful not to burp aloud. "I think even I am feeling hungry. I can sense some discomfort in my stomach. Hope we get something soon from Doctor Harrison's kitchen."

"Chef Harrison!" they all corrected him.

"Fine!" he acknowledged.

As they chatted to pass the time, Martha said, "Even I am sensing some discomfort in my stomach. Darling, did we have something we weren't supposed to at lunch?"

"Yes. Each other." Kory said, and they all laughed aloud, including Martha.

It was a matter of moments as the food trolley pulled towards the table that Nathan reached out, holding his stomach in pain. He was alarmed, looking at Gwen.

"Gwen!" he shouted.

The rest of them, keenly looking at the kitchen staff bringing the food, turned to her to witness a horrid expression of pain on Gwen's face as she held the empty wine bottle and stared intently at it, terrified. She was perspiring and fell to the ground with a thud.

"Call the ambulance!" Nathan commanded the staff, and they acted swiftly with practised precision.

He reached out to Gwen, forgetting his increasing pain. "Gwen! Speak to me!"

He could only hear her mumbling, and she seemed to have difficulty opening her eyelids. He held her head on his lap and spoke to the staff.

"Don't waste time waiting for the ambulance. Let's take her in the car."

"Sir, the ambulance has an inbuilt ICU. I suggest we wait for it. They're on their way already."

"Gwen, wake up. Don't lose us." Nathan, too, felt his pain increase. He looked at the others, who also seemed in pain, except for Kory. She stood there in total shock. He looked at her blankly for a moment when her eyes met his. His eyes expressed more than words could. However, she was too lost at the moment to register anything.

With every passing second, the pain increased. Only a few minutes had passed, but it seemed like hours. Nathan's staff got to Gwen to check her pulse. "She's very much alive, sir. Help is almost here."

Martha and Albert held each other. Her strict demeanour had taken a backseat, and she was sobbing. "Albert, I cheated on you."

"What?"

"I don't know if we will make it through. I just wanted to confess that I cheated on you with a younger colleague, Shawn. But I swear I came out of it because of my love for you. I love you, and if I could have changed the past, I promise I would have. Please don't hate me." She cried, holding him tightly. He knew she meant every word, but it was difficult for him to reply. He held her back and patted her head, forgetting his pain for now. It wasn't as unbearable and he hoped help would arrive soon.

They heard the wailing of the ambulance. The resort staff carried Gwen outside to meet the ambulance at the main entrance. Nathan tried but could not stand. Albert looked at him and got worried. He left Martha for a moment and came to Nathan's aid. Kory had already reached out to Nathan to support him.

"Hey, try standing up, buddy," Albert said, patting Nathan's cheek. They made Nathan stand up and supported his shoulders as the hospital staff entered.

As they rushed towards Nathan, shouting instructions at each other, he fell to the ground, dead.

****

Several hours had passed.

The world had gone upside down for this group.

Claire fainted when she heard the news on the phone. On regaining consciousness, she'd revealed her engagement with Nathan to her family and then about his sudden demise. Her family didn't know how to react, but they could see that she was shaken to the core.

"It's all because of me!" she cried out loud with a few close relatives around. She would not listen to Henry, and when Bianca came to Claire, she held on to her, sobbing.

"I had wished that he'd die, Bianca. I manifested it in cold blood. And you know why? So that Henry would sympathise with me and marry me. I am evil, Bianca," she cried, holding her.

Henry and a few close ones around were too stunned to say anything. They were more concerned about Bianca and how she would react, considering the wedding was in a few days.

"No, Claire. Primal emotions just washed you away. That does not make you evil. You are a kind person, and I am sorry for your loss. I truly wish that the real evil gets what it deserves." Bianca embraced Claire while the latter continued to sob uncontrollably.

****

Matthew, Cassandra and Jeffery immediately travelled to Palm Beach when they heard the news.

Matthew hadn't spoken much since he heard about his son's death. He opened his mouth only twice, and on both times it was to ask Cassandra, "Are you sure?" He was in denial. He was in shock.

Jeffery was terrified and once had a panic attack during the journey, worried about his only daughter.

Cassandra had hit a wall while trying to console Matthew and hence resorted to giving some relief to Jeffery. "My people have brought the kids to our hospital in Palm Beach, Jeffery. I have passed on strict instructions already to get the best doctors to attend. I am sure your daughter will be fine. Have faith."

Jeffery clasped her hands, holding them to his forehead and broke down. "I cannot lose my daughter. I love her too much."

On reaching the hospital, Matthew refused to look at his son's dead body. Cassandra had to identify him for verification purposes when the police were present.

Kory sat in a corner, still too shocked to react to anything. She was fiddling with her thumb and saying some prayers to herself. Her eyes were wide open and strained. She had been asked to take some rest but still kept herself awake.

"Ms. Kory?"

Startled, she saw a man and a woman in uniform towering over her.

"Yea... yes?" she uttered.

"May we ask you a few questions?"

"Can you please... later?" Her teeth were chattering.

"Ma'am, I understand you are in shock. But we are running against time," said the man.

"Please..," she cried, and the woman nodded to the other, and they backed off.

The two cops walked towards the doctor's office on the other floor.

"Please be seated. Doctor Ed will be back in a moment."

They nodded and chose to remain standing while they waited.

"Ben, Tracy, good early morning." A plump Dr Ed walked towards them. Evidently, he was summoned in the middle of the night to address this high-profile situation.

"Hey, Doc," said Ben.

"What do we have, Dr Ed?" asked Tracy.

"Well... nothing unusual. Typical modus operandi of poisoning." He seemed to refer to a report while speaking with them.

"I request you not to be so dismissive when you speak with the victim's family," said Tracy.

Dr Ed eyed her through his bi-focal spectacles and smiled. "I will take that at face value. Considering Mrs Cassandra's father owns this hospital, I could be fired immediately."

"What do the medical examiner's reports say?" Tracy pressed him.

"Out of the four chalices, we have found a smaller portion of poison in the three chalices and a disproportionately high portion in Gwen's chalice. Poor kid. She went into a coma before I could reach the hospital."

Tracy had her eyebrows in a knot. "Then how come Nathan died?"

Dr Ed nodded and continued, "Nathan's blood levels indicate a higher concentration of poison that led to a quick death."

"I don't follow." Tracy looked confused with Dr Ed's words.

The plump doctor continued. "Albert and Martha's blood levels indicate only a minor consumption. They are out of danger. They've been moved to the general ward. You should be able to speak with them soon."

"Will Gwen make it?" Ben interjected.

"Though we've managed to push out the poison from her body, her body is not responding the way we'd expected her to. I am afraid that some poison may have spread to her brain."

"What next for her then?"

Dr Ed smiled. "Mrs Cassandra has asked some young doctors to intervene."

"Why?" Ben asked the obvious question.

"I guess she isn't very happy with the progress that an old man like me has shown in saving Gwen, though I am trying my best. I don't complain, though. I just hope the patient comes out of danger."

"Let's hope so," Ben added.

"What about the murder weapon?" Tracy checked.

Ben burst out laughing, attracting attention from a few around. "It's poison, Tracy. How can you not..."

"The carrier of the poison, you mean?" Dr Ed clarified with Tracy.

Moving her tired glance from Ben to Dr Ed, Tracy nodded.

"No. The forensics team didn't find any container filled with poison. The killer must have gotten rid of it immediately."

"That's... not easy. We'll take a look at the murder scene again," Tracy confirmed.

"You suspect someone?" Dr Ed asked.

"We cannot remove anyone from the list of suspects. This is a high-profile case. The Commissioner is behind our Captain, and we cannot leave any stone unturned," Tracy said as a matter of fact.

"As long as you don't suspect me, I am fine. I will let you know if I come across something," said Dr Ed, as his eyes continued to scan the reports for any observations.

The cops assumed that the conversation was over and got up to leave.

As they reached out of his earshot, Ben spoke, "He is quite old, isn't he?"

"Yes."

"Poor thing. It would surely hurt my ego the day I am replaced in some case by some young stud."

"May happen sooner than you think," said Tracy.

He laughed at her jibe but soon realised she didn't mean it as a joke.

"Tracy!" They heard a faint voice coming from the other end of the corridor. They turned to see Dr Ed trying to get their attention.

They jogged their way back. "Yes, Dr Ed?" Tracy asked, and Ben raised his eyebrows at him.

"Indeed, I am getting old. However, it seems funny that even you two didn't register it when you read the report summary."

"What is it, Doc?" Ben was impatient with the old doctor's time-consuming methods.

"If you see here..," Dr Ed indicated a comment in the report he'd just underlined, "while Gwen's chalice contains a dangerous level of poison, the wine is quite diluted."

"She had more ice. So what?" Ben shrugged.

"I...don't know."

"Dr Ed.." Tracy had turned a page in the report she was holding, a curious expression suddenly taking over. "The wine bottle.."

"Yes...it has no trace of poison."

"What!" Ben exclaimed in disbelief.

"How's that possible?" Tracy was surprised.

Tracy and the doctor looked at each other, and an unsaid understanding passed between them that this was more twisted than they'd assumed earlier.

CHAPTER 16

"Fuck!" I shouted, pulling my hair on both sides, similar to what Claire had done the night before Nathan's death. I went to the washroom, and had I not anticipated how I'd look, I would have shouted 'Ghost!' and run to Shenoy Uncle for help.

I splashed cold water on my face. "How the hell am I going to complete this book?" This was a complex story, and I had no idea why or how Krishav trusted me to complete this. I went to bed, knowing there was no point in trying to sleep. The sleep would have to choose to come to me. Till then, I mulled over the script I'd read. I must admit I'd read it in a hurry out of sheer excitement, not waiting to observe the minor details in any mystery.

I tried to reason and made a mental note of all possible suspects. I realised the list was huge. I might as well add my name to it. "Argh!" I shouted into the pillow.

How can I think like Havish while all I have are a few of his books referencing his persona? How can I replace a best-selling author? How can I write a genre I was introduced to less than two days ago? How would I know who he wanted to frame for the murder in the book?

These questions haunted me through the night. While I had no ready answers, I was quite sure of one thing. There was no way I could put myself in Havish's shoes to complete this novel.

I woke up in the morning with a mild temperature. I felt less guilty about calling the showroom to inform them that I was still unwell. I slept well during the day, catching up on lost sleep.

It was only in the afternoon that I could think straight at all, though I'd not wanted to think much and put pressure on my fragile brain at present. It may only be a slight exaggeration if I were to sum up that the last two days had packed more punch than perhaps the previous two years.

Yes, let's think about it. Firstly, I concluded that Havish was a writer of pathetic humour based on his two books. Then, thanks to Sujna, I was convinced that Krishav was a serial killer on the hunt. Then, it was disclosed to me that Havish was a mystery genre writer. Then I was told that I write good mystery (what a revelation that was!). Then I heard that Havish was Rāghavānka, the best-selling mystery author. Then I was told I was supposed to pitch in for him not to complete some random romance or humour story but a complex mystery. Then I read the bloody script, which is so complex that I am in self-doubt.

It was as if I had gone through a few life-changing events in rapid succession that I could not undo. They would stay with me till my last breath. I felt slightly helpless and more lost. At the same time, I knew this was something I had to sort out.

I refrained from calling Sujna or Krishav for the day.

While I was still not feeling my best the next day, I stepped out of the house. I needed to spend time with people to clear my head. It did help. All the conversations and familiar transactions at the showroom helped ease my nerves.

I didn't get into any false notion that the task at hand was easy, but at least I was able to face that fact with less anxiety.

***

It had been over a week since I'd read Havish's incomplete story. On my weekly off, I stared blankly at the laptop screen. The intention, like it had been every single day for the past week, was to start with the second portion of the story.

"Chuck it!" After staring at it for half an hour, I pushed it away and switched on the television to see if I could watch something interesting. I'd convinced myself to watch some thriller or murder mystery that might inspire me to start where Havish had left off. I wanted to get into the groove, as some say, but I never understood it. After searching for some such shows on all online streaming platforms, I decided that there was no good material to watch on such a topic. I slowly diverted to a drama with good reviews and started to binge-watch.

By the time I was done with the latest season, which ended with a cliffhanger at the end, I saw that it was late evening and the sun was taking leave for the day. "Even this television show had to leave me hanging in the air! The universe is conspiring against me."

As expected, I felt guilty for having wasted the whole day instead of focusing on the job at hand. I think I hated Havish even more right now. At least earlier I hardly knew much about him, so there was more indifference. But now he'd snuck into my life in a tricky way and gotten under my skin like a bed bug. I think it was his form of revenge in some way.

I got a call, and it was Krishav. "Hey, I've been busy for the last few days, Ankana. I couldn't return your call."

"Ah, yes. I just called yesterday to say that I am overwhelmed."

"That's normal. Let it sink in. It may seem complex, but it will get easier once you get used to the idea."

"Exactly what I've been telling myself for one week, Krishav. It's just not working. I think you will kill me if you get to know that I've not even written a word from the time I agreed to complete the novel."

"That's okay, Ankana. You have to believe me when I say it is a matter of time. And you know what? The biggest mistake you are making is not starting to write."

"Huh?"

"Just start to write whatever you think should be the next chapter. Chances are that you may not like that. So what? You can delete it and start afresh. I am no writer, but I've read about many successful writers who rely on their subconscious to write the story. Thus, they don't necessarily think about every sentence and word that will come next. They just start writing, and the words come on their own."

"Hmm... that sounds encouraging."

"Also, some say it is better to write in a notebook or paper than a laptop."

"Really? How does that make a difference?"

"I don't know. I guess that helps to get the flow of the writing. Once you are sailing smoothly, then you can shift to a laptop, right?"

"Well, nothing goes in trying," I said.

"I will catch up with you next week. By then, I hope you will have written something at least, and I repeat that some of it may not even make it to the novel. But it will have a part to play in getting you into action."

"Okay, boss."

"Great!" He hung up.

Trust me, the next day, I did try some things that Krishav mentioned, okay? I even walked to the nearest bookstore from my showroom during the lunch break to buy a notebook. It was damn confusing whether I should be buying the one with narrow lines or broad ones or blank ones and what size should the book be. I was irritated with Krishav for not being specific. I decided to buy one of each variety, and when I returned to the showroom with a mini bundle of books, all eyes were on them, wondering what I was up to.

The same evening, I wrote a couple of paragraphs describing the features of the two cops, Ben and Tracy. I imagined Ben to be chubby and Tracy to be athletic. I described their uniform and how they walked or jogged, and also contemplated if I needed to end the story by having these two come together romantically. I realised I was going all over the place and cringed after reading what I had written. "Eww... if Krishav hears of this, he will find a skyscraper and throw me down its terrace." This way of writing wouldn't work at all in the present context. I scrapped the page and didn't attempt anything further for the day.

The next day, before I started, I called Sujna and explained my situation without giving her all the story's details.

"Why are you hell-bent on getting the cops into a romantic relationship?" she laughed.

"I don't know, man. It sounded natural at the time. But I am getting nowhere."

"Should you not get the story's skeleton set before you begin the dramatisation?" she spoke like an expert.

"It went over my head. What do you mean?"

"Describing the details of the characters, etcetera, would be getting into the story's nuances, wouldn't it? Some authors do it in detail, some do it broadly, and some completely leave it to the readers' imagination. However, in case of a murder mystery, before you choose a style of writing, should you not zero in on the murderer?"

"Hmm…"

"So once you get the main skeleton of the story right, you can think about how you want to dramatise the same story. I thought that's how you would have written the first two books," Sujna spoke very convincingly.

"That's true. While I didn't have these terms you mentioned in mind, the flow of my books was similar. I had the end in mind and a couple of major incidents that I wanted to include in the story, and then the story emerged."

"Precisely!"

"I don't know why I am forgetting the basics while trying to look at Havish's work."

"Don't worry. Attempt it again and look at this approach or any improvisation on the same approach."

"The biggest thing bothering me right now is that I don't know how to think like Havish. I don't know who he might have wanted to frame as the murderer. I am feeling very lost."

"Won't it help you get to know his style and thinking of the characters or plot better when you read his other books under the 'Rāghavānka' pseudonym? You've read only one completed work of his, and now this is unfinished, right?"

"You are right. I will get those and start reading them soon."

I did as I agreed with Sujna the next day. I took an auto-rickshaw from my showroom to get to a good bookstore. When I entered the store and saw that Rāghavānka's novels were put up at the centre and arranged nicely, pretty much with a celebratory tone, my heart skipped a beat. I bought all four of his books, though I already had one as an e-book with me.

The rest of the week went by just reading his books. One thing that stood out for me in these mysteries was that the detective or the police who solved the crime were all different in each of the books. There were no common characters. Thankfully, that would work well for me as the readers didn't know any of the characters from Havish's incomplete novel.

When Sujna and I had talked about this, it all seemed to make sense. Yet, when I sat with the incomplete novel again to make sense of it, I was still getting nowhere.

It was clear that I was not cut out for this. I just could not think like Havish. I had been stalling the whole thing till now instead of accepting the fact and moving on.

Chapter 17

It was a month since I'd agreed to Krishav's proposal. It was evening, and the staff started to leave the workplace one after the other. It was then that Javed came to me with two cups of tea.

"Hey, Javed! Why are you getting tea?"

He smiled and came to my desk. "Ma'am, I know you like this roadside masala tea a lot."

"That's true. I am not complaining at all. But why did you put so much effort into it? You'd have to walk a lot to get to that tea vendor, no?"

"Yes, but that's okay."

I sipped the tea, and he was right. It tasted good. I smiled at him.

"What's up? All okay with you?" I inquired.

"First class, ma'am. But you don't seem to be fine. So, I thought I would try to cheer you up." He smiled, showing all his teeth.

"Oh god! You are… thank you, Javed. That's nice of you. But you didn't really…"

He shrugged, not letting me complete it. We sat in silence, sipping tea. He finished his tea before me. "Ma'am, I know I must not speak out of turn. You have not been your usual self for around a month now, since the time you had fallen ill. I know that it is more than just your health. It must be something personal that you cannot share. I will pray to god that everything falls in place at the earliest."

Here was someone who came from a different culture, religion, language, social status, and perhaps many other things that could be listed to show us our stark differences, yet he struck the right chord with me better than I could imagine.

I just smiled at him. "It's nothing too personal as such, Javed. But yes, not something I can share."

"I understand, ma'am."

"It's a problem that I am facing, and I don't think the answer is simple."

"I can only imagine. It would have been good if I could have been useful to you. I guess that is not the case."

I looked at him for another moment. "Actually… let me ask you this."

"Yes, ma'am." He sat straight in his chair attentively.

"If there is a story… no… okay… let's say…" I was having difficulty in framing what I intended to say.

Javed sat there patiently without batting an eyelid, waiting for me to complete my sentence.

I took a moment to gather my thoughts. "Let's say that I have started writing a poem, right?"

"Okay…"

"Due to whatever reason, I am unable to complete it."

He nodded without giving out any expression.

"Then, I ask you to complete the poem."

"Oh, okay." He seemed more interested now.

"However, you are supposed to do it without discussing with me about the poem's first half. How can you end it like I wanted to? How can you think like me?"

I waited to see if he would have any answer. He seemed to be deliberating something.

Javed then said, "It's not possible, ma'am."

"What?"

"It's impossible to complete the poem in the same breath, passion, meaning, ending, and other finer elements that could be associated with the person who started the poem."

"Oh, okay." I was disappointed, but then, it wasn't fair for me to expect him to have an answer to the question I'd been grappling with long enough.

I didn't realise that he was yet to complete.

"But is that condition essential?"

"Sorry? What condition?"

"Is it essential that I put myself in your shoes to complete the poem? Can I not do it in my way?"

"Say more."

"A poem or any work of art is an emotion, as we all know. It is a creative emotion. The best part of creativity is that it is unique to each creator. Without knowing what you had in mind for the whole poem, and without having access to you, it is not fair for you to assume that I can imagine what you had in mind."

"Hmmm..."

"But then, if you gave me the task of completing that poem, it means you chose me to do it in my way and not necessarily copy your style, words, feelings, or even the end you had in mind.

"I will honour the fact that you chose me. But I will not be able to copy you. In fact, I should not copy you. It is an insult to you and me. I will try to add the best I can offer. However, it is up to me to ensure I link the remainder of the poem to the concept of the first half. In this example, the poem would be whole only when both the halves that have been put together sound like one to the reader. It is up to me to carry on the spirit of the poem being accepted as one whole – one soul when the reader looks at it. The end may or may not be what the first poet wanted it to be. I may try to decipher from the first half and attempt it. But I will never know that. However, even the final reader doesn't know that. What he does know or care about is that it is a beautiful poem at the end of the day."

I kept looking at Javed for a long time, which unsettled him.

"Sorry, ma'am. I know I talk rubbish when I get carried away. My wife keeps saying that always. I am sorry."

"Javed."

"Please pardon my random monologue. It was never meant to..."

"Javed!"

"Ye… yes, ma'am."

"You are the best! Thank you." I smiled at him. It confused him at first, but he figured he'd somehow helped me.

I came home with a renewed vigour. While I still had no idea how to end the story, I felt a new confidence today.

The biggest mistake I had been making until now was that I was trying to think like Havish. I had gotten lost in the following sentence or chapter he'd wanted to write or whom he attempted to frame as the murderer.

I decided to use the facts given in the first part and try figuring out who the murderer would be. If it meant I had to fill in voids created by Havish, I would do it in my way. If contradictory facts were intended to confuse the readers, I would weigh them the way I should and then try to decipher how that would pan out. If I couldn't get into Havish's mind to figure out who the murderer was, that was fine. I would reconstruct the facts and arrive at the murderer in my way, even if they might not be the one Havish intended to frame.

I just had to be overtly careful of one thing. I could not ignore the simplest of facts mentioned till now, for that was the only line of sight the reader and I would have.

I told myself that each sentence, which may seem like a plain reference, is usually placed by the author for a reason, and having read Havish's other books by now, I knew that's what he would do as well. I needed to involve myself in the story more than I had until now. I couldn't just read past the sentences but live each sentence and imagine it like a reader and an author, an author who is not Havish. Where would I place those clever gems that the reader would miss, and at the end, when the truth is revealed, they would appreciate how it was hidden in plain sight all along?

I opened the laptop to look at Havish's story, which I was running away from, giving myself and others several excuses for over a month. For the first time, it didn't scare me.

I read each sentence, imagined it, questioned it, and lived it. It was gruelling, to say the least. I had hardly finished a few pages, and a long time had passed. However, I was satisfied with this approach. I dedicated time to do this daily and would give it additional time over my weekly offs.

After being diligent for a fortnight at this, I had separated some facts after going through the script with a fine-tooth comb. These facts didn't add up in my mind, or I could see they were left by the author to be used later, or perhaps I had just assumed that they were vital while they were actually nothing.

But that was okay.

Chapter 18

My initial sense was that someone didn't want Gwen and Nathan to get back together or, at least, was super pissed that they had slept together. Was poisoning them – killing one of them and making the other battle for life – an act of revenge?

Let me come to the final drink they all had together.

Nathan pops open the bottle as per the tradition of the Grayson family. There are no issues there.

Hence, somehow, the murderer sneaked the poison into the four chalices. Three rounds of serving took place. Once Nathan finished, the next one was by Gwen, and the last time was when Kory jumped in to serve everyone. Nathan and Gwen were the victims of the poison. Dr Ed confirmed that the bottle was poison-free; Nathan's blood and Gwen's chalice had higher levels of poison. Does that make Kory the obvious murderer?

Kory? As I consider Kory's actions throughout the story, she's in the background. Is it perhaps a way of hiding the killer from the spotlight during the story and showing her true intent only in the end? Suspicions about her are that she comes to the Grayson Villa earlier than expected, is the only teetotaller, and enthusiastically serves everyone the last round of drinks. Most importantly, she had access to the storeroom keys; the same storeroom with the chalices in them.

No motive has explicitly been stated in the story for Kory to be the killer. Was she some secret lover of Nathan and jealous when she saw him sleeping with Gwen in all their glory earlier that morning and sought revenge? Or was she to gain something by killing Gwen and Nathan? If I think about it, the author had placed motives for

Albert and Martha. Even his father has motives, yet Kory is cleverly left out. That's suspicious. Does that mean the author planned to introduce her motive at a later stage once the death had occurred? That, in my opinion, would be shoddy writing, which would disappoint the readers. Thus, I shall stay with the motives that can be derived based on the facts mentioned in the story.

But then, if we think of it, Albert and Martha were clearly out of danger. They were hardly affected by it as they were moved from the hospital's ICU to the general ward.

Martha? Martha had a motive. She didn't want Nathan to disclose the secret of her disloyalty. No, that's ruled out. She confesses to her husband about her adultery. If not anyone else, she surely thought she was about to die. Unless, of course, the author was trying to pull a fast one, and she had administered the poison and pretended to confess her guilt, all the time knowing that she and her husband would anyway be safe. No, that doesn't make sense. If she knew Nathan would die, there was no threat left for her actually to confess to her husband.

Albert? The spotlight moves on Albert. He, too, had a motive to get rid of Nathan because of the money he owed. Throughout the story, while his hatred towards Nathan is visible, I wonder if he had the finesse to sneak poison into the chalices, as his character comes across as brash. But it could be a cover for his true colours.

Moreover, he seems surprisingly in control of himself while Gwen and Nathan struggle due to poison. He tries to help Nathan to get on his feet. This means that Albert wasn't as affected by the poison. Hmmm... here's a clear suspect.

Gwen? She is the most sorted one in the Villa. She counsels Nathan after the argument between him and Claire in the beginning;

even after they end up making a 'mistake' by sleeping together and Nathan is panicking, she is the one who asks him to take it easy. In the end, she is the one fighting for her life. It will be a drag to push her as a suspect.

Should a hard and fast rule exist that only those at the tea table could have done this? There could be others who were operating from the shadows.

Matthew? Could a father do this to his son? Nathan's father, Matthew, calls out of the blue to express his love that morning. Strange. Could it be possible he was trying to give a false impression that he was a caring father while he was the one behind the poisoning? He had a motive. Because of his son, he had to face Jeffery's wrath. Also, this could get him sympathy from Jeffery. Hmmm... that doesn't seem meaty enough as a motive. He speaks about his initial disapproval of Nathan's engagement and admits that he's reconciled over it. It's just too complicated for him to have carried out the act while staying in New York.

Oh, wait! What if Kory was Matthew's secret lover and was only carrying out the instructions he had laid out? No, that's too far-fetched, and again, something like that being introduced post-death would mean the author is relying on readers' stupidity. That was not Havish's style. Nevertheless, I shouldn't remove Matthew from the list of suspects yet.

I've not considered other names yet, though it looks pretty difficult to make their connection with the murder.

Jeffery? Nothing stops him from going after the guy who was with his daughter for six long years and called it quits. But then, he was already getting revenge by making Matthew's life hell.

Titus? Uncle Titus seems to be the most elusive one of all. There appears to be no motive, and nothing much has been said about Titus throughout. Anything said has only a positive angle, and Nathan always believed him to be good. At the same time, Matthew shows hatred towards Titus in his conversation with his wife. Perhaps there is a side of Titus that only Matthew knew, which wasn't pleasant. It's possible, but it does not look likely. While it's said that the wine bottle is poison-free, could there have been a way wherein the initial doses from the bottle had the poison, and then it disappeared? No! That's not fiction. That's fantasy.

Amelia? What does look likely is Amelia's involvement. She seems to have this aura of a carefree girl who loves Nathan like a brother. Based on her conversation with Nathan on the phone on the day of his death, it is evident that she knew he was supposed to be at the Villa that day. Also, isn't it peculiar that she tells Nathan – "Cheer up now. It's not your last day on Earth"? That's too fishy to be ignored. By saying that, what if she is implying the contrary, that it is indeed his last day on Earth? What's her motivation? And if I somehow believe she hypothetically wanted to murder Nathan, how did she poison the chalices from so far?

Claire? I am not sure about her, though. Yes, she seems to get into random fits of wanting to kill her fiancé. I seriously don't consider those haphazard thoughts she had about him to be enough motivation to travel for a hundred miles from Highlands to Palm Beach in the car she'd slept in to kill her beloved fiancé in a drunken stupor late in the night. That's too far-fetched. In the morning, she recollects a nightmare where she ends Nathan's life. That comes across only as symbolic and cannot be real, or can it?

Chef Harrison? He, too, had access to the Villa. He had access to it even before Nathan and others arrived. While I know it is not right to use my heart here to arrive at the murderer, and I should rely on facts and my brain, I just don't want to believe that a sweet man like Chef Harrison could have anything to do with Nathan's murder. Oh, man! I am so biased.

Nathan? Amidst all this, I forgot one person who could be behind all this. Nathan, the man himself! I wonder if I should focus more on the suicide angle here. Imagine all the guilt he might've been carrying on his shoulders that his father had to cut a sorry face and face a big backlash in business because of him. It has been highlighted that his father blamed Nathan initially for all the loss he had to face.

Add to this the fact that now Claire wants to end the engagement. He surely must have been devastated by all this. All of it was coming together on one day to blow his top off. It is mentioned that he had the urge to jump off the balcony at the very beginning of the story when he was smoking. Gwen interrupts his thoughts and distracts his intentions.

If it indeed was a suicide, why drag Gwen along? Of course! It is because of Jeffery, Gwen's father, that Matthew had been put in a tight spot that threatened his main business, besides the emotional trauma that his ill-expressive father may have gone through.

So yes, there seems to be a motive to commit suicide and drag Gwen along. But in such a state of mind, would anyone be able to make such a watertight plan and execute it with cold-blooded efficiency? Also, he ends up poisoning Albert and Martha as collateral damage. These are plot loopholes, as far as I am concerned.

Theoretically, I listed the probable suspects, their possible motive, ease of committing the crime in the given circumstance that required caution and finesse, and finally, the probability of them committing the crime based on the facts highlighted in the manuscript.

Based on this initial list, one thing was evident. It seemed that more than one person could be involved in this crime.

The married couple came to my mind as the first duo.

But then I could see that Kory lacked only the motive. Hence, she might have teamed up with other suspects on my list to send Nathan packing. That seemed more likely than pinning down only on Albert and Martha.

Kory could have partnered either with Albert or Martha. From an execution standpoint, Kory was at the epicentre of the crime, if I chose not to consider Albert and Martha.

Chapter 19

I called Krishav the next day after sleeping over the list I'd made.

"I think I have your killer, Krishav."

"Who's that?"

"Take a guess."

"Don't tell me you think it's Nathan who committed suicide."

"Not actually. That's one of the possibilities after looking at certain details in the manuscript. At least, that's what Havish has ensured. But I don't think that's the case."

"Okay, so who?"

"No more guesses?"

"Ah, come on! When I read it earlier, I could see everyone as a suspect. So, I am not sure. Even if you name someone, I only care about how well you frame that person in the story to ensure everything adds up."

"I think it is Kory."

"Hmm…"

"What? No reaction?"

"Isn't it too obvious?"

"I agree. But what is not obvious is that she'd partner with one of the others to commit the murder."

"Ah! Say more."

"See, she has the means to pull off the murder, but the story doesn't provide any motive at her end. It must be that someone else who has the motive convinced her to carry out the task. If the police try to get to her, they could be fooled into believing that she had no motive to kill Nathan at all."

"Hmm… I like that. Who would be the other one then?"

"Frankly, I don't know yet. But I am warming up to Albert."

"Yes! He seemed to be quite fit at the time his wife and Nathan were struggling after consuming the poison, no?"

"Exactly!"

"Okay, good. So you have the two people you need. Will you be writing the rest of the novel, then? I guess from here, it is a simple task."

"Sort of, but not that easy. I may have to invent a few things from here to fit the story and the clues to put the two behind bars."

"Understood. Once you finish the draft, let's look at it."

"Sure, will you be editing it initially?"

"I am not too worried about editing. Your language is fine based on what I've read before. I am more concerned about how the end product will look. It needs to tie in with the first half."

I was reminded of what Javed had told me.

"Give me a few weeks to invent storylines on Kory and Albert."

"Yeah, no problem. I suggest you take a month or two from now as the target to complete the novel."

"Are you insane? I am no magician. I may need much more time, considering I have a full-time job."

"Fine, fine! I was testing to see if you could do what Havish used to."

"And what was that?"

"He used to finish a complete novel in two-three months."

"How's that possible?" I asked incredulously.

"I know some writers who can complete it faster. I guess each one has a different style and speed."

"That sounds fishy."

"Rubbish. Just because you cannot do it doesn't make it impossible, no?"

"Yeah, fine."

"It was his second book as Rāghavānka that Havish finished in two months. He was in Mangalore when he finished it.

Unfortunately, it was the same time your mother expired, and he hit a lull, taking much time to edit."

"Oh!"

"Sorry, I don't know why I brought that up."

"No, that's okay." I paused to think of that day. "You know what I did when he visited me then?"

"You asked a relative to send Havish off."

"You guessed well."

"It's not a guess. I was with him."

"Eh... what?"

"He was put up in my house while penning the second book. He was nervous to visit you. So, he asked me to accompany him."

"Wow! You've known about me since then?"

"Yeah, sort of."

"You must have judged me then, I suppose."

"That would not have been a fair thing to do."

"What else would you expect me to do when he doesn't visit all his life and chooses to visit only when Amma was no more?"

"Hmm... not completely true, Ankana."

"Sorry?"

"He'd told me categorically that he'd visited at least thrice over the past years when your mother was alive."

"What!?" This was a revelation.

"Yeah, just that your mother didn't want to meet him and sent him away every time."

"Oh, I... wasn't aware. I thought..."

"Maybe your mother believed it was best not to share it with you."

"Hmmm... he used to travel to Mangalore often?"

"Not actually. Once in a while. That last time was an unfortunate coincidence."

"Sorry, I ended up speaking to you about things unrelated to our job."

"No, that's fine. I guess I am one of the sources for you to seek inputs about Havish."

"Okay… enough information about him for today, I suppose." I tried a tired chuckle. "I will keep in touch with you then."

"Hey listen, Ankana."

"Yes, sir."

"So will I formalise it then?"

"Oh!"

"Don't tell me you still have doubts, please!"

"No, no. I don't. Sure. Please send me whatever documents I need to sign. I am keen to start working on this story now."

"Great!"

I hung up, and it was then that I felt overjoyed. It was all unofficial while I was trying to help out Krishav until now. Now, I would be formally getting into writing the novel. This was going to be my first published novel. I was very excited.

***

It was a nightmare trying to build a convincing scene where Kory and Albert would strike the deal. I tried to imagine how Albert would offer her some money. Havish's part of the novel suggested that Kory didn't come from a rich family. But that scene came off pathetically, and I deleted it.

Then again, I tried to create a romance between the two and almost puked at the idea. To imagine them making love was revolting. No, there couldn't be such a relationship between them. I was secretly impressed with Havish's characterisation with these roles. They were actual people to me now, and I could sense their presence when I closed my eyes. Thus, I knew that Kory and

Albert, if they were actual living individuals, would never have slept together.

George R. R. Martin once said, "A reader lives a thousand lives before he dies. The man who never reads lives only one." If only one wondered how many lives a writer lives before he dies.

***

It had been almost a month since my last conversation with Krishav. Thankfully, I had made some progress. I would say it was better than I had expected from myself. While the scene about Kory and Albert making a deal had reached a dead-end, I decided to start writing about the story past that deal. That seemed to be going much better.

I was pleasantly surprised with my writing speed. With this flow, I could complete the remainder of the novel sooner than my committed timeline.

The contract from the publisher took time to reach me. Though it was evident, Krishav was kind enough not to disclose how much effort he had put into convincing the publisher about me. Hence, when he was happy with my progress till now, it relieved me greatly.

I would be a published writer, which motivated me to push myself.

Chapter 20

I was penning the book's last chapter less than three months after I started writing. I had no idea that I had it in me to write this fast. Amongst a few other scenes I had to revisit or complete, I remembered the deal-making scene between Kory and Albert. Again, however, my pen stopped moving when I had to write about them. I took breaks, listened to songs, watched some shows on Netflix, and went for a long walk, but this overwhelmed me for no reason.

I cursed myself for returning to this scene instead of finishing the novel in one go. I'd pretty much wasted the whole day stuck with these two irritating characters.

"Come on, Albert, go for it. Say what is needed to convince Kory to partner with you to kill Nathan! Don't be shy. She likes you. Well, she doesn't. But that shouldn't matter." I wasn't going mad as such, but I thought saying such things would motivate Albert to have the required conversation.

"Kory, I see you want to make some quick bucks. No? Okay, fine, don't make money. But don't you find Albert attractive enough to do something big for him?" Argh! For all you know, Kory finds Martha more attractive than him.

It would have been easier had Kory partnered with Martha for this. The thought evolved as I sat on my bed, resting my head on three pillows. Then I thought I should at least make a hypothetical map of how the same story would look in case Kory partnered with Martha instead of Albert.

"No!" I admonished myself. I was almost done with the novel, and trying to create something new at this stage would be a nightmare!

But then, a part of me told me it was just for fun. When that part of your mind gives you any such advice, ditch it and move on in life, and don't do what I did!

I opened a blank page in the notebook I was using to put together the story's skeleton, recollecting the story in my mind and connecting all conversations that involved Kory and Martha in Havish's part of the story. I was surprised to realise that they seemed to share a better camaraderie involving a good mix of love and hate than Kory and Albert.

"Shit! Did I miss a trick here?" I asked myself.

To ensure I hadn't missed any other critical aspect about Martha or Kory, I read Martha's lines from Havish's portion again. It was easier, considering Havish's story was on the laptop, and I could search for Martha's lines without much effort.

There were a few grammatical errors that I was tempted to correct, but I had to refrain from doing it, remembering my conversation with Javed. That part of the novel was frozen, and it would be wrong to touch anything there to paint my picture over Havish's words. If the editors believed that any correction was necessary, they would take it up.

I was reading the scene at the beginning where Martha gets out of her new car as Nathan comes to receive the couple. She says, "You said it will be the four of us". I saw the error in the reference, which I had to correct.

"You are such a doofus, Havish! How can you make such a simple summation error? I'd have thrown you out if you worked under me and made such a silly error." I corrected the number to five.

How did I miss that, though I've been through the manuscript several times? Unless… wait. Maybe what Martha says in this context was not an error.

Martha mentioned that she expected it to be just the four of them. She'd obviously counted herself, Albert and Nathan, without a doubt. So that meant either Kory or Gwen weren't expected to be present? That's a… new line of thought.

But then, in the following line, Albert is surprised that Kory is already there. Which means she, too, was expected to be there, but she'd arrived earlier. My whole premise of framing Kory was that she was present at the Villa earlier than required to set up Nathan and Gwen's murders.

However, I had completely missed that if I accounted for Nathan, Kory, Albert, and Martha as the four, Gwen was not even supposed to be present at the Villa! Hmm… that's interesting.

That explains why in the opening conversation between Claire and Nathan, the former was surprised that Gwen was present at the Villa. It wasn't because he wanted to hide anything. He genuinely didn't know that Gwen would land up there.

In fact, even in the conversation between Jeffery and Matthew in New York, Jeffery was slightly surprised that his daughter was at Grayson Villa.

I wondered if Havish had put these here only to mislead the readers or if there was something more. Did I need to consider Gwen as a suspect? No! That didn't make sense at all. She was the one left fighting for her life at the hospital, remember?

Hmm… for that matter, technically, even Albert and Martha were admitted. I agree; it was fair to qualify that they seemed to have a minor poisoning case compared to Gwen, who was in a coma. Havish hadn't indicated if she would even survive.

Let's for a moment ignore the point that she was battling for her life at the hospital and look at some hints that may exist in or around conversations about Gwen, for I seemed to have unconsciously ignored all of it.

I searched for all the references about Gwen and read them in a new light. I saw nothing odd about her at all. I reread the part where she and Nathan got carried away and did it.

Gwen also didn't have anything apt to wear for the pool. This, again, might only suggest that hers was a last-minute inclusion to travel to Grayson Villa.

Nathan had asked her to look into the room she used to occupy earlier to find her swimwear, and she said the wardrobe was empty. He then sent her to his room to check his spare wardrobe. Nothing was amiss here as well.

Hmm… the remaining four played at the pool for some time, and there were inquiries from others as to why Gwen was taking so much time. What was she doing at the time?

And once she returned to the pool, amidst all the wooing about her attractive body, Nathan said that her bikini looked new. Hmm… new? She must have lied about not having her swimwear. She just wanted an excuse to access Nathan's room alone. Also, she had enough time and the complete set of spare keys from Nathan's room to get into any room to plant anything she wanted to.

Later in the middle of the night, when Gwen woke him up by asking for the fourth room's keys, no wonder he was frustrated that the room keys weren't arranged in order, or perhaps, she'd intentionally messed them up when she visited his room earlier.

Gwen knew Kory snored, which she stated to Nathan during this conversation. Hence, she used that as an excuse to enter Nathan's room at night, and by messing around with the room keys, she increased her chances of getting to stay in Nathan's room for long.

Why did she want to stay? Hmm… the sex then wasn't just a coincidence. She'd probably planned it. After the conversation she'd overheard, she tried to understand how he felt about Claire. She'd wanted to know his opinion about Claire before venturing deeper. When she didn't get a satisfactory response, she got touchy with massages and stuff, leading to wild sex.

Ah yes! There it is! While Nathan felt guilty in the morning, she asked him if they could continue where they left off, and he disagreed. If she'd intended to murder him, it must mean that the break-up they had after six years of the relationship must have hit her hard. It was a betrayal for her. She'd come to the Villa with a plan to kill him for vengeance, but on overhearing his conversation with Claire, she saw an opening. An opening for them to be together again. She pushed for it all the way, but even after sleeping with her, Nathan told her that it was a 'mistake'. That was the last straw.

The final evening, when the five of them get together at the table, Gwen insists on Nathan getting the special chalices for the drinks. Hmm… this was important. All chalices, in the end, had portions of poison. Did it mean that the previous night, when she had access to Nathan's room and his keys, she ventured into the storeroom to coat a layer of poison on the complete set?

However, in the end, Nathan died, and Gwen had a higher portion of poison in her chalice, and she was also fighting for her life.

Before the sad turn of events, Martha complained about the warm weather, while Gwen was wearing a full-sleeved top with a cuff. Perhaps she had concealed something with her? A second serving of poison that could kill, maybe?

Nathan was the one serving everyone first, and Gwen carried out the second serving. Kory carried out the final serving. Only during the second serving could Gwen have sneaked a potent dose of poison into Nathan's chalice when everyone was distracted after she spilt wine on the table.

Kory jumped in to serve the final round of wine. This non-poisonous serving from the bottle should have then only restored all chalices to a similar proportion of poisonous remains. How did Gwen's chalice end up with a higher dose of poison, with her in the hospital fighting for her life? She would be easily caught, as one cannot fake a coma. Even Dr Ed confirmed that she had slipped into a coma. Did someone else double-cross her and put her life at risk?

Havish had neatly left that inconclusive. He'd done this to show the readers that while Tracy and Ben were searching for the murderer, they might not think of Gwen as the suspect the way I hadn't earlier because of the 'victim bias'. She was a victim, so there was no question of her being the murderer. I liked Gwen as the murderer, barring these not-so-small details I had to account for.

I was both proud and miffed with myself. I was proud because I believed I had finally managed to get the real culprit; well, at least the real culprit the way I see it after looking into facts mentioned in Havish's part of the story. I was miffed, obviously because I couldn't answer the last few open-ended points about Gwen.

I was concerned that I had to rewrite a good part of my completed story. I didn't know how to explain all this to Krishav.

I took my phone to call Krishav, thrilled, excited and nervous about my findings. But then I thought I should not jump the gun every time this way. I'd already goofed up earlier by making Kory the killer, though 'Kory the Killer' did sound good as a phrase—something like how some characters in *The Lord of the Rings* sound: Gandalf the Grey and Aragorn, son of Arathorn.

What I meant was that I wanted to be very sure that I'd not left any stone unturned. Hence, I had to hold on to my excitement and call it a day.

Chapter 21

I slept very well, I must say. All the intense thinking I'd done for the book or the thinking on rewriting the book had made me quite tired, which helped me sleep like a log.

In the morning, I knew I'd done the right thing by waiting before calling Krishav. It was a working day, so I took my laptop and notebook to the showroom.

As it was the middle of the week, the customer footfalls in the showroom were minimal. I hardly had any work and thus thought of eye-balling Havish's manuscript for one final time to search for clues I'd overlooked. I didn't want some fans of Rāghavānka, a.k.a Havish, to make a big deal of some minor detail or fact that was missed or used incorrectly, creating bad publicity. Of course, I might have been overthinking this, but it was better to err on the side of caution.

As I began to read, I told myself that I would try to focus on characters that seemed meaty when I started with the book but had fizzled out when Nathan took his last breath. I wanted to know if they were there to serve some big purpose or only to fill pages, as some authors might do to reach a certain thousand words in a novel. Fine! I had also done that for the two books I'd sent to Krishav.

Amelia was one such character I'd expected, or rather hoped, would have more to do in the story, but somewhere, I felt she was under-utilised.

I thought the character Amelia was too straightforward to have anything to do with murdering her cousin. She was put there as a character that could help as Nathan's conscience-keeper or a good little-big sister, who was far more sorted than her elder cousin, and thus, she was used in times when he had to bounce a few emotions off her. Also, she was there to help be the bridge for Claire to settle into this "mad rich family", as was said somewhere in the story.

She was even daring enough to admit to Claire that her family, especially Matthew, was unhappy about the whole thing. Here it was: "He can be all expressionless, but his eyes never betray him."

This rang a bell in my mind somewhere. I recollected reading that on the engagement day, when Claire looked around, she saw a disgusted expression on Matthew, and here it said expressionless. Havish might have made a mistake in reference, making the characters expression-full and expressionless as per his will.

But then, I stood corrected as I returned to address the engagement scene. In my mind, I had converged two different references. One sentence said that although Matthew was expressionless, Claire's instincts told her he wasn't happy with the engagement. So here again, it was proven that Matthew wasn't used to expressing emotions quite easily. There was another sentence before this that mentioned Claire registering an expression of disgust for a fleeting moment when she looked around after accepting Nathan's proposal.

I must be ageing. I didn't know why I had been missing all such important points. This meant that Claire saw someone expressing disgust, and unlike what I had assumed at the back of my mind, it couldn't be Matthew, for there were several instances later where Havish had informed his readers that Matthew was expressionless.

Strangely, Gwen wasn't even present at the engagement. This is where I felt like kicking myself. It was pretty dumb of me that I'd already finished one version of this story in which I was obsessed with finding partners in crime instead of just an individual murderer. How did I not even consider that possibility in this new version?

Argh! Thank god I didn't call up Krishav last night and blabber about Gwen, only to tell him the next day that she might've had an accomplice.

But who else was present at the engagement? I wondered because not even a single person from the engagement gathering was present at Grayson Villa during the crime, except Nathan himself. Kory, Albert, Martha and Gwen– none of them were present at the engagement.

Holy crap! Amelia? No! I am so disappointed. Come on, Amy! I trusted you, and you broke my heart.

Amelia was present at the engagement, yes. But was she Gwen's accomplice? That seemed so uncool and yucky. Also, all other leading facts I had considered in the story didn't indicate any wrongdoing on her part.

Wait, who else was present at the engagement? Uncle Titus? No, that guy was just thin air. I am not sure why he was even present in the story. Maybe to pass on the wine bottle and get his nephew popped off.

Cassandra? Hmmm… she hardly had an active role in the story, like they say, a 'blink-and-you-miss' role. I don't think she would have anything to do with her own son's murder.

Curiously, Matthew mentions to Jeffery that he heard from Cassandra that Gwen was in Grayson Villa when Cassandra had called to check something. "What else are you involved in, Cassandra?" I whispered aloud. But again, the same thing– why would a mother randomly try to get her son murdered? Should I focus back on Amelia?

Cassandra seemed quite dedicated to her husband throughout the story. She had been married for twenty-five years, considering she mentions the silver jubilee anniversary not long ago. She highlighted in their interaction that she cared a lot about him and would do anything to help him return to his usual self. Ah! And she did mention that Nathan should have thought about Matthew before getting engaged to Claire.

But wasn't Nathan around thirty years old? That came up when Kory and he were at the pool. Did this mean Nathan was five years old already when Matthew and Cassandra married? Impossible! Matthew was quite old school that way, like his father, Ned Grayson. Cassandra was not Nathan's mother! As they say in the Grayson family, it might have been a marriage of convenience. In all probability, she was Matthew's second wife!

Matthew was angry with his son for a long time as his break-up with Gwen hit him hard. He seemed to have told his wife, as highlighted in their conversation, that he wished he had never had a son like him, and Cassandra confirmed that he'd been saying that a lot, many times.

Cassandra would probably go to such an extent to comfort her husband, who seemed to have been stripped of his pride. Again, the same logic would work. She knew that if Nathan died, the problem was solved. It would be easier to convince Jeffery or make him sympathise with their loss. Matthew would regain his credibility if the original relationship between Jeffery and Matthew was re-established. Cassandra and Gwen seemed to have a decent relationship, considering they called on each other. Should I plainly assume that Cassandra and Gwen were in it together? What would one gain from the other? Gwen wanted revenge, and Cassandra's part of the deal may have been that Gwen convince her father to continue supporting Matthew in the business.

How could Cassandra help Gwen with the murder?

Oh! Matthew had to go through some health checks, which Cassandra seemed to have insisted happen in the central New York branch of her father's hospital chain. Then, some medicines were sent out to Grayson Villa on the day of Nathan's death. Does that mean the package had the poison that was administered? No, wait.

If that were the case, the whole episode of Gwen going into the storeroom the previous night to poison the chalices would fail.

I was sure there was some reference to what those medicines were called. This happened when Nathan took Kory to the storeroom to get the chalices. Yes, the only reference here seemed to be Thiopental. The sad news was that the internet showed Thiopental was only an anaesthetic. So, nothing out of the ordinary on that one. If I read the conversation between Matthew and Nathan on this topic, it seemed like Matthew had shipped it to Grayson Villa so that his son could bring it home from there.

I couldn't see how Gwen needed any help from Cassandra to carry out this plan. She could do this alone, and she did. And as her karma, she was now admitted to… a hospital owned by Cassandra's father!

Shit! Gwen must have consumed less dosage of poison, exactly like Albert and Martha. She could act as if she was very ill, and the last bits in Havish's story clearly stated that Cassandra had replaced Dr Ed with some new doctors to attend to Gwen! That meant Cassandra had reasonable control over what went out to the police. That made sense now. Cassandra wasn't supposed to help Gwen commit the murder. She was supposed to protect her from becoming a suspect. Removing Gwen from Tracy and Ben's suspect list would be easier if the hospital manipulated the reports.

I could work with this detailed sketch and complete the story very comprehensively. I was now ready to call and update Krishav, which I decided to do while still in the showroom.

"What? Kory shouldn't be the killer?"

"No, Krishav. That would be Gwen and Cassandra. And sorry, I hadn't considered some aspects in my first version, which led to this slip."

"But Havish's portion says that Gwen is serious… I don't get it."

I took time to walk him through all the details I'd mentioned in my story sketch.

"Wow! That is super convincing, Ankana! Gwen would be easily saved in Cassandra's hospital as she might be faking a coma, if that's even possible. This version sounds more comprehensive and water-tight."

"Isn't it?" I was excited.

"It must be frustrating to rewrite most of what you had already completed, though," he chuckled.

"I know, but that's okay. I am looking forward to revisiting the story now. It's just that I am worried if we will extend beyond what we'd committed to the publisher," I voiced my concern.

"I will manage that. Don't worry about it. You focus on getting this version going now."

"Great, Krishav!"

"Also, send out the version you've already written anyway. I will try to validate if there is any big gap in your style compared to Havish's and if that needs addressing. Then you will be able to incorporate that while you begin work on the final version of the story."

"Done!"

***

Writing the final version of the book was a beautiful journey.

It spread well over a few months, and I enjoyed every bit. I would look forward to it when I came home from work, and impatiently waited for the weekly offs or any holiday to live in the world of Grayson Villa and help make the book turn out better.

Sujna had come down once in between to the showroom during lunch. We'd stepped out to the nearest eatery, which was quite crowded. We had to share a table with a couple seated before us. But we honestly didn't mind.

"You've put on weight in these couple of months, stupid." I hugged her sideways.

"Shit! I was hoping that was just my imagination. Don't tell me!" She searched for the mirror in her purse to look at herself.

The couple in front of us seemed shy and kept whispering to each other, giggling in between, in a world of their own. They hadn't touched a thing that had been served to eat and drink yet, and I was feeling extremely hungry looking at the spread of food and soft drinks.

I turned to look at Sujna, scrutinising her cheeks. "Relax, all you did was travel and eat. You will be fine once you are back to your routine."

"Since when did you become a fitness expert? I thought you'd been into writing. Yeah, how's the book coming along?"

"It's been all over the place, and hence I have been very busy. I have a couple of open points to close. I should be done soon."

"No wonder you've not been calling me frequently."

"Sorry." I pinched her cheeks.

"Wait, wait." She held my face in both her hands.

"Okay, Sujna. I can understand you want to kiss me, but that just used to be a joke. I..."

"Shut up! Of course, I know you didn't joke about it and meant whenever you said that. I am just seeing a new glow on your face." She let me go.

"Really?"

"I think you seem to be in a good place, mentally."

"Well... I don't know. Maybe. It is somewhat embarrassing to admit that I enjoy writing this more than my other two stories on romance."

"Ha ha!" we laughed.

Our food and soft drinks were served, and there was a moment of silence when we both gobbled up. Sujna's glass was placed next to the couple's soft drink. I was irritated that the waiter had not filled the drink to the brim in Sujna's glass while the other glass was full. When the waiter came around the next time, I opened my mouth to speak and immediately froze. I held Sujna's glass, which was at room temperature, while the other glass had water droplets surrounding it. It was cooler because of the ice cubes put earlier in it, which had now melted.

Shit! Gwen must have used an ice cube or a small ice container as the carrier of the lethal dose of poison that killed Nathan. Once she was done administering it to Nathan during the second serving, she had to get rid of it. She collapsed to the ground after the third serving but left the ice container or cube in her own chalice. That was what Dr Ed found as a high concentration of poison in her chalice and the diluted wine!

***

I was now done with the draft of the entire story and was reviewing it keenly. I had also sent the same to Krishav a week ago, and he'd called to tell me that he'd read it once, and it looked pretty good. He wanted to send this to his editors before he could send it to the publishing house, but I requested some time from him so that I could review it for one final time. He'd told me I was getting unnecessarily worried about it and should take it easy. Nevertheless, he agreed to my request.

I had made a list of items I had to check in the draft, and I'd already done that many times. All the items in the list that were coloured red in the beginning indicated that I had to address them, and all had turned green, except one.

I was still irritated with that medical package sent from New York to Grayson Villa. This was an unnecessary detail. There was no action to be taken from my end on the part. I just had difficulty convincing myself to colour it green. I smiled at my obsessive behaviour.

I again went to the internet searching for Thiopental. I spent some time on it and got no different result. It was an anaesthetic. I went deep into it and looked at its practical usage. That's when it helped. I saw an article telling me how to use that in this story. After all, I had cracked what I believed was a thick brick wall. I jumped on my bed and punched the air, feeling fulfilled. It meant I had to make only a minor tweak in the manuscript. I was sure Krishav would be supportive when I explained it to him.

I went to bed, content. I could not keep myself from smiling half the time and couldn't recollect the last time I cried tears of joy, but I did have them now. In my imagination, I thanked all the characters in the book for helping me figure them out. When it came to Cassandra, I said, "Such a bitch! But, well played."

I don't remember when I drifted off to sleep.

Chapter 22

Thoughts… they can be so scattered at times. They are all over the place. They are sometimes like pieces of a puzzle lying on the table but draw no interest, for it makes no sense in that scattered form. Some compare thoughts to monkeys that jump frequently from one branch to the other without gathering the essence each place offers. Similarly, our thoughts don't stay in one place to gather the meaning provided to us. Thoughts are like those dry leaves shed in autumn, carefree, in their own world; the wind carries them on its lap and lands them on the ground, unhurt. Each leaf in itself means nothing. But then you look at the ground to find all of them coming together to form a pattern. Ah! That is beauty. The pattern is the key.

Thoughts can be scattered like pieces of clothes that look shabby. Only if we can gather our thoughts like the thread that gathers the pieces of cloth and makes them whole once they are woven together-that's beauty, yes.

Threads may remind us of kites. Again, leave it for the wind to carry it, and the kite shall follow the wind like a child following her mother. Little does the kite know that the womb of the wind is big enough to accommodate the whole world. A kite, like thoughts, needs a fine thread to keep it grounded. Let the kite, like thoughts, wander in the sky aimlessly, for that's what it was born for. Never forget the times when there was a fear that the kite would go so far that there would be no coming back. There will come such times. And then, the thread takes prominence. When you know that it is a matter of time before the kite will be lost forever, hold that thread. It will then know its source. It will then know that its journey was supposed to be only temporary, and its home calls for it. No matter how far the kite has flown, it should always remember that it must return. It may be a faint pull on the ground, but for the kite? The kite feels it like a tug in its heart.

"*Ahhh!*" I woke up with a start, with goosebumps on my body, shivering and strangely sweating at the same time. It was getting very difficult to breathe. I wanted to shout, but my voice didn't come out. I desperately reached for my phone. I was terrified. I didn't know whom to call to express what I was going through. It was after all… a thought, wasn't it?

I saw that it was four in the morning. A vehicle passed by on the road, and its light flashed in my open window, making me shout with surprise. I had finally found my voice. I was able to breathe with less difficulty now, but I kept shivering and madly looking around with fear.

I tried to get out of bed, but my legs lacked strength and I almost fell. With some difficulty, I moved to the window and closed it.

I came back to my bed and found my phone. I struggled to get a proper grip. I was about to dial Sujna's number but stopped short.

I dialled Krishav's number instead. It rang multiple times, but he didn't pick up. "Pick up, damn it!" I shouted and called again.

This time, he received the call.

"Ankana… don't tell me you discovered another twist in…"

"Ka… Kau…" I was just unable to speak.

"What happened, Ankana?" He sensed my discomfort in speaking and the short breaths.

"I… didn't know who else… you are… were… a friend," I stammered.

"Get hold of yourself, Ankana, please. I am getting worried now."

"I think… yes. I am sure…"

"Should I call for an ambulance? You don't seem…"

"It just came… yes. I am scared…" I was crying now, and my words were understandably difficult for him to decipher.

"Ankana, you are having a panic attack." His voice was tense.

"I… closed the windows… no one can hear… me."

"Please listen to me. Close your eyes and take a deep breath."

"Door's closed also… night."

"Please close your eyes and take deep breaths. Do it, please!" he said in a commanding tone.

"I really…"

"No, don't talk, Ankana. Do as I say. I promise I will listen to you. First, please do as I say. Don't talk. Take deep breaths. Close your eyes."

"Ok…ay."

"Deep breaths. Yes." His voice had a calming effect, and I could breathe properly, although my head seemed to be spinning.

It worried me that I heard nothing from him for some time.

"You there? Krishav?"

"Yes, I am right here and not going anywhere, okay? If the call gets disconnected for any reason, I will call you back. You don't have to worry."

"No, listen…"

"Calm down, Ankana. I will listen to you."

"Shut up and listen…" I was getting back into panic mode.

"Okay, okay…"

"Can I… trust you?"

"I… yes, Ankana. You can trust me."

"I called you… because… I… don't know whom to… trust."

"What is this about, Ankana?"

"It's about… wait." My fear and tears were replaced with anxiety. "Who all have you spoken to about the book?"

"Havish's book, right? Only to the publisher for now."

"Sure, right?"

"Yes, Ankana. You are letting the story overwhelm you. You are doing just fine…"

"Please listen… please." I was sobbing again.

"Sure, tell me. What about Havish's book? Did you have a bad dream?"

"Uh huh." Tears were flowing down, and I was having a lump in my throat again. I was unable to say a word.

"Please calm down, Ankana, and take your time. I will listen to whatever you have to say. There is no hurry."

I regained my breath. "Krishav…" I cried again but didn't stop. "Havish's death…"

"Yes, Ankana."

I took a deep breath. "I don't think it was an accident. I… think he… he was… murdered."

***

There was stunned silence at the other end. However, he spoke immediately, "I am still here, Ankana. I haven't gone. I… am just unable to…"

"I know… it's okay. Don't tell anyone."

"You keep walking in the bedroom for a while. It helps with the panic attack."

"Did you hear what I said?" I was anxious.

"I did. You relax for now, please."

"Okay… don't tell anyone. Is someone in your room?"

"No, I am alone at home and won't tell anyone about anything we discuss. Okay?"

"What if the phone's tapped?" I started breathing in gasps again.

"No, no, Ankana. Stay with me. No one has tapped our phones."

"You don't know that," I said.

"I… should I send any of my friends in Mangalore over to your place so that you have company?"

"Yes, I need someone. I… will call Sujna."

"She's in Mangalore, right?"

"Yes..."

"You don't worry about anything for now, okay?"

"You understood what I said, right?" I wasn't sure he had heard me correctly, and I didn't want to repeat anything as I was paranoid that anyone else might overhear.

"Yes, I understood. I just... don't know what to say right now."

"I know you don't believe me." I could control my voice better for now.

"It's not like that."

"You think I have gone mad writing the book."

"Of course not!"

He was feeling helpless and struggling to keep me from getting further anxious. But in that moment, I was feeling way more helpless than I can express in words.

CHAPTER 23

I could hear Sujna speaking to someone over the phone. She was trying to keep a low voice, but as I had slept holding her tightly, her subtle movements woke me. My heart was still pounding heavily. However, I could control my emotions and thoughts better than a few hours ago.

Krishav had ensured that I call Sujna up in the early hour so that she could come to my place immediately, and till she came, he tried to keep my mind engaged with simple topics. He didn't utter a word about what I'd told him in my anxious state. Perhaps he didn't want me to get upset or lose my mind. Once Sujna reached my place, he spoke to her, maybe briefing certain dos and don'ts. He told me he would see me soon. I'd just held Sujna and gone to sleep.

"Oh! Sorry, I woke you up, dear," Sujna apologised, sensing my movement.

"No, I just… who was it?" I asked.

"Krishav had called to confirm that he'd just landed. He's on his way from the airport."

"What?" I was confused.

"Yeah, he told me when I got here that he would board the early morning flight from Bangalore."

"Oh god!" I ran my hands through my unkempt hair.

"Listen, whatever it is, it'll be fine." She smiled as her hand replaced mine on my head. She was seated next to me on the bed. Krishav had said nothing to her when they'd spoken earlier, and I could not articulate anything when I asked her to come over immediately.

"Krishav told you not to ask anything, right?" I asked, looking at the ceiling fan.

She nodded, which I could see from the corner of my eyes.

"I… whatever." I let my head rest on her lap, and wrapped my hands around her waist.

"It's fine, Anku."

I shook my head while resting on her lap. She just patted on my head. I admired her patience. She had come at a god-forbidden hour of the night to be with me, knowing nothing about what was going on, and remained calm though she was in the dark.

"What did Krishav say on the phone when you'd just reached in the morning?"

She hesitated, but only for a moment. She could see that I was in better shape now than when she'd come in. "Nothing much. He was crisp in saying that you just had a panic attack and were better now. Yet, he warned me not to ask a thing about it. He told me not to speak anything for the time being. And, as I just mentioned, he said he would take the next available flight to Mangalore."

"Hmm…"

"So, it's nearly ten in the morning, and I am quite hungry. Do you want to go down to the nearest hotel?" she inquired.

"No!" A sudden fear gripped me. What if someone was waiting for me outside and would kill me as soon as they saw me? What if I was abducted? What if… but unlike a few hours ago, I was able to control my anxiety.

"Fine, Anku. I will order something in, okay?"

"Sorry, Sujna. I just…" I took a few deep breaths. "Let's go to the nearest hotel. I think I do need some fresh air." I smiled, after what seemed to be a long gap.

"Great!"

We had our breakfast, and she suggested we go for a walk in the nearby park, which thankfully wasn't closed after the typical 'morning walk' hours. I felt much better after this. The only thing was that I could still sense my heart beating rapidly and my body warming up, as if I had a fever.

Once we were back, I could see that Sujna had difficulty going on without being let in. Thankfully, Krishav reached by then. The initial formalities kept them busy because the two were meeting each other for the first time. However, Krishav could not converse properly, perhaps because of what I had told him early this morning.

After a bit of chatter, there was a prolonged silence. Sujna wanted us to tell her something at least, and Krishav waited with bated breath to see if I wanted or had already informed Sujna about anything.

"Sorry, Sujna. I didn't tell you earlier anything about why I was in a desperate state this morning."

Sujna nodded, comforting me. She knew I must have had my reasons.

"And sorry for the scare I gave you in the morning, Krishav."

"That's okay, Ankana. You know that if you don't speak more, I might have a panic attack right now." He tried to make us laugh, which worked on me at least. Sujna, who was trying to be brave and comforting, was now having difficulty playing that role. She was indeed worried, and that was showing on her face.

"As I said, Krishav, it is a thought. But a very strong one."

"I am sure it is, considering how you sounded this morning. So don't worry about whether I believe it or not. Just tell me what made you think that. I am not able to see how."

"Here's where you will tell me the context, guys," Sujna interjected, waving her hand at us.

"Sujna, I think Havish's death was not an accident. I think he was murdered."

I saw her eyes go wide. "What… how? What are you saying?"

"Sujna, first, let me tell you the story I helped Krishav with."

"Sorry, what? Ankana, this is no story time. You just said…"

I raised my hand. "There is a reason I am saying that. Allow me to share the story."

"Is that allowed? I thought you were not supposed to…" She was confused, her eyes shifting rapidly from me to Krishav and then back to me.

"It's all right, Sujna. Go on, please, Ankana," Krishav said.

I summarised the story and got it to the endpoint, which even Krishav knew.

"How's any of this linked to…?" She was unsure why I was talking about the book. I could see that Krishav, too, had the same question in mind but waited.

"Krishav, I'd told you earlier that the medicines sent from New York, which Kory left safely in the storeroom, were bothering me, right?"

"Right," he nodded.

"It was Thiopental."

"Right," both said, and Krishav continued, "You already confirmed that it was no poison."

"That's true. But then, last night, a simple thought came to me. Matthew, Nathan's father, had required some basic health supplements based on his conversation with Cassandra, as recorded in the book…"

"Yes."

"Then what was Thiopental doing there in the first place? It is an anaesthetic, and Matthew didn't need any anaesthetic as a health supplement."

"Hmmm…" His eyes were looking through me in a daze. He was trying to think as well.

"So, I deep-dived into all the possible uses of Thiopental."

"And…," both said in chorus.

"It is a barbiturate drug. It is used to medically induce a coma under special circumstances."

"So?" He wasn't able to follow.

"In this story, it seems to be an intentional move by Cassandra to travel to New York and go to her father's main hospital facility, where she could get her hands on this drug and get it to Palm Beach. Perhaps it was imported from another place."

"Why is that?"

"This drug was scarce in the US a few years ago because its sole manufacturer ceased production. New York was one of the places where it was easier for her to procure it."

"Okay…"

"Cassandra got this drug transferred to Grayson Villa, not to use it during the murder, but after."

"How?"

"Once people from Cassandra's hospital picked everyone up from Grayson Villa, including the Thiopental, and reached the hospital, Gwen was not put under Dr Ed's charge. Some of the other doctors, whom Cassandra had under her influence, put Gwen in a medically induced coma before Dr Ed could reach.

"Thus, even if the police would want to have a second opinion about the whole incident, which was likely considering they'd know this hospital belonged to Cassandra's father, even the second opinion would suggest that the patient was in a coma due to the poison consumed by her, which strengthened the case against Kory or someone else, leaving Gwen out of contention."

"Medically induced coma… isn't that a risky process?"

"It used to be a risky process in the past. However, based on my research last night, medically induced coma isn't as difficult nowadays. Of course, the basis of my research is only the internet."

"This is all fine, Ankana. But how's this connected to Havish's death?" Krishav asked, and Sujna nodded too.

I waited for it to dawn on them.

"Unless you are saying… no… no way, Ankana."

Sujna was curious. "What is that? I don't understand."

Krishav continued to look at me. "So you are saying that Havish's wife, Rupa's coma immediately after the accident was an artificially induced one?"

"Yes."

"Oh!" Sujna was surprised.

"Come on, Ankana! This is just speculation. How can you just... I mean on the basis of some theory that emerged in the story..."

"Think about it, Krishav. How many days did Rupa spend in a coma?"

He thought for a moment and said, "I guess anywhere between five days and a week."

"And a medically induced coma isn't recommended for a prolonged period. It can be around a week."

"That can just be a coincidence, Anku," replied Sujna.

"Guys, there is surely more to it."

Krishav seemed more irritable right now. Perhaps he was kicking himself for having come all the way from Bangalore only to hear me share my thoughts about Havish being murdered without any concrete proof. Looking at the discouraging expressions of the two people I perhaps trusted the most at the moment, I was beginning to doubt myself. It was so clear when it came to me. There was a strong conviction about the whole thing in my mind back then, which seemed to weaken at the moment.

"At least tell me how it happened?"

"How what happened, Ankana?" He was losing his patience.

"Do you know how Havish's accident happened?"

"Yes, of course. Havish and Rupa were on their way to Madikeri to spend the weekend. On the way, after their car overtook another vehicle near Channapatna, it went off the road into the steep farmland next to it. Havish died on the spot, and Rupa survived with injuries."

I was desperately looking for something I could hold on to but couldn't put my finger on anything.

"So, how was Rupa taken to a hospital?"

"Listen, I don't know the minute details, Ankana. I think I was right. You have gotten too involved with Havish's book; naturally, it's tiring you out. It is also my fault that I pushed you too much for this. I am sorry if that was the case. It would help if you stopped trying to draw a parallel between the book and real life. I don't think any crime has been committed in real life," he said it slowly, purposefully, as if talking to a child.

"Come on, Ankana!" I thought to myself. The pattern seemed too accurate here to be a coincidence. Something must be there that I could hold on to. I wondered why I was latching on to the coma situation alone. I had a few other questions as well.

"Uhh… which hospital was she taken to?"

"I don't remember the name of the hospital, Ankana." He was indeed irritated. "I just remember it was in Vijayanagara because I'd gone there the next morning. Rupa's cousin, Rakesh, is the Administration Head there. Hence, I…" All three of us froze for a moment. Krishav held himself back from saying anything.

I probed, "Did you say you went to see Rupa the day after the accident?"

"Yes. The accident had happened the night before."

"Which means the hospital you found her in was the first hospital she was admitted to?"

"I… guess so. Why?"

"If the accident occurred in Channapatna, isn't it strange that they didn't get Rupa admitted to some hospital nearby, considering the urgency of treatment? Why did they bring Rupa all the way to Vijayanagara in Bangalore? The distance must be more than thirty kilometres."

"It's more than fifty kilometres," added Sujna.

Krishav slowly nodded. He was thinking. “See, Ankana. I understand that there seem to be missing answers when we sit here and discuss. However, I am sure that if these questions are asked of the right people, there will be simple and relevant answers that will disprove your theory.”

“I understand that’s a possibility,” I agreed.

“And you cannot just go around accusing others here without proof. This is not a book. This is real life.” He sounded serious. “If there is no reality in your story, then a defamation case can cost you money and result in imprisonment. I am saying this because I know a few people in the literary field who have been involved in such cases.”

Sujna and I nodded, slightly scared.

“Also, let’s hypothetically assume that what you say is true. Then, if there is some wrongdoing, it means that such people can go to extreme lengths to harm you as well.”

“Oh!” Sujna said.

I was getting more anxious. This seemed too big for me to get into, and what if Krishav was right? What if all these were just a figment of my imagination? I didn’t want to think that was the case. But just because I think that’s how it is doesn’t make it real. Should I back out? That option sounded very wrong in my mind.

“You need to be careful,” Krishav said, looking down at the floor, and I nodded. He paused, as if contemplating something, and repeated, “*We* need to be careful.” He looked at me.

His words released the weight on my shoulders, and I smiled, hesitantly acknowledging that.

Chapter 24

"Firstly, we are not professional investigators or police. We should stop acting like one and take help wherever needed," said Krishav. Sujna and I nodded in a dumb manner.

"We will need the right people who can check on facts and help us clarify if there is any truth in the theory we have." He looked at me.

"You are still not convinced?" I asked.

"Just because I'm convinced about something doesn't make it the truth, and just because I'm not convinced about something doesn't make it false," he replied, and it made sense.

"So, what next?" I wanted to understand.

"I don't know either, Ankana. I am thinking of whose help we can take to find out more about the facts of the case."

"Shouldn't an FIR be lodged in the police station for such cases? At least that's what they show in the movies," Sujna remarked.

"It works surprisingly well in the movies. We have to see how it works in reality. I think I know one person who can help," Krishav said, deep in thought.

"Like, do you know the Commissioner of Police or some big politician or industrialist?" Sujna seemed curious.

"No, Sujna. Again, this is not a movie; we don't have such influence. I'm speaking of..."

"Even as a literary agent, you don't come across such influential people, Krishav?" I was surprised.

"No, guys!" He stopped and tried to calm down. I think he had almost branded us as bimbos in his mind, but was courteous enough not to say it. "I don't get to have such luxuries. I only know a few big people in my field who might know such influencers. I don't think we can take such routes at this point. We need to be very discreet here. No one should even know that we are trying to unearth something. As I clarified earlier, we still don't know if there is any wrongdoing. We are just trying to get to the bottom of it. Is that fine?"

"Yes," I said more readily than he'd have expected.

"You said you may know someone?" Sujna probed.

"Yes, and he's not some commissioner in the police. He's a constable."

***

"Senior Constable Joshi here."

"Uncle, Krishav this side."

"Who Krishav? I don't know anyone with that name," the voice replied curtly.

"Rudramma's grandson, Uncle."

"Oh god! Krishav. Sorry, I didn't recognise your voice. How are you doing? It is a pleasant surprise to receive your call."

Krishav had made that call on speaker mode, and the sudden change in Joshi's demeanour made Sujna and I exchange glances and smiles.

Krishav, without referring to the case, asked in plain words that we would need help getting the facts of a specific case discreetly. Joshi agreed so readily that I wasn't sure if he understood what we were asking of him. Even Krishav tried to emphasise why it could be difficult, but Joshi had already decided to help us.

"Just tell me which case you are talking about. I will get the details for you."

"Uncle, there was a death some months ago of a certain Havish. It was an accident on Mysore Road, near Channapatna."

"Hmmm… I don't know much about it, Krishav. Let's do this. I will try to find out the whereabouts of this case. I will need to know in which jurisdiction this accident was registered first. Let me do that and get back to you. You text me the details that you are aware of."

"Sure, uncle. We can meet when you have some updates about the case," Krishav answered.

"Done."

"Sorry for the trouble, uncle."

"Come now, Krishav. You are Rudramma's grandson. All you have to do is order."

"Please don't embarrass me, uncle. Thanks a lot. As I said, no soul should know about it."

"You don't worry about that. I will call you back in a couple of days."

Once the line was disconnected, I said, "What would we have done without your grandmother, Krishav?"

"I sometimes wonder that myself," he said, not completely jesting.

"Was she some don?" Sujna inquired politely, and the two of us laughed.

***

"Eww… why are all the men staring at me lewdly?" I was creeped out. It had been two days since our conversation with Uncle Joshi, and I'd come to Bangalore.

"Yeah, not sure why Uncle Joshi asked us to come to such a shady place. I guess ladies do not regularly visit it, hence the stares. You don't keep looking around now," said Krishav.

There was a sleazy Kannada song being played in the bar, if I could call it that.

The waiter came to us to take our order.

"You have coffee or tea?" I asked, and he gave me a nasty stare.

"We are waiting for someone. Will order in a bit," Krishav said, and the waiter asked him to hurry up and left us.

Krishav turned to me and asked, "You are a teetotaller?"

"Of course not!" I said, almost sounding offended. "I mean, there needs to be the right ambience. I surely won't be able to drink in and around such a crowd." I made a face.

"Right."

"Don't tell me you're a teetotaller? Like Kory," I said and laughed.

"Ha ha! I have wine sometimes, nothing else."

"Don't worry, we will ask Uncle Titus to send a big bottle of his vintage wine for you." I was having fun.

"You have gone mad with the book, haven't you?" he asked.

I just shrugged and laughed in response.

Someone tapped on Krishav's shoulder. It was Senior Constable Joshi.

"Hello, uncle." Krishav got up to greet him.

"Please sit," Joshi said, taking Krishav's hand and shaking them excitedly. I could see the joy in his eyes even with the dim lights in this dingy place.

He looked at me and then at Krishav, who introduced us. "Oh! You are Havish's sister?" Joshi seemed suspicious.

Krishav took a moment and explained the reason crisply.

"Then how come you are interested in finding out if it was a murder?" His voice was reduced to a whisper while he said the last word, but I could understand it easily.

"Sir, I thought it was the right thing to do. If some person is responsible for this, they must be punished," I blabbered, not with much conviction.

Joshi nodded, considering my words. He didn't buy it. If I were any other person, he'd have readily dismissed me. However, I was with Krishav, the descendant of Rudramma, and that outweighed everything else.

"Here's what I have got from the FIR. Such information is confidential, so I had to bribe a few people. However, even in the end, I could only write a few lines down. I couldn't take a picture of the same." He tried to pull out his handwritten notes.

"Uncle, did someone wonder why you were trying to snoop around?"

"No, nothing to be worried about. Here, let me read.

"To summarise, Havish and his wife Rupa were on the way to Madikeri late at night. It was around one o'clock when…"

"What? One o'clock in the night?" Krishav interrupted, sounding surprised.

Joshi and I looked at Krishav with a puzzled expression on our faces.

"Is that an issue?" I asked.

"Havish was a morning person. He'd wake up around four in the morning to exercise and write. It just sounds odd that he'd drive at such an hour."

"Unless there was a necessity," I said blankly.

Joshi resumed. "It was around one o'clock in the night that Havish tried to overtake a vehicle from the wrong side and lost control, and there was an accident. That led to the car being thrown out of the road and into the sugarcane field at a slightly steeper altitude. As the car was at high speed, the accident caused Havish's immediate death and severely injured his wife, Rupa. The post-mortem report, which is compulsory in case the victim dies within twenty-four hours of the accident, clearly states that Havish was not drunk. Hence, it was a clear case of hit and run," he concluded.

"Did someone from the accident spot call up the police station or an ambulance?" I asked.

"That… is not clear in this report."

"Would you have access to the post-mortem report?" asked Krishav.

"No, Krishav. All those are very difficult to get."

"Uncle, if we have to bribe a few people, can we do that and try to get some more information, please? What we have seems insufficient," said Krishav.

Joshi seemed to feel bad that his work wasn't sufficient to help us out. He thought and said, "I was told by a few colleagues that a certain sub-inspector named Patil was showing interest in the case. His superiors asked him to let the case go, as they thought it was a simple hit-and-run.

"So Patil may have some information, but he is strange. I will see what else I can do by talking to his juniors."

"Thanks, uncle," Krishav said, taking out some money to give to Joshi.

"Eh… please, Krishav. What are you doing?"

"Uncle, you said you may have to bribe some people. I thought…"

"Please! Don't ever do this with me. I cannot accept a single rupee from you. Please don't insult me like this. My payment will be complete when you are happy with the information I get," he said, smiling.

"Okay, uncle." Krishav backed off, knowing that Joshi would be hurt if he persisted.

***

"That was hardly anything new," I complained.

"Not entirely. Until now, when I'd heard that the accident had occurred at night, I assumed it would be earlier. I cannot imagine

Havish driving at one o'clock in the night. Ankana, once when we had to travel to Mumbai to meet a director…"

"What? A director? Like a movie director?"

"Yeah, well, last year, someone in Bollywood had shown interest in making one of Havish's books into a movie. Hence, we had travelled."

"Wow!"

"Anyway, I still remember that it was last-minute travel. He refused to take a late-night flight, though our options were limited, stating that it upsets his biological clock. We had to end up postponing our meeting with the director as we didn't get any other flight that suited our timing."

"That's curious. I now understand why you reacted like that when you heard what Joshi Uncle had to say."

"I hope he will have more concrete information for us to dive into," Krishav concluded.

"Hmmm… let's see. Anyway, I'll get a cab now."

"Cab? Where to?"

"Eh… I… yes, that's a good question. In my eagerness to meet your Uncle Joshi, I forgot to book a hotel room for myself." I'd come to Bangalore only that afternoon.

"What? No, Ankana. Relax, will you? Please stay at my place for a few days till we get this sorted out. I have a couple of spare rooms. You could have invited Sujna as well. If only her work had permitted…"

"No, that's okay, Krishav. I will…"

"Nope, you are not doing anything like that. I am not doing any favour here. You don't have to think it burdens me. Also, it's better if we stay close, right? What if there is some attack?"

That got me, and I was momentarily worried about that possibility. Then I looked at him, and he was laughing.

"Krishav!"

"Sorry, sorry. I just wanted to see your face after saying that. Enough of the drama. Please stay at my place for a few days, Ankana."

"Fine."

* * *

The next morning, Krishav had to leave for some work. I stayed put in his house, which was relatively smaller than what I'd imagined it would be. It was kept quite tidy for a bachelor, though. No wonder he had three people as domestic help. It had been difficult to explain to each of them who I was.

I was sure that in the maid community in and around Krishav's area, the news would spread like wildfire that some chick was staying with him.

There were enough resources at his place to keep me occupied. There were all possible online streaming services on his television, enough genres of books on the big bookshelf, and perhaps the best variety of restaurant spread that I'd seen in my life in the area. I made good use of all of it until it was time for me to get to completing the story based on the Thiopental angle I had unearthed. As it was a minor alteration, I finished it soon.

Immediately after that, I got a call on my phone, and it was Krishav.

"Yes, Krishav?"

"Ankana, can you get a cab and come to the same place as yesterday?"

"You mean that dingy bar?"

"Yes."

"Why?"

"Not completely sure. Uncle Joshi called me and said that he's managed to get some more information."

"That's good. But what's with such secrecy? Can he not come to your house?"

"Ugh! We will request him to meet at a less shady place next time, okay? Can you leave soon? I am on my way already."

"Oh, sure. I will leave now."

The bar had fewer people, as it was still early evening. Krishav and Joshi Uncle occupied the same table as the previous day.

"Come come, Ankana," Uncle Joshi called me excitedly to the table.

Krishav was having a glass of wine, and as I sat next to him, I saw that Uncle Joshi was having something that looked wicked in a glass, and it smelled too strong.

He seemed slightly embarrassed. "Hope you don't mind," he said with glee, referring to the weird liquid in his glass. I just smiled and nodded, making a note in my mind that I would ask him what it was so that I could try it when I was alone in Mangalore.

It looked like the two were waiting for me to arrive and hadn't started to speak on this topic yet.

"I will send you his biodata, Krishav. Please see if you can forward it to someone in MNCs. As I told you already, he is a nice guy. English may be a problem, but he will surely work hard." They were discussing a different topic, which they wanted to conclude before moving on.

"No problem, uncle. I will send it to some of my friends working in Corporate."

"Sure, but you also send it to MNCs," he emphasised.

"Uncle, both mean… sure, I will do that," Krishav said with a smile.

"*Haan*, sorry. We were speaking of my nephew while waiting for you, Ankana. Anyway, I got hold of another senior constable who had worked for sub-inspector Patil to wrap this case up. There seems to be nothing much recorded that is important. They have treated it like any normal hit-and-run case. So he told me that it is better to let it rest."

"Oh!" Krishav, too, wasn't happy with the progress.

"The only additional information I could get was that immediately when the accident occurred, the wife was apparently still conscious. So she called her brother for help. He then spoke to his hospital and got the ambulance to get her to safety."

"That is ridiculous, no? Wasn't it common sense to get her admitted to any nearby hospital?"

"Yes, but maybe in a panic they took her to a hospital in Bangalore."

This wasn't convincing, but I knew we had hit a dead-end with Uncle Joshi.

"We won't be able to extract anything else, uncle?" Krishav, too, sounded desperate.

"To get involved any further, you have to get it through official channels, Krishav. That will attract attention, and it is not recommended if you don't have any solid backing."

"One-quarter rum!" the bartender shouted.

"That is for me. Let me get back." Joshi Uncle left the table to collect it.

"What to do now, Krishav?"

He, too, seemed low. "We cannot ask for this case to be reopened until we have evidence."

"I am sure once the case is reopened, we can have access to many other things that can point us in the right direction."

"As of now, nothing is conclusive about this being a murder. We are only working on probabilities. It will get us nowhere."

"Is it possible for us to ask Uncle Joshi to introduce us to his other colleague whom he'd approached for information? We can directly…" I stopped speaking as a man pulled a chair at our table. I thought he wanted to take the chair away, but he sat with us instead.

I was super frustrated with such behaviour. Before I could say something, Krishav said, "Excuse me. Can you please occupy another table?"

He looked at Krishav and nodded but continued to sit in the same place and posture.

I wasn't sure if he understood us. I tried, "Boss, did you hear what he said? Other tables are empty. Leave this table at once and occupy another."

By then, Uncle Joshi had come back with his quarter of rum. He gestured to Krishav as if asking who the other man was, to which we both shrugged, stating we had no idea. Joshi Uncle raised his hand, gesturing that he would manage it.

"Hello, brother. Do you know who I am?" he said, winking at Krishav and me.

The man at the table removed his dark glasses, though it didn't make sense why he was wearing them in the first place, and left them on the table.

He then looked up to meet Uncle Joshi in the eye.

"Yes, I do."

It was as if, in a moment, Uncle Joshi's high disappeared. "Pa… Patil sir," he said, without blinking.

Patil nodded indifferently and gestured for Uncle Joshi to exit the place, which the latter did without any protest, leaving his glass of rum at the table.

Chapter 25

Krishav and I were initially nervous about saying a word, waiting for Sub-Inspector Patil to make the first move. He wasn't in his uniform.

"I've seen you. No?" Patil spoke, looking at Krishav.

It seemed as if Krishav had recognised his face. "Yes, sir. I remember now. I saw you once in the hospital and at Havish's house. I was Havish's literary agent and friend."

"Hmm… and you would be?" He was looking at me. It looked like he used his thick moustache to camouflage his boyish face from criminals so that they took him seriously. I didn't know how much it worked on them, but it worked perfectly on us now.

"I… am Havish's sister, Ankana."

His expression gave away his curiosity. "Strange, I don't recollect recording any statement under your name. I don't think I've even heard of you before."

"Havish and I were estranged since a young age. He was my half-brother."

"Oh!"

He paused, clearly assessing something about me.

"Why all the interest right now?"

"About?" I tried to play innocent.

"About asking Joshi to get all the facts related to the case."

"What is wrong with that?" I spoke with a certain confidence, which surprised even me.

"It is a closed case, Ms. Ankana, and it is wrong for a civilian to poke her nose in matters related to the law."

I stayed quiet for a while.

"Sir, we didn't intend to cross any line. We were just not sure if the case was closed in the right manner," Krishav said.

"What do you mean? It is closed as any other simple hit-and-run case. What is not right according to you?"

"I don't think you have the authority to cross-question us." I looked directly into his eyes, and Krishav's change in breathing suggested that I shouldn't have said something like that.

"Okay. But I do have the authority to take action against Senior Constable Joshi, who has crossed his line in trying to access reports beyond his reach. I assume you will be fine with that, won't you?" he said, with a calm arrogance that took me by surprise.

"No!" both of us said in unison.

Krishav continued, "Sir, please don't drag him into this. He didn't do anything."

"On the contrary, Mr Krishav, it seems like you have dragged him into this, though he had nothing to do with it."

Krishav opened his mouth, but Patil raised his hand, indicating that he should shut up.

He now looked at me. "And Ms. Ankana, this is India. People fear police more than rowdies for a reason. We can misuse power better than most." At that moment, I thought he was drunk on power. He immediately continued, "And I don't say that with pride." That made me wonder if I had read him correctly.

"But sir, what wrong have we done? We were doing some harmless investigation on our own."

"It's a simple question, Ms. Ankana. What are you trying to gain by doing this? Why are you trying to get your hands on the facts of this case?"

"We just… thought it is possible that…," I attempted.

"What's possible, Ms. Ankana?"

"That… there may have been some foul play."

"Surprisingly, you weren't even in the picture until after Havish's death, and now you have sprung from nowhere stating possible foul play. Let's think about this. Isn't it funny that you are trying to prove that something is wrong months after the case is closed? Maybe… I don't know… you have a plan of your own," he said, chuckling at the last bit.

"Sorry?" I was not sure I understood his words.

"I am trying to understand your motive, Ms. Ankana."

"Sir, it is possible that someone has misled the keepers of the law. Also, it is possible that…," I contemplated and went ahead, "that there is a murderer out there, running scot-free."

He raised his eyebrows, not expecting me to say something like that.

"So, you are doing this to bring justice to Havish, though you've been estranged since childhood?"

"Well, yes."

He smiled sheepishly. "It looks like you want a piece of Havish's property. So, you want to reopen an already closed case, introduce new variables, confuse people, and maybe gain sympathy from Rupa in due course to get a share for yourself."

"Sir, that's not the case," Krishav stepped in.

"Mr Krishav, you are a clever man. Let's not try to act all naïve. You, too, know what I mean. I have seen plenty of such instances in my career."

"Mr Patil, it looks like you don't even know the basics of how rights of property work." I was angry, and Krishav was trying to pull my arm. But I was not going to be stopped.

"No matter how much Havish benefitted from his writing profession and his corporate career that ended a few years ago, there was a portion of wealth that he inherited from his father, *our* father. This means that I have no need to blame or frame someone for Havish's murder to get my share of the wealth. If it was money I was after, I could have hired an average lawyer and gotten at least half of my share. But, as you can see, I have done nothing like that. Instead, we sat with a senior constable, trying to figure out if something may have seemed wrong at the death scene or before. This means we were only trying to get to the truth in a non-controversial way," I paused after this monologue.

He took a long pause and a big puff from his cigarette. "So you knew that already."

I realised that he was testing me, and if I was not wrong, I had passed it.

I just shrugged.

"You said there could be a murderer running free."

"Yes, sir. We believe that is a possibility."

"What proof do you have?"

"Sir, we don't have any proof."

"Do you have a theory?" he asked.

Krishav and I looked at each other. Patil understood.

"Hmm… what is that then?"

I saw an opening. "Sir, I am happy to share that. But is there any way you can help us?" I pleaded.

He looked at me and shook his head slowly. "No, I cannot help you officially."

Krishav and I stared at Patil, who looked at his watch and then lit another cigarette. I wasn't happy being a passive smoker, but I kept that opinion, under the present circumstances, to myself.

Patil finished his cigarette and looked at his watch. It seemed stupid and annoying to me.

"I will see what I can do to help you unofficially. It's past six now, and I am off duty." He looked up to both of us in turn.

Krishav and I looked at each other, confused. Then, a faint smile formed on the face of the thick-moustached Sub-Inspector that made us smile back.

Chapter 26

"You surprised me by stating that you think Havish was murdered. Why's that?" Patil sounded very curious. He had toned down his voice and somehow appeared more human now.

I said, "Based on what we heard from Uncle Joshi, I thought you believed that something was not right in this case, and that's why you were getting deep into it before being discouraged from going on any further."

"True, I felt there was something that didn't make sense. However, my suspicion was not about Havish's death at all. I mean, I never once thought it was a murder. Else, I wouldn't have let the case close."

"Can you please say more? What didn't make sense?" I questioned.

"I was somewhat suspicious about Rakesh. I wasn't convinced about travelling back to Bangalore to admit Rupa to the hospital instead of trying to admit her to any hospital near Channapatna. In fact, Maddur and Mandya would have been much closer than Bangalore, and they have some good hospitals."

"That's true."

"I suspected that Rakesh had intentionally delayed in helping Rupa. If she met her end during the transit, I thought he might have stood to gain somehow. Hence, I was livid when she was put in such danger that she went into a coma the same night, and I made some noise. That's when my higher-ups told me not to make a big deal of a simple hit-and-run case. When Rupa came out of the coma in a week, I was left with no other option but to close the case."

"Do you think anybody influenced your seniors to direct you?" Krishav asked.

"No, no. You might have heard in the corporate world that the reward for good work is more work?"

We nodded. I was unable to understand the reference.

"It is true in the Police as well. I don't mean to boast, but because of some issues that were sorted under my charge, my superior kept my table full of things that required my attention. Hence, he didn't want me to waste my time on an open-and-shut case."

"But, did you not get to question Rakesh about his approach of getting Rupa to Bangalore?"

"I did that. When I had to visit the hospital, I met Rakesh, who was talking to the doctors about Rupa's health. You must already know that he is the Administrative Head of the same hospital. After speaking with him, I didn't feel there was a need to remain suspicious. He was surprised when I inquired about it. He said that Rupa had made a desperate call for help. It would have been a nightmare for anyone to track her down in the farmland. He said that he had thankfully asked her to share her GPS location, which she did before she lost consciousness, and he dispatched an ambulance immediately to get her to the hospital. His claim also was that he believed her to be severely injured and couldn't trust any hospitals around the area of the accident to be able to save her. Again, though this point wasn't very compelling, it was a statement I couldn't argue with. Moreover, it was a weekday, and there was no traffic on Mysore Road at such an hour at night. They would have gotten her in record time to save her life instead of trying to figure out which was a better hospital that could help her survive."

"What about Rupa, sir? Did you get to ask her anything at all since her recovery?"

"I was relieved once I heard that she'd gained consciousness. Even though the facts and the probabilities derived from them suggested that Rakesh might be right throughout, I still wasn't very convinced.

Once she was fine, instead of sending my constables, I visited the hospital myself to take her statement formally."

"Did you believe there was anything important to support her statement?"

"Nothing. After all, the lady had survived a difficult accident and lost her husband. I didn't want to make it difficult for her. That's also one of the reasons I wanted to go instead of sending my constables. Some of them do not have a good emotional quotient and might end up traumatising the victim even more," he chuckled and continued, "Rupa said that Havish was returning from a lecture at Delhi that night."

"Oh!" I reacted.

He added, "You both know that Havish left his corporate job and took up writing full-time. Even though he may not have come up with any new books for a long time, he used to go to institutions to give lectures that combined his writing and corporate career.

"I wonder how a writer who'd seen average success was getting such opportunities. Anyway, I got someone from my department to call up that institute under Delhi University the next day. That was needed to record the chronology of the events. They confirmed his visit. They said it was a huge success. The students had liked his lecture so much that they almost mobbed him with questions. In the excitement, he missed his scheduled flight and had to take another one later that night. Delhi University had appointed a student to oversee Havish's requirements during the visit. We got that confirmation from him."

"That's something we didn't know," Krishav said.

"Doesn't that sound suspicious? Why would Havish come home after taking a late flight and randomly decide to take his wife to Madikeri?" I interjected.

"Yes, sir. And as I was telling Ankana, based on my interactions with Havish, he was a morning person and slept quite early," Krishav added.

"What's there to be suspicious? I was surprised, yes. But Rupa explained it to me. She said Havish was very happy that evening when he returned from Delhi because that lecture had been his best yet. Hence, he wanted to sort of celebrate in Madikeri. She had mentioned this to Rakesh the same evening in a conversation, and hence, it was already recorded in the case file even before Rupa came out of the coma."

"Was there any record of a hotel or resort booking in Madikeri?" Krishav asked.

"No. I had that covered. As it was a spontaneous decision, there was no room booked. Considering it wasn't the peak vacation season, Havish was confident of getting a room even at an odd hour like that."

"Anything else that Rupa had to say? As in, about the accident itself."

"She could only remember that Havish was driving fast, against her request. She repeated that he was thrilled and had difficulty curtailing his emotions. Then, they tried to overtake another car from the wrong side, which led to confusion and a collision. Havish lost control of the car, and it went into the farmland, off the road."

"Does she remember which car that was?" I asked.

"No, she doesn't remember. It all happened so fast that she couldn't register half of it. And I cannot disagree with that statement."

"And they got Havish's body as well?"

"Yes."

"Shouldn't they have waited for the police to arrive? He was already dead, and nothing could be done by getting him to the hospital."

"See, that's debatable. You are technically right. They got Havish's body along with them. It helped as the post-mortem could be done here."

In Patil's theory, Rupa seemed to be just a victim.

"Even after all this, sir, you felt it was important to note that Uncle Joshi…"

"Sorry, is he really your uncle?" Patil interrupted.

"No, he's Krishav's family friend," I corrected and continued, "you noted that Uncle Joshi was snooping around on this closed case. You felt it was important to track him down to us and have this conversation amidst your busy schedule." I was curious.

He smiled knowingly. "It is difficult to put my finger on it. For some reason, I feel that something in this case is still amiss. I have been feeling that for all these months."

"Some case points indicated that?"

"No, rather… I don't know. Call it a policeman's hunch."

"Then why did you close the case?"

"I already told you. Besides, the law doesn't work on hunches, but only on facts and proofs."

"It's the hunches that can drive you towards proofs, no?"

"Ha ha. Well said, Ms. Ankana. Anyway, when I discovered that Joshi was trying to check on something, I got curious."

"Understood."

"Besides, it looks like I am the only one answering all the questions here."

"Sorry, that was not the intention."

"Let's come back to the same point you've avoided discussing. You roused my curiosity during the conversation by stating that you sensed this was a murder. Why do you say that? What's your explanation?"

"Sir, to begin, our theory differs greatly from yours," I said.

"I assumed that. Who do you think was behind the murder in your story? Rakesh?"

"Could be, yes. Along with… Rupa." I paused.

He immediately reacted. "That's ridiculous! She was severely injured in the accident and could have died. You already know that she came out of a coma after nearly a week. How can she be a suspect?" Patil had raised his voice a little.

Krishav said, "Sir, you know Havish was a writer. He had left an incomplete manuscript with me. After Havish's death, I'd asked Ankana to look into it and see if she could complete it."

"You are a writer as well?" Patil was surprised.

"I'm a struggling author if you can call it that, sir," I said.

He nodded.

I continued, "In that story, a certain set of clues suggest the usage of a strong drug that can artificially induce a coma. Thus…" I waited for him to digest it.

He realised that it was an intentional pause. "I don't get it. So what if… oh." It seemed to have come to him.

"I didn't think of that at all," Patil said to himself.

"I mean, it is still a theory, sir. We are not sure about it yet," added Krishav, exhibiting the doubt that he still had.

Patil nodded, scratched his cheek and was deep in thought for several moments.

"That is surely interesting. How did I not think of that possibility? Yes, I have heard certain instances where it is essential for a doctor to medically induce a coma so that the patient can be saved from brain injury."

"Correct," I added. This guy seemed smarter than he let others believe.

"That's a good thought, Ms. Ankana. But as your friend says, it's still a theory."

"I know, so we wanted to gather as many facts as possible to test this theory."

"You are missing another angle here, Ms. Ankana. If there was anything fishy about Havish's death, then it would have shown in the post-mortem report. It was all clean. We didn't even have a reason to suspect anything." He shrugged, but it wasn't convincing.

"Right, sir. I understand. You mean the same post-mortem report produced at the hospital where Rakesh is the Administrative Head," I replied.

"That..." Patil closed his eyes and took a deep breath. "Hmm..."

"So we don't know if Havish had been poisoned or drugged. What if the accident was just a setup?" I spoke with new theories and sounded desperate.

"No, that would not be possible. Police got access to the car in the middle of the night itself. Immediately after the ambulance was dispatched from Bangalore, Rakesh called the police to inform them of the location. The local police reached the spot immediately. The car, indeed, had met with a severe accident. The next day, the nurses and the driver in the ambulance very clearly described how they removed the unconscious Rupa and Havish's body from the car to get to Bangalore. I visited the spot a couple of days later to look at it. So, the poison theory doesn't hold good. Nevertheless, yes, you are right. We cannot be sure if some facts were tampered with in the post-mortem report."

"How difficult is it to have another post-mortem done on Havish's body?"

"That is almost impossible. We cannot do anything like that without getting a court order," Patil replied in a resigned manner. "Apart from that, I am not sure whatever we are looking for would be possible to detect in a new post-mortem report, considering months have passed."

"Hmm… some poisons or strong drugs can be detected even months after death."

"Going to court means making this formal, Ms. Ankana. Then, we'll have to discuss a very different approach than the one you're following presently. You would be openly accusing someone without any proof. That could backfire very badly," Patil warned.

He continued, "Think about it. The accident was a real thing; even an amateur could look at the car's big impact and how they were thrown off the road. The couple was found in the car; one of them was dead and the other injured. All other stuff we speak of is fictional. Even if we hypothetically assume that Rupa wanted to do something like that, it would be practically impossible for her to cause such a fatal accident while assuming that she would be alive by the end of it. Unless we have missed something big, it sounds like a story."

Krishav and I nodded.

"We may not be able to go any further unless something concrete comes up. Otherwise, it is better to stop thinking about it as a murder," he ended.

Patil left us unsure about the whole thing, and though he'd shared his contact, he parted with no promise of meeting again.

CHAPTER 27

Krishav and I sat in silence for a few minutes.

"Is it all just in our minds then, Krishav?"

"I don't know, Ankana. Sometimes, I feel that it's as if we are hoping that it should be murder. It might not be the case."

That pricked me, but I knew he was right. Was I just another impulsive girl, like most audiences of horrendous reality television shows, who only craved for controversy and unrealistic probabilities? I was expecting just that, no? I expected some kick that I had managed to solve a murder mystery in real life, though the plausibility of it was bleak and even unreasonable. For all I knew, Rupa was a victim, unlike Gwen in the story I'd completed. Why did I have to try to draw parallels and frame Rupa?

Yes, some events did seem odd, like Rakesh sending an ambulance to get Rupa all the way to Bangalore. If I think about it, would I have done any different if I had a loved one involved in a life-threatening accident and thrust the responsibility to some small hospital in a small town to save them? And just because Havish had mentioned some indication of a medically induced coma in his book, it couldn't transpire into a real life incident just like that. Rupa was indeed involved in the accident. She was in a coma, and it was a mere coincidence that she was out of it in a matter of days, which happens in any usual case. Instead of being relieved for her, here I was, trying to frame her for murder.

Murder has never been my favourite topic. I've always avoided the dark subject subconsciously, and only when I agreed to complete Havish's book did I even open my mind to experimenting with the topic. That helped me realise one thing. Of all things, murdering someone is not easy. The very thought can send shivers down the spine. To assume that the same thing happened to Havish was perhaps a superfluous fragment of my imagination, and I should be happy that it didn't happen.

Krishav and I reached his house, and conversation remained minimal during our dinner.

"Sorry, I made too much fuss about the whole thing," I said, dissecting a piece of *rasagulla* at the end of the meal.

"You don't have to apologise, Ankana. It was a thought... a solid thought that came to you, and you gave all you had to validate its truth."

"I was thinking... I will leave Bangalore tomorrow."

"Why? Please stay for some more time."

"No, Krishav. My manager reached out the last time I took an unplanned leave to focus on writing and told me nicely that I cannot take things for granted. I don't want to push it unnecessarily."

"Hmm... I understand. But Ankana, we may have to travel to Delhi once to meet the publisher. He'd expressed the same in the last two meetings I had with him. He seemed keen to connect with you."

"Is that necessary? I can have a video chat with him if need be."

"No, don't do that. It isn't a routine that you get to meet the publisher. It wasn't ideal that you weren't a part of the last two sittings. They were fine with me being there because of the unique situation we'd agreed upon. Otherwise, they expect the author to be there."

"Hmm..." I wasn't too keen.

"Come on, Ankana! Such meetings can create opportunities in this field. Don't tell me you've changed your mind on making writing as your career."

"Sure, you... let me know when we need to travel then." I smiled.

"I will do that. Maybe in a couple of weeks. Let me keep you posted."

I mulled over the statement he made without speaking about it. Did I really want to make a career out of writing?

I decided not to worry too much about my passion for writing and go with the flow. However, I knew I had to put some effort into my showroom work to regain the credibility I had with my supervisor.

"You want me to book a bus ticket for you, or will you take a flight?"

"Huh?" I said, coming out of my deep thoughts. "No worries. I will take a flight." Though I couldn't afford to fly down as often, the reduced flight rates in the past year ensured I could indulge a bit. And more importantly, I was tired of Bangalore. I wanted to return to my city, whose comfort I was presently missing.

"Makes sense. You will save a lot of time." He was busy serving himself another portion of the dessert. I felt he'd put on some weight since we'd met months ago.

"How far is Havish's… Rupa's house from here?"

Krishav looked at me with a slight surprise on his face. "You want to meet her?"

"Maybe… I am feeling quite guilty about the whole thing, you know?"

He smiled and nodded. "That's… brave of you."

"Yeah, why not?" I laughed.

"What? I mean it in a nice way."

"Fine, I believe you."

"Hmm… I have an idea. I think there is an afternoon flight that you can catch. We can leave for brunch at the CTR hotel in Malleshwaram later in the morning. From there you can rent a cab to the airport. Rupa's place falls on the way, near Ramaiah Hospital. You can spend some time there and reach the airport directly."

"Sounds good."

"Yeah. I have her number as well. I'll share that with you."

"Done."

***

"The dosa is almost soaked in butter!" I raised my voice.

"Is that an issue? We can order one more butter dosa without… eh… butter, if that helps," Krishav said, making a face, contemplating if the hotel would prepare such a dish.

"Of course not! I love it!"

I didn't know I had the appetite for two of those rich dosas; evidently, even Krishav didn't. After that, we bid farewell, and I travelled to Rupa's place in the cab. Krishav sent me the precise address, so I had no issue locating it. The locality was quite posh and impressive. "Hmm… sometimes I think I should have staked my claim on my father's wealth," I murmured to myself.

The door to the house was open, and as I rang the bell, a gentle voice said, "Who's it?"

"Ma'am… Ms. Rupa, this is… my name is Ankana. I am… was…" I'd thought multiple times about calling her before coming, but every time I picked up the phone, I wasn't sure how to introduce myself or what I'd tell her. That, precisely, was happening to me right now.

"Havish's sister?" There was excitement in the voice.

"Yeah."

"Please come in. I am in the living room," she said.

I felt relieved, for I'd anticipated a probability of her asking me to get out and never show my face. We writers, I tell you, have a dangerous imagination.

She sat at the big teak table in the huge living room. My whole house could've fit into this, and here, I didn't have to use too much of my writer's imagination.

"Hmm… hello, Rupa," I said, trying to put up my best fake smile, which came out due to the awkwardness of the whole situation.

"Please sit down, Ankana. How are you doing?" She had a lovely smile.

"I'm fine, Rupa." I was still hesitant. "How about you? Are things… better now?"

She took a deep breath. She chose not to say anything but just nodded and smiled.

"Listen, I am sorry I didn't come earlier. I was just…"

"That's okay. You don't have to explain anything. I know that you shared a complex relationship with Havish. It is not my business to probe or judge."

"Thanks for… understanding."

"How rude of me! What do I get you to drink? Will you have tea or coffee? Or wait, I'd made *akki rotti* this morning. May I please serve?"

"No, nothing. I had brunch at CTR just before leaving."

"Oh, you were in Malleshwaram?"

"Yes, I was staying at a friend's place. I am actually on my way to the airport. I am travelling back to Mangalore. I thought I should drop by to say 'hi' before leaving."

"That's very nice of you." She was elegant in her mannerisms. Along with feeling like a moron, I also felt utterly ill-mannered.

"Not at all. I should have…" I left the sentence unfinished.

"At least you must have something to drink, Ankana."

"Don't bother, please. I am completely fine."

"No, no. Nothing doing. Coffee or tea?" she insisted.

The day had gotten warmer than I'd anticipated, and I was in no mood to have something hot before hitting the road again. "Hmm… I can have some juice."

"Oh dear, I think I finished the stock of the packed juice yesterday. Let me try to make some from fresh fruits. Could you please hand me…," she hesitated sadly, pointing towards the crutch leaning on the wall.

"Hey, sorry. Do you still have trouble due to the accident?" I jumped to help her.

"Yeah, well. The doctors say it should be much better in the upcoming months."

"Can I make something instead?"

"Now come on, Ankana. That will be very…"

"No, seriously, Rupa. Please don't be so formal. And you don't have to worry about my culinary skills. I am used to making coffee at home; I mean instant coffee." I laughed nervously, and she joined in, perhaps out of courtesy.

"Fine. You can find the fruits in the fridge."

"Cool." I opened the fridge and found packets of curd. "Or… may I please make buttermilk?" I asked.

She smiled, almost unable to contain her laughter.

"Why? What happened?" I asked, confused.

"Even Havish liked to have buttermilk instead of fruit juice. Sorry, I just happened to remember. I will be shameless and ask you to make two glasses." She laughed. Thankfully, it wasn't just me being silly. She must have been nervous about meeting me for the first time, especially when I came unannounced this way.

I made my way to the kitchen, and she followed me slowly with the help of her crutches.

On the way, I noticed the transparent shelf, where I saw a few silver-coloured chalices. I smiled, for it reminded me of the four chalices in Havish's story. However, these differed greatly from what I had imagined while reading.

"I hope I don't offend you when I say that I notice some resemblance between you and Havish."

"Oh, really? I never thought…" I shrugged. Yup, definitely

awkward. "How come you stay alone?" I immediately added more so that it didn't sound rude: "I mean, is there no house help?"

"I do have a maid. She comes in twice a day—morning and evening. She left only a while ago, clearly leaving the main door open."

"Ah, no wonder."

"When it comes to cooking, I always prefer to do it myself. I am a bit orthodox that way. I don't let maids enter the kitchen."

"Hmm… hope me entering your kitchen is not an issue." I felt odd.

"Come on, Ankana! Of course not."

Preparing buttermilk seemed to need more effort than I'd anticipated, especially in someone else's kitchen. But I was finally done.

"Hmm… this tastes different from the one I generally prepare."

"I don't think you add coriander, or maybe it's the garlic?" I attempted.

"Yes, I think it is garlic. It's good. I will surely try it next time."

We chatted for some time on simple topics, and I had a good mind to say that she should meet another guy and move on, for she was still young and had a long life ahead of her. But I knew the line I wasn't supposed to cross and kept the thought to myself. Who knows? I might stay in touch with her and have a camaraderie later to allow me to make such suggestions.

"Rakesh was telling me about you. I understand he'd coordinated with you when you were here."

"Ah, yes. How's he?"

"He's doing fine. He is one of the few who visits me often. He was to visit this morning. I don't keep close with many other relatives."

I was about to say that I agreed with her and implemented that approach in my life too, when I realised that I was technically her relative and had landed at her place unannounced.

"Nice chap," I said and smiled, remembering my naughty dream about Rakesh. I wondered if I should explore that path, which I had almost forgotten in all my assumptions about Havish's death for a while.

"Havish spoilt me that way. I used to mingle a lot with people. But he was quite reserved. He didn't like it when people visited us, and he hardly visited anyone. Because of him, I always had to think twice before inviting guests home."

Come now! How many more similarities between him and me? "I am sure he wouldn't have liked me visiting," I said, immediately realising I should not have done that.

"Nothing like that! Though he kept things to himself about you and your mother, whenever he spoke about the two of you, it was always in a nice way."

"Hmmm..." I was pleasantly surprised. I noticed she didn't delve much into things when she saw that I felt uncomfortable, which made me like her even more.

After a while, she looked at the clock and asked me, "What time is your flight?"

"Oh, yes. It's... umm... nearly three hours from now."

"I don't intend to sound rude, Ankana. But it may make sense for you to start your journey to the airport. Otherwise, you will cut it too fine. The office traffic must have picked up by now."

"No, not at all. Thanks for letting me know. I didn't realise how time flew while speaking with you. I hadn't intended to spend so much time here."

"Why, I'll take that as a compliment!" She smiled radiantly. Oh, it's a pity I am not a guy. Else, I'd have fallen for her smile. Wait! That would make me even more similar to Havish.

"Please do come to Mangalore when you feel better. It would be nice to host you."

"Sure, and the same holds good for you as well. I hope you will visit me the next time you're in Bangalore. If you can plan the visit, it would be nice if you could stay with me for a few days."

"Thanks, Rupa. You take care."

We parted on good terms. As soon as I sat in the cab, another car approached us and parked in front of us.

Rakesh got out and came walking towards me. I felt a strange tingling in my guts and further down.

"How glad am I to see you, Ankana! This is a pleasant surprise."

"Hey, Rakesh, yes. Nice to see you as well. I thought of visiting Rupa."

"Why don't you come in?"

"Eh… no, Rakesh. I have a flight to catch. Maybe next time."

"Sure, you have a nice journey." He smiled and joined Rupa at the door, waving to me as I left.

"Awww…," I said as I got comfortable in the cab.

"What happened, ma'am? All okay?" asked the driver.

"Ahem… yes, of course."

Chapter 28

I never thought that I could hate my job until this day. After a long gap, I'd returned to the showroom and thought I would at least be reasonably excited to be back, but man, was I wrong.

The tasks seemed too mundane, and I wondered how I used to like the same or at least used to be okay with them only some time ago. Krishav had spoilt me literally for literary stuff.

Even at the end of the day, there seemed no motivation to return home. A few days ago, I used to jump at the opportunity of going back home and working on the unfinished mystery. But now, it felt like a big void in my life.

I wondered if I should resume writing my novel, the one I'd left after finishing only a quarter. When I did that, it felt repulsive. The story was so predictable. Then I thought of the other two novels. Even they weren't magnificent. The themes were too common, but as Krishav had mentioned once, maybe it was just the parts where I included an investigation that I liked and perhaps wrote well.

I was now having an identity crisis when it came to writing. Shit! Krishav had guessed this quite comprehensively.

Instead of dreading writing things I didn't like, I thought I should try reading more on mystery. I explored many stories and other authors. I couldn't help but identify the places in the stories where they had gone wrong or had made too simplistic assumptions to suit the story. No wonder not many successfully drew a crowd when writing a mystery.

I wondered how my book, which I'd co-authored with Havish, would fare amongst the readers. That was an excitement that kept me going.

In a week, Krishav called me.

"Will you please get permission from your supervisor so we can travel to Delhi next week?"

"Sure, I know he will not be happy. But I am looking forward to the meeting."

"Great."

"Eh, listen, Krishav."

"Yes?"

"You know we'd briefly spoken about my earlier two books."

"Yes."

"Would you be able to…"

"Oh yes, sorry. I'll arrange for a good critic and an editor to assist you. Some big parts may need to be changed, but I hope you do not have to derail the plot. Once that is done, we can see if publishers are interested."

"Hmm… okay."

"I will get your ticket booked from Mangalore to Delhi, and I will come from Bangalore. We can meet there directly."

"Cool, see you next week then."

***

The representative from the publishing house, Mr Sharma, seemed to be an old gentleman dressed in a crisp suit and groomed to perfection, giving me the feeling that I was underdressed. I might as well have worn Gwen's two-piece bikini.

Thanks to Krishav, who was merely dressed in formals, I felt I could continue sitting in front of this complete man.

"I read the story. It was difficult to say that two different people had penned it," said Mr Sharma at a speed of ten words per minute, making it difficult for me to remember the first few words of the sentence by the time he had finished speaking. Fine, I am exaggerating. Ten words per minute is unreasonable. He was trying at least fourteen per minute, I think. Don't try it at home, it's too dangerous.

"Thank you, sir."

"I have asked my people to fast-track it from here so that it hits the bookshops sooner than the standard process," said Mr Sharma.

I wondered briefly how easy or difficult it would be for Mr Sharma to fast-track his sentences.

"That's great news, Sharma," Krishav said, as if he were speaking to his classmate, but the latter didn't seem to mind.

"Readers will be delighted to know that Rāghavānka is back." He seemed genuinely excited, which made my heart throb faster. The ability to make a reader wait desperately for your story—what a power a good writer could command.

"That's kind of you, sir."

"My editors will get in touch with you starting next week. Is that okay?" Mr Sharma asked me.

"Why next week, Sharma? Ankana can make time this week itself. She is excited too," Krishav said and looked at me.

"Yea... yes, sir. Of course." I wanted to kick Krishav. Then I thought that he was right. I was keen to start soon.

"Also, now that you're here, please meet one of the three editors working with you before you take our leave, Ankana."

"Three editors?" I was surprised.

"Krishav mentioned that this is your first book. Each book goes through multiple editing steps. The final editor, Ritvik, is here today. Coincidentally, he's edited Rāghavānka's last two novels as well. Hence, I thought I should have him do it this time also.

"Oh, that's nice... sir."

Mr Sharma called Ritvik into the room, and we did a quick round of introduction. Mr Sharma asked Ritvik to take me around the small office, and Krishav stayed back in the cabin, still speaking.

When we reached Ritvik's desk, I said, "You have to come to the office regularly, is it?"

"Yes, we do. Rather, I feel more like it."

"Oh, I thought your job doesn't require you to…"

"I feel more productive in this ambience. So, I come to my desk daily unless something at home needs me to work from there."

"Nice!"

After hesitating, he said, "I am sorry to hear about Havish."

He didn't know about my equation with Havish. "That's okay."

"One of the most wonderful people, I must say."

"Was he?" It was a reflex.

He seemed surprised at my reaction. He continued anyway. "Yes, of course. He was the easiest writer to work with. And trust me when I say that because I have been doing this job for over a decade. All the writers are timid when their first book is being edited. Once their book manages to sell decently, and I mean it need not even be a bestseller, the change in attitude is unbelievable."

"Oh, really!" That was news to me.

"It was never the case with Havish. I was nervous when I had to do the final editing of his third novel under the Rāghavānka pseudonym. Though I had the experience, I knew this one would be a big deal, and it was. I could still call him any time or day, and he would be there to help. Always respectful and joyous."

I wouldn't say that I was not shocked when I saw Ritvik tearing up.

"Hey, that's okay, Ritvik." I put my hand on his arm and patted him a few times.

"I am sorry. I am usually not this emotional. I feel so stupid." He wiped his tears away and cleared his throat.

"You must have admired Havish a lot." I thought that was the only appropriate thing to say.

"Yes. He was surely an inspiration. I mean, think about it. His books were doing so well, and he could come out of the shadows and claim that stardom any time. Yet, he chose to remain behind the scenes and still gave some excellent stories for people to read."

I felt a sudden weight on my shoulders. This was a senior editor who had such an expectation. What about the final readers?

"I am worried that I might end up disappointing you with my work!" I exclaimed.

"Why would you say that, Ankana?" He was genuinely surprised.

"I have a very big pair of shoes to fill, and I might not have done a…"

"Of course you have!" he said.

"What do you mean?"

"I've already read the final manuscript you sent a few weeks ago."

"Oh, you… have."

"And I could not have expected a better version. I couldn't point out where Havish's writing stopped and yours began. It was wonderfully synchronised. The only part I could notice where there was a difference in writing style was that Havish would unintentionally end up sounding funny in some parts. In your case, it is more on the serious side."

"Ahem… wow… okay." I was thrilled. I was tongue-tied with embarrassment and surely was blushing. I didn't know what else to say to keep the conversation going. "So you got to meet Havish… at all?"

"Yes, I met him whenever I had to travel to Bangalore or when he travelled to Delhi."

"Oh really! That's some bromance you speak of," I said and regretted talking bullshit like that.

Ritvik didn't seem to mind and giggled like a school kid. "It was more of a fanboy moment for me when I used to be with him.

However, he never let that happen. He always said that he looked up to me, for I made his stories more beautiful. Talk about modesty."

"Hey, come on! I am sure he meant every word of it."

Ritivik half-nodded and half-shook his head, smiling. I didn't know what to make of it—but I smiled anyway.

I looked at Mr Sharma's cabin. It had a glass covering, and I could see that Krishav was in some serious discussion. I turned to Ritvik and wanted him to return to his desk, for I couldn't do more socialising than I'd already done. But he stood there expectantly, so I had to search for topics to make conversation. I thought of something he'd said and figured out the next topic of discussion.

"Hey Ritvik, you said you met Havish every time he travelled to Delhi."

"Yes, Ankana."

"So when he travelled for the last time, did you…"

"Yes, I did. I accompanied him to the guest lecture late afternoon that day. While there was no formal reason for me to meet him, I didn't need one."

"Oh, okay."

He seemed to get more sombre as he thought about it. I guess I had scratched open some unhealed wound.

"It may seem stupid. You know, it feels like I could have played a role in preventing what happened." He was looking at the foot of the chair.

"No one could have done anything, Ritvik."

"Technically, he should not have travelled that night at all. I should have continued to…"

"Sorry, what?"

"He got held up at the University seminar at the college and missed his flight."

"Yes, and he was to come on the next flight on the same night."

"No. There was no other flight available. He was told that he could travel only on the next morning flight. He was in a fix, considering he'd already checked out of the hotel. I asked him not to worry and to stay with my family for the night. I had often spoken about him to my spouse, and I was sure she'd be happy to meet him. That's how I'd convinced him about it, and he was fine with it. He called his wife right then and informed her that he wouldn't be able to make it that night and would get the morning flight back to Bangalore."

"Then what happened?"

"He just kept stating that while he appreciated my gesture, he usually was more comfortable at his place. So I asked the Delhi University representative, who was helping Havish out with his stay, to try one final time in case any flight had a seat available. I had said it only casually and assumed that at such short notice there would be no other option but to take the morning flight."

"Okay…" I listened intently.

"That boy returned fifteen minutes later and said there was one flight with a last-minute cancellation. Thus, a seat was available. But he had to hurry, as the boarding was almost complete. Havish had to run helter-skelter, and he made it just in time. I wouldn't be surprised if he was the last person to board the flight. Considering it was a private airline, I suppose they waited for a couple more minutes."

I was having a lot of difficulty containing my emotions.

"Would you…" I took a deep breath. "Do you recollect if he had called up his wife again to inform the change in his plan?"

"Eh… I don't think so."

"Meaning? You don't think he did that, or you don't think so because you don't remember?" I was being curt, which he didn't seem to register.

"Until the University boy returned, Havish had already assumed he wouldn't travel that night. Once the boy came, he rushed to get on the flight. I was with him throughout. The University had given him a huge memento that he couldn't carry around, and I helped him. Yes, correct. Once he cleared the security, he had to carry his luggage and the souvenir and rush towards the aeroplane. I don't think he could have practically called anyone meanwhile. And you know how it is once you get on a flight; they don't allow you to use the phone, right?"

"Hmm..."

"Ankana, are you okay? You seem to be shivering."

"No, I am fine. What time was that flight?"

"Hmm... yes, it was the eight-thirty p.m. flight."

"Okay..."

"Please sit down." He ensured I sat and asked the office boy to get me a glass of water.

I sat on the chair, squeezing its sides in a vicious grip.

Chapter 29

"Ankana, it need not be a big deal." Krishav was trying to convince me.

"Of course, it is, Krishav. This is a new twist. Rupa didn't know Havish was coming home the same night."

"I understand that he may not have had the opportunity to speak to Rupa before he boarded, not even when he was on the flight. He could have called once he landed, no?"

"Think about it, Krishav. I checked the flight details. It was a direct flight from Delhi to Bangalore. It landed only after eleven in the night. Thus, he may not even have called her, assuming she might be sleeping."

"Okay, fine, let's assume that. So he didn't call her and directly went home. So what?"

"Krishav, think. Maybe, on reaching his house, he saw something he wasn't supposed to see. He then freaked out and rushed out of his house. I don't know why he chose to go to Madikeri, but please stay with this line of thought. That is when this accident occurs."

"That's too convenient."

"No, Krishav. This is too odd to be a coincidence."

"Even then, many things don't make sense."

"Krishav, come on. There are many layers to a problem. Let's solve one after the other."

"Okay, what do you suggest we do now?"

"I think we should at least inform Patil about it."

"This is a small update to what we already knew. I feel Patil would have moved on from it by now. He seemed to be a busy man."

***

We'd checked into the airport and parked ourselves near the boarding gate. I tried calling Patil, and as Krishav had guessed, he didn't receive my call.

My flight was scheduled for departure an hour from now, and Krishav's was fifteen minutes later. We'd reached much earlier as we had no other place to visit after leaving the publishing office. Reaching early and sitting at the same airport that Havish had visited the night he died made me uncomfortable.

I sat without speaking to Krishav, shaking my leg vigorously, not knowing what to think or do.

My phone started vibrating, making me gasp with surprise. It was Patil. I received it eagerly and told him what I'd found.

"That's odd. Can you be sure of it?"

"Sir, we can safely assume that Havish didn't inform Rupa before the flight took off. He didn't call her when he landed because it was well past eleven at night. You can verify that by checking the call records."

"Hmm… that could be a good possibility. But again, we cannot do it without a court order, which can happen only if the case reopens."

"Sir, I know some facts aren't adding up, and things look hazy…"

"Ms. Ankana, wait. Listen to me carefully. Remember what you said the first time we met? Hunches drive us towards proofs. Facts and proofs are playthings for the police to worry about. You are not the police. You don't worry about fact-finding for now. Trust me, I have seen weirder cases, and facts add up in the end. Imagination is your forte. Use that. Get to a theory, and let's see how facts add up to that. No matter how strange, don't curtail yourself due to lack of facts, okay?"

"Yes, sir." What he said gave me tremendous confidence.

"I will check on you again in the morning. Let me sleep over it as well." He disconnected.

Krishav looked at me. While he didn't hear what Patil had to say, he'd learned to read me enough to know I was not to be disturbed. I put my head down, held my head with both hands and closed my eyes. I wanted to think, and my head ached badly. I stayed that way for some time and felt my throat dry up. I lifted my head to see that Krishav had got me water in a paper cup. I took a gulp, didn't worry about thanking him, and returned to my thoughts. I stayed that way for several minutes, and when I rose again, I was sweating a lot.

"I will have to come to Bangalore," I said, looking at him blankly.

"What happened, Ankana?" Krishav asked, worried.

As I left him to run to the ticket counter to see if I could swap my ticket from Mangalore to Bangalore, I turned back and said, "I have a theory."

***

It was a hassle to get my tickets swapped. I created a bit of a scene by adding some news of a close fake relative being admitted to a hospital in Bangalore. I managed to get the Bangalore ticket by paying the difference. It was a bit of chaos; there never was a chance for me to connect with Krishav, which is precisely the way Havish wouldn't have been able to communicate with Rupa the night he travelled from Delhi to Bangalore.

The flight was a quiet one. My seat was far from Krishav's, and I could sense that he was desperate to understand what was happening.

Once we landed in Bangalore, we took a cab to Krishav's house.

"Come on! Give me something at least," he pleaded.

"Not here. Not now," I said.

The driver looked at us through the rearview mirror and gave a sly smile. The whole thing scandalised Krishav, and he was about to explain to the driver that we weren't a couple. I had to hold his arm and make him relax so he wouldn't say more than he needed to. It was one of the reasons why Krishav remained silent and, if I am not mistaken, maintained a gradually increasing distance from me in the car.

I texted Patil, "I have a theory. Can you speak in some time?"

His response was quite immediate. "Sure, I will wait for your call."

I showed it to Krishav, which didn't help to reduce his curiosity.

When we reached his house, I ran to the living room as Krishav bolted the doors. I called Patil on his phone, and Krishav was all ears.

"Yes, Ms. Ankana?"

"Thanks for taking the call. It is slightly late."

"No, that's okay. Should we get Mr Krishav on a conference call?"

"Eh, no. He is with me. I mean, I am with him. We both are at his house." None of the sentences came out as I expected them to.

"Okay…" He seemed taken aback but tried his best to stay calm.

"So, the theory?" Krishav asked, without caring to greet Patil.

"Okay, here it goes. Havish doesn't get to inform his wife that his flight will land the same night. This means she wasn't expecting him. The theory here is that she was doing something... or was with someone when Havish came home. I guess it must be an affair, and it must have been with Rakesh."

"What? Rakesh is her brother!" Krishav interrupted.

"No, not brother. He is a cousin. He is her first cousin if I recollect correctly."

"Yeah, but still. That's the same as a brother." Krishav was hell-bent.

"Krishav! You are in India. We have a multitude of cultures. In our culture, it is normal for cousins to marry. An uncle of mine married his first cousin. Irrespective of that or any moral judgement about blood relatives sleeping with each other, this is my theory. So, let's say Havish comes home late at night, opens the door softly with his keys, only intending not to disturb his sleeping wife, goes to the bedroom and sees the two of them in a compromising position.

"He raises hell at both of them, and they cannot deny anything, for they are caught in the act. He asks them to leave the house, and she refuses, pleading with him to forgive her. Then, he decides to go to Madikeri. I don't know why he chose Madikeri and I disagree with the logic Rupa told you, sir. But let's assume he wanted to spend time in Madikeri.

"This is where it gets tricky for me to imagine what happened. I guess that Havish leaves Madikeri alone in his car."

"What!?" both Patil and Krishav interrupted.

I raised my hand, asking Krishav to wait.

I continued, "Rupa and Rakesh knew that if they let him go, he would file for divorce and leave Rupa penniless. All said and done, Havish's net worth was at least a few crores of rupees. And I'm unsure if he had a life insurance policy, too.

"So the two lovers followed Havish in Rakesh's car. My assumption here is that either they knew exactly where he'd be going to in Madikeri, or they knew how to track him. Maybe his GPS tracker was live, so Rupa could find out where her husband was going. It was natural for Havish not to have checked such things when he was fuming about being cheated on.

"Somehow, they caught up to him on the road to Madikeri, near Channapatna, or even before, because he must have stopped the car to refuel or to eat something. I guess that he may not have had anything to eat since the time of his journey.

"When they chased him down, they waited for the right moment. Once they got a good stretch of empty road, they overtook him. Not knowing that it was Rakesh, Havish let him overtake, and that was when Rakesh's car collided with Havish's, making his vehicle fall off the road. When they checked, I assume he was already dead, or perhaps… they ensured he was. Rupa got into the same damaged car and maybe tried to get some bruises so that it looked like she was with Havish when the accident happened.

"I don't think she was injured at all. I can say this with more conviction now that I think about it. I visited her only last week, and she claimed that she couldn't exert herself much due to her injuries, yet she was exerting herself unconsciously at times. More importantly, she hesitated a bit when she asked me to hand over her crutch. At the time I thought she hesitated because she felt helpless. I realised only now when I gave it some thought. The real reason for her hesitation must have been that the crutch was kept quite far away from her seat. Which meant that she had travelled to the seat without the help of a crutch!

"Returning to the night of the accident, Rupa settled in the damaged car, and Rakesh called the hospital to send an ambulance."

"That does sound convincing, Ms. Ankana," said Patil, and Krishav nodded.

"Wait, what about the medically induced coma? How did that come into the picture?"

"That's simple, Krishav. If I am not mistaken, in a passing moment, Havish must have shared the core idea of his book with Rupa, in which no one doubts Gwen because she was victimised and put in a medically induced coma. Rupa may have shared that information with Rakesh, which they ended up making use of. No one questioned Rupa's integrity because she had met with an accident along with her husband and was also in a coma fighting for her life."

"That is some good theory, Ms. Ankana." Patil was impressed.

"But, sir, how do we build facts around this? Or at least how do we bridge the loopholes in this theory?"

"If we prove that Rakesh or someone else was at Havish's house when the latter came home, that will be a great input to reopen the case. If I recollect correctly, Rakesh had specifically said that he was at his residence in Bangalore when Rupa called in the middle of the night for help."

"Now, how to do that? I am sure we cannot expect people to be on the roads at such an hour in the night and ask them that."

"No, that wouldn't have worked even in daylight. We cannot establish a crime based on lousy proof. We need something concrete. I noticed that Havish's house was in a posh locality."

"Yes, that's true. As I said, I visited Rupa only last week."

"Won't the houses there have security cameras?" Patil asked.

"Hmmm… they should have. I didn't notice. But people in such localities surely would have," I said, feeling positive.

"Here's the thing, Ms. Ankana. Those CCTVs technically override their memory every two or three weeks."

"Oh!" I was disappointed.

"Hold on. Those are the basic versions. Then there are slightly high-end CCTVs where the recording is stored for at least two months, extending up to three."

"The incident happened around six months ago."

"Yes, that's the sad part. However, there are high-end CCTVs that have unlimited storage capacity. Your task is to track if any house nearby has such a high-end CCTV that we could use to prove your theory."

"That's a bleak chance." I was disappointed.

"I know. But do try. There may be some offices or workplaces in the area. Such establishments may have those high-end CCTVs."

"Hmm… makes sense. We will try, sir."

"And that's not all. The second thing is that even now, it is a theory. Hence, you still need to act discreetly. I can help you only offline and not on duty."

"Understood, sir."

We disconnected the call.

"Why do we get to do all the difficult jobs?" Krishav cringed.

"Wait a minute." I gazed intently at Krishav.

"What's that?" He seemed concerned.

I went to his glass shelf, got a cap that was put on a stuffed monkey, and returned to place it on Krishav's head. "You look like a top-notch CCTV salesman," I said.

"Over my dead body, Ankana!"

Chapter 30

We rang the doorbell.

"Hello, sir. I am from Ankana & Co., an upcoming CCTV manufacturer. We wanted to showcase our product to you, which I am sure has much better features than your existing CCTV."

"Eh, bro. I don't have a CCTV."

"Oh, not a problem, sir. Thanks for your time."

"No, wait. I have been thinking of getting a CCTV."

"Sure, sir, I will return tomorrow."

"What? Wait!"

Krishav rushed down the stairs with me beside him, as I laughed uncontrollably once we were out of earshot of the potential CCTV customer.

"This is ridiculous! I sell great manuscripts to big publishing houses, and here I am standing with a second-hand CCTV set, trying to make fake sales. This is such a demotion!"

"I will try the next one. Don't you worry, Krishav."

"Aren't you a salesperson in the showroom?"

"Huh, no! I am the store manager."

"Yeah, whatever."

It was afternoon, and though we had covered a good number of households and a few business establishments, some didn't even entertain us, and many didn't have CCTV. Most of them with CCTVs had the basic one that would rewrite the old recording every two weeks. A few had a slightly advanced version, storing the recorded data for up to three months. In one such place, a woman latched onto us. She wanted to check our ID cards so she could complain to the authorities, stating that her CCTV had stopped working months ago and she wouldn't fall for such fake products again. We had a tough time convincing her that we weren't troublemakers and had to run away.

We had covered more than enough houses, and it was well past lunchtime. As usual, my head began to ache badly. We had made no progress and were way behind, not even covering a kilometre yet.

We decided to take a break for lunch and went to a sandwich place.

I was feeling discouraged.

"We are just wasting our time, aren't we?" I asked, assuming it would be rhetoric.

Krishav mulled over the question momentarily. "No, I think we are on to something."

"What? You believe it's possible?" I was genuinely surprised. Krishav had supported the whole cause from the beginning but was unsure of it the entire time, and hence, his admitting that we were on to something came to me as a breath of fresh air.

"I do. I admit that I wasn't entirely sold on your idea when you shared your bad dream or vision. But too many coincidences aren't making sense. I am sure there must be something. We should keep at it. No matter how tough the wall is, if we are persistent, we will crack it. It is a matter of time."

I suddenly wanted to hug him. Having realised by now that he was not a touchy person, I just smiled at him.

"I must say, you don't behave like a professional salesman," Krishav said.

"Of course, I don't intend to."

"Come on! You need to play the part."

"Ha! I saw how well you acted when that irritating woman came after us."

"Ha ha! I thought she'd call the police when she realised we didn't have an ID card to show which company we were representing. You could have shown your company's ID, no?" he asked.

"Eh, no way! My supervisor is already angry at my attendance over the past few months. If that woman had caught on to the office address in my company ID, she'd have reached my supervisor directly, who'd have come down from Mangalore to take me to task."

"We still have a lot of distance to cover. However, the roads start spreading out in a bit. Not sure if that is going to help our cause."

"True. We will take stock in a couple of hours."

"Should we get some fake ID or something?"

"No, come on. Not all salespeople have ID cards. We cannot take one aunty so seriously," I opined.

"Hmm..."

"What? You have a crush on her or something now?" I teased him.

"Really, Ankana? You could surely do much better. Even Havish's earlier books had better humour."

"Ouch! That hurt." We laughed.

As we returned from the eatery, I said, "That advanced CCTV Patil spoke of may not even have come to India, no?"

"Not sure. I got to know... or well, even thought about various CCTVs only once he told us. But I agree with you. Either they have not come to India, or perhaps they are unreasonably costly, so people don't go for them," said Krishav.

"True. Even the semi-advanced ones, if I can call them that, hardly a couple had those installed. Not even business establishments had them. I was surprised."

"True. Had we investigated the same a few months ago, maybe those couple of houses with the semi-advanced ones could have been of some help, as they would have stored information for up to three months."

"Yeah, if that were the case, I would have offered that aunty dinner with you at one of the restaurants nearby in exchange for her help."

"Still a bad one, Ankana."

"Ha ha!" I poked him in his arm as he tried to escape.

He walked ahead of me, and I was a couple of steps behind him. He stopped in his tracks, and I bumped into him. "Dude, stop thinking about that aunty now!" I shouted.

"Of course, we need to think about her!"

"What? Krishav, are you trying some reverse psychology with me?"

"What did she say about her CCTV, Ankana?"

"Nothing. She just said it stopped working a few months ago."

"Precisely!" He seemed excited.

It dawned upon me. "Holy shit! Then, no new recording could have overridden her old recording!"

"Yes! If lucky, that night's clipping may still be with her."

We rushed back to her house, unsure how to seek her help. There was no use trying to act smart. I thought of an idea. I called Javed from my showroom, explained the situation briefly and told him what we intended to achieve. He, being a sweetheart, readily agreed to play along.

I rang the bell this time.

The aunty was fuming this time when she saw our dear faces.

"What does this even mean? How dare you both come back? You ran away last time."

"Ma'am, please hear me out. Yes, we got scared earlier. Then we spoke to our manager about what you said. He was unhappy with how we reacted and reprimanded us for our behaviour."

"Good. You deserve it."

"Ma'am, please don't say that. He warned us that we must solve this issue, or he would cut our commission by at least half." I made a sad face, which shockingly came naturally to me.

"Oh!" She was indeed surprised. Not bad.

"My humble request to you is to give us an opportunity."

"I don't know who you people are. Why should I do it? For all I know, you both might be rapists."

"Please don't say that, ma'am. My colleague may look like one, but we are in a bad situation. Talk to our manager if that helps to sort this out."

I showed her my phone, in which I had edited Javed's name as 'Senior Manager Javed', and dialled that number.

"Sir, yes. Ma'am is right here."

She made a face, wondering why she should speak to him, but went along, seeing me begging.

"Hello!" She was curt.

We obviously couldn't hear what Javed was telling her. But she started replying in '*hmm...s*'. It was a matter of a minute before she started to enjoy talking with him. I was zapped but kept a straight face.

Krishav nudged me.

"What?"

"What do you mean I look like a rapist? I am offended."

"*Oh ho* Krishav, sorry. I was playing along. Chill for now," I requested.

"Okay, fine, sir. That's helpful. Sure. I will give the phone to this girl," said the aunty and handed the phone to me.

"Yes, sir," I said once I got hold of the phone.

"Such a nice lady, ma'am. You were talking ill about her?"

"Ahem... yes, sir."

"Okay, she will hand over her CCTV set to you."

"Eh, what? sir?" I didn't understand.

"I said she will hand over her CCTV set to you."

"Okay..." I couldn't fathom how that was possible.

"But we have to hand over the CCTV set that you are carrying right now as a warranty, which she can use while we try to sort out the issue with hers."

"Oh, sure."

"I told her that the piece you have with you is the most advanced in the market, ma'am. She bought that lie."

"Ah, sure, sir. Understood."

"You may have to install it and all. She will then hand over the old set to you."

"Done, sir. Makes sense." I disconnected the call.

"So, you install the new one that you have," she demanded.

Thankfully, I'd checked some internet videos this morning, and we were able to get the CCTV installed on her premises. We also showed her how it worked, which made her somewhat less grumpy. She then handed over the piece she had and took both our phone numbers and Javed's with a timeline of a few days for us to return it in its working condition. We promised her the same and left.

"Yes!" I jumped in glee once we had walked for some distance.

"How did Javed manage to do that?" Krishav was stumped.

"Not sure. Maybe he just praised her using some of his Urdu poetry, and she fell for it."

"This is gold. Let's hope this at least clarifies what we need."

Krishav called up Patil, though it was only late afternoon. When he learnt that we'd acquired a CCTV set, he was excited and came over to Krishav's house soon after.

Before playing the recording, I was shivering and understood what having one's heart in the mouth meant.

"Calm down, Ms. Ankana. Firstly, let's hope we have the right date's footage. Then whatever it has to show, at least it will clear all your doubts," said Patil.

I nodded. I struggled to decipher how to search and play the footage. Seeing my struggle, Patil took over, and he navigated easily.

He opened the folder with the name of the month we needed, and there was a file with the required date. Both Patil and Krishav let out a heavy breath. My pulse quickened.

Patil focused on the footage a little before midnight, ideally when Havish should have returned home from the airport. He forwarded it with reasonable speed as we watched for anything strange. The footage ended, and there was nothing in it.

He then played the footage of the next date, which showed the recording starting at midnight. I was surprised by the clarity of the video. We had put it on the television that Krishav owned, and it was very easy to identify objects on the screen.

Just after midnight, there was an incoming cab, which excited both Krishav and me. "There, there!" we screamed.

"Relax, both of you," said Patil, who was in complete control of the situation. He'd been in such situations enough times.

He returned to the moment on the screen when the cab could be seen. Krishav immediately recognised that the one seated next to the driver was Havish.

"We are lucky to have this quality. The normal ones are too blurred. You would not have been able to recognise him at all," said Patil.

The cab went back almost immediately after dropping Havish.

Patil continued forwarding the video at a high speed. We could see that Havish's car had moved out of the locality hardly fifteen minutes after his visit.

"Shit, we cannot see his face," said Krishav, as the footage now showed the back of the car.

"Hmm… that's okay for now," Patil said.

He again forwarded at a decent speed. I could hear my heartbeat. And then it happened. Another car went in the same direction in a matter of minutes. We couldn't see anyone's face, and only the back of the car was visible, but I immediately recognised it. "That's Rakesh's car! I recently saw him come out of such a car when I met him in Bangalore."

I hugged Krishav immediately after that and held him tightly for a moment.

Without showing any sign of getting awkward, Patil moved back to the footage from the previous date to track Rakesh's arrival. He noted that Rakesh's car had come in approximately when Havish boarded his flight.

"Hmm... here, we can see Rakesh coming in his car just after nine at night. That's a big car he drives around."

"Phew!" I had parted from Krishav and was now wiping my sweat. My eyes were slightly moist.

Patil looked at us and smiled for the first time today. "This... my friends... is evidence. While this is not good enough to prove that Rakesh and Rupa murdered Havish, this is good enough for us to reopen the investigation. And then, who knows what all we will find?"

"Will we be able to appeal to redo the post-mortem of Havish?" I asked.

"Yes, in sight of possible tampering of the evidence, the court may grant that without much fuss."

"Also, will we be able to verify any traces of chemical remains in Rupa's blood, if necessary?" I spoke, looking blankly at the television.

"Why just that? I am sure there is a medical record that Rakesh has made about her in his hospital stating that she has sustained a lot of injuries. We will be able to re-examine most of them. For example, you mentioned that you doubted whether she had any problem with her leg while walking. That can now be tested and proven otherwise."

"Also, Rakesh said that Rupa had called asking for help from the accident spot to his residence in Bangalore, but I believe he was with her. Now that the case would reopen, can we trace where that call was made from?"

"Yes, we can attempt to do that."

"And sir, you saw Havish's car just after it met with an accident, right?"

"Yes, I did."

"If Rakesh's orange car collided with Havish's car, then we should be able to trace orange remnants on Havish's car, no?"

"That's a good point." Patil thought about it. "Funnily enough, Ms. Ankana, when I was handling the case, I had not seen Rakesh in this big car. He had a red hatchback. Maybe he intentionally refrained from using the car involved in the accident."

Krishav added, "Nowadays, you can check which part of the car has been repainted, replaced, or repaired recently. Car service providers consider those basic technology, especially during used-car dealings."

Patil nodded. "Agreed. You are right. Rakesh won't be able to bluff his way through. It should be simple for us to prove it was his car."

"I thought as much." I looked at Patil, who seemed to have gained some admiration and respect for me. He took our leave, saying there was much work to do.

For some reason, I couldn't speak much for the rest of the evening. I couldn't describe the feeling I was going through. It was somewhat new. All I could say was that I felt light and heavy simultaneously.

CHAPTER 31

Two weeks later

The first thing Sub-Inspector Patil verified when the case reopened was the call made by Rupa and received by Rakesh, who had used the same mobile tower, establishing my theory that they were together at the accident spot, tightening the case against them.

Patil was able to prove that Rupa and Rakesh had committed the crime. Rupa was informed that if she cooperated, there could be a possibility of reducing her sentence.

On this day, Rupa was recording her statement, and Patil had invited Krishav and me to remain in the background.

"I liked Havish, no doubt. But deep down, I knew that he was not the love of my life. He loved me; I wouldn't say unconditionally, but deeply. Rakesh and I were never close in our younger years. We'd grown closer as the years progressed.

"It was only a matter of time before I would have broken up with Havish and settled with Rakesh. Then, one day, Havish proposed to me out of the blue. On the day he'd received the news that his books as a mystery writer had sold record-high copies. I am a practical person. Rakesh and I discussed and decided that I should go ahead with the marriage, make it look pretty for a few years, and then divorce Havish amicably, so that I could get a share of his wealth as part of the alimony settlement.

"We had managed it well for a couple of years. I'd ensured that we didn't have kids so that there would be no complications when we separated. Maybe in half a year, I thought, I would be able to push for divorce. Rakesh and I were contemplating the reason we'd quote.

"One day, Havish came to me, excited. He'd just come up with the idea for a book. He told me how the murderer would try to get away because she'd be portraying herself as the victim. I got curious and asked him for more details. He explained about medically induced coma to me then and how a particular character, Gwen, aided by Cassandra, tries to escape the murder of the lead character, Nathan. That sounded wonderful to me. I asked him if he'd finished writing the book, and he said he'd just started it. I promise that till such a time, I hadn't thought of any murder at all. But that story appealed to my dark side. I imagined him to be Nathan, and myself to be Gwen.

"The next time Rakesh came home, we made love on my marital bed. I shared this information with him. He, too, felt that it was powerful, but then we laughed it off.

"A few weeks later, when Havish asked me to accompany him to an institution in Delhi, I declined, as I knew it would bore me. When he called me that night, stating he had missed his flight and would try to book one in the morning, I asked Rakesh to come home to spend the night with me.

"You know the rest. Rakesh came home, and we made love that night, not worried about Havish coming home. It was around midnight when I heard the main door open. Havish was about to enter the bedroom when I ran to him, hardly covering myself. Rakesh had rushed to hide in the bathroom, and I knew we were poorly stuck this time.

"I tried to act normal the whole time, but Havish sensed that something was wrong. I knew that because he seemed quite excited when he came, stating that the lecture had gone well and was his best yet, but then his behaviour changed in minutes. He was sensing something wrong. I got him lemon juice and added a heavy dose of his sleeping tablets in it. I hoped he would soon fall asleep so that Rakesh could escape unseen. Fortunately for me, Havish had the drink without thinking twice.

"It was a matter of time before he observed Rakesh's shoes and trousers thrown carelessly on one of the chairs in the living room. I had no time to clear those without being noticed. Havish understood and rushed into the bedroom. I am sure the room reeked of sex. He saw that the bathroom was locked and tried opening it. It wouldn't. He forced it open and found Rakesh there. He was disappointed and angry at the same time.

"He didn't speak a word. Somewhere, I feel it would have been easier had he spoken then. It would have de-escalated the situation, but he left the house, bottling up his rage. He hardly took anything with him besides his Delhi luggage and car keys.

"Rakesh and I knew this was the end of things. He was not keen to let go of crores of rupees, which also applied to me. Rakesh asked me to check Havish's GPS tracker, and I could still track Havish's movements. He was always bad at technology. There were days when Rakesh and I spent time together, although Havish was in the same city, because I could track his live location. Rakesh asked me to get some clothes handy, and we left immediately after Havish. I knew he'd be going to his Mysore grandma's place. That was the place he always went to when he wanted some time for himself. Madikeri was the location Rakesh and I made up to divert attention to a vacation destination.

"Havish never drove very fast, and Rakesh caught up with him by the time he'd reached Ramanagara. We noticed that he'd taken a break at a café. Perhaps the sleeping drug was making it difficult for him, and he'd stopped at the café to have coffee or something. That was when Rakesh made a plan to kill Havish. I tried to stop Rakesh, I swear. I told him that we cannot kill someone. But when he spoke of letting go of the property and the lifestyle, I got convinced more easily than I thought I would.

"Rakesh, having used this highway for years frequently, more or less knew the big stretches where we could take such an action. We missed a couple of them due to bad timing. But Rakesh kept at it. The greed in his eyes was evident. I wondered if it was his greed or if I saw my reflection there. I can only say that we were not ourselves, or perhaps that was what we truly were deep down. I guess that's what it takes to kill someone.

"When we approached Channapatna, we knew that was a good chance. Rakesh tried overtaking Havish. Havish had no idea that we were following him, and he was still under the influence of sleeping drugs that made his motor skills very weak, which he may not have registered earlier due to his rage. Rakesh saw the right opportunity and rammed into Havish's car, which sent the latter into the farmland.

"I was sure that even Rakesh would injure himself during the act, but he was in total control. Our airbags didn't go up, as we were still moving. I hurt my temple slightly and got a sprain in my hand. After stopping the car and ensuring no one had witnessed our act, we ran to check on Havish. I was prepared that we may have to finish him if the accident already hadn't. I thanked my stars that he was no more. Rakesh checked his pulse and confirmed the same.

"Rakesh asked me to call him on his phone so that there would be a basic proof of me reaching out to him for help. Then, I had to climb into the almost upturned car. Rakesh suggested I try to injure myself more so that there was enough blood. I did that and also used Havish's blood to smear on myself. The thought now seems scary, but I didn't feel a thing back then.

"Rakesh called up folks in his hospital and informed them to send an ambulance. He made me send him the GPS location that he forwarded to them. He also called up the police station and asked them to help immediately. He then told me to act as if I was unconscious. He was confident that no one else would find us deep in the farmland except the ambulance he'd called for, which had the specific location details.

"He immediately went back by the same route to the hospital, cleaned up, and received me and a few others when the ambulance reached. He had a good influence on some people there, which he made the best use of. An experienced doctor helped me get into a medically induced coma, which scared the hell out of me. Before I went into the coma, Rakesh told me that he'd take care of everything.

"When I came out of the coma after a week, he filled me in on everything. He told me that he'd got the post-mortem done for Havish based on his instructions, and also, there were reports made to prove that I had experienced certain deep injuries.

"He then informed me that while he'd asked Havish's sister Ankana to visit so that it looked natural, he was sure she wouldn't. She had surprised him by turning up at the funeral. Hence, once I was in better shape, Rakesh spoke to her about my health, while all we wanted to check was if she was interested in the property. Thankfully, she didn't seem to be. She didn't even want to see me, which worked well for us.

"Rakesh had temporarily stopped driving the car he used for the accident. Only recently did he get it repaired and repainted. The day Ankana visited me unannounced, I was taken completely off-guard. I believed I had made an excellent host. I later realised a few mistakes. I shouldn't have pushed the lie about the crutches, as it would have been easier for her to see through it if she wanted to. I believe I was sort of desperate for her to think that I was the victim. I remembered that it was time for Rakesh to come home. I was worried that he'd let slip something as soon as he entered the door, revealing the truth of our relationship. So I politely asked her to leave. Thankfully, she met Rakesh only when she'd stepped out, which didn't cause any awkward moments.

"Little did I expect that Sub-Inspector Patil would be on our tail. He seemed to have his hands on things I hadn't fathomed. I confess to all I just said and regret the role I played in the murder of Havish."

There was basic chatter in the room as a few officials left.

"Sub-inspector Patil." It was a policeman with a lot of grey hair. I assumed he must be someone senior.

"Sir?"

"This is another feather in your cap."

"No, sir. It would be unfair for me to take the credit."

"How do you mean?"

"I couldn't have solved this murder if Havish's sister hadn't helped me see things." His eyes darted towards me.

Only then did Rupa turn to see that I was seated in the last row. Two policewomen escorted her.

"How?" asked the senior policeman.

"Her imagination, sir."

"My boy, you must gather evidence to prove a crime, which you did well. How does imagination play a role?" He almost ridiculed.

"With due respect, sir, proving a crime needs the right facts and evidence. Solving a crime needs great imagination," said Patil, saluting his senior, and looked in my direction. I looked back at him. There was no smile or gesture. We communicated through our eyes, where most words failed. The senior guy didn't seem to understand anything. He patted Patil on his shoulder and moved out of the room.

Rupa passed by me as the policewomen were taking her away. She stopped when she came closer.

"I heard from Patil that you managed to solve Havish's unfinished mystery exactly how he'd planned." She was staring at me. I refused to make eye contact.

The policewoman who held Rupa by her shoulder nudged her to move. Rupa stayed still, looking at me. "You know, Ankana… your brother would be proud that you could complete his…"

Everyone in the silent room heard a thundering whack by the time I registered that it was I who'd slapped Rupa across the face with a rage I didn't know existed in me. Rupa fell across the other side, losing her balance, though she had the policewoman holding on to her. Only Krishav tried to move. Perhaps he was worried I would jump on her to get into a cat-fight. I didn't. Everyone resumed what they were doing.

Still reeling with shock from the slap, Rupa went with the policewomen without making any further fuss.

***

Two months later

I had not returned to Bangalore since my slapping episode with Rupa. I didn't have it in me to return anytime soon after all that had unfolded since my last visit.

The week following Rupa's confession, Ritvik sent me the novel after the final editing. It was ready to be published. I requested that he make one last change to it. Once Gwen is found guilty and confesses her role in Nathan's murder, I put in one scene where Amelia lands a slap across her face so hard that it reverberates in the big hall. He did it without any fuss and agreed that this seemed to give it an apt ending.

After two months, I was returning to Bangalore because my book, or my co-authored book, was made available in the stores. I heard it was going down very well with the fans. Krishav had invited me for a small celebration. Sujna, too, was to join, but she would arrive a day later because of her work. I think she was still making up for her long vacations by working overtime.

I was seated on the bus next to a lady busy with a novel.

She saw that I was trying to read the title and smiled at me.

"You're into romance too?" she said, looking expectantly.

"Hmmm… not entirely. You must try mystery. Totally worth it." I smiled at her.

"Is it? I was never drawn into that genre. Nevertheless, can you suggest any author that I can try?"

"Rāghavānka." I was grinning.

She made a face but pulled her phone out and searched for the name. "Oh! These are some good reviews. I think I will try one of these books."

"You won't be disappointed." I smiled at her.

I reached Bangalore and soon travelled to Krishav's place.

"Hello, bestseller!" He reached out to give me a celebratory hug, which turned awkward as he wasn't used to hugging people.

"Nothing like that."

"Now, don't try to be too modest here. It doesn't suit you. Your book is doing well."

"Nice to hear that."

"When is Sujna coming?"

"She'll be here at the same time tomorrow."

"Ritvik, too, is travelling to Bangalore to attend a publishers' conference. It is actually on the weekend, but he's asked permission to travel earlier so that he can join us."

"He's a sweetheart, isn't he?"

"Yes, nice chap."

I settled on his sofa set and wanted to switch on the television.

"Seriously?"

"What?"

"Your book is doing so well, and I am ecstatic. But you want to watch some stupid show instead of telling me how you're feeling?"

"I am happy, yes. How else should I feel? We should also credit the brand Rāghavānka that Havish created, which is helping with such good sales, no?"

"Of course. But that usually helps the pre-release bookings. Though it's been weeks since its launch, the book continues to do well. Thus, that credit is yours too."

"Fine. Thank you, Krishav." I bowed dramatically.

"You're too coy! Just like your brother. I mean, Havish. And anyway, you were a part of the brand Rāghavānka already. So you might as well…"

"What do you mean I was a part of that already?" I didn't understand his reference.

He looked at me as if I were the one pulling his leg. He then noticed that I was being honest.

"Shit! You've not realised it, have you?"

"Now, what have I not realised?"

"You haven't registered it, Ankana!"

"Okay, bye. I am watching *Rick and Morty* now. Don't disturb." I thought he was pulling a fast one on me, so I started the show on Netflix.

"You don't know why Havish chose the pseudonym Rāghavānka?"

"Duh! Of course, I know. Rāghavānka was a great Kannada poet in the late twelfth century. He penned *Harishchandra Kavya*, one of the most popular works in Kannada literature. I did pay attention in my school life, you know?" I mocked him.

"Eh… Ankana."

"What?"

"Look here."

"What is it, Krishav?"

"What was your mother's name?"

"Ragini. You know that. Why do you ask?"

"So RAG from Ragini, HAV from Havish, and ANKA from Ankana make it what?"

I still thought he was playing the fool when things dawned upon me. I sat up abruptly. "Seriously!?"

"This is unbelievable! You cracked two murders. One in the book and one in real life, and you couldn't crack something this simple?"

"I… Rāghavānka was a blend of our three names?"

"Yeah! Havish had told me as well. He always cherished the time spent with you and your mother as his best years. I thought you would have understood it from the very beginning. I told you that he loved you. He tried reaching out…" The rest of what Krishav said was a blur to me.

Early the next morning, I went to the cemetery where Havish was buried. It was humid, with dark clouds lingering in the sky, similar to the day he was cremated. It was quite deserted, and I searched for his grave. When I found it, I stood in front of it like that little girl in front of her elder brother. I knelt in front of his grave and touched the epitaph on which his name was carved.

The knot in my throat gave way, and tears rushed down as the rain washed them away. I cried like a little girl who had lost her brother. I cried for all the love he wanted to shower on me that my arrogant self had deprived me of. I cried for losing my only close relative, whose voice I'd not heard in ages and surely wouldn't hear anymore.

It was Krishav's hand that rested on my shoulder. I stood and embraced him. "I am so bad, Krishav. I never understood my brother. He loved me so much, and I gave him nothing in return. I blocked him out of my life, and now I cannot reach out to him when I need him."

Krishav patted my back. "Why do you say that, Ankana? I am sure that in his own way, he'll always be with you."

***

Later that evening, Sujna tried to click a selfie with four of us in the frame, but it wasn't happening.

"You have put on a lot of weight in the past month, Krishav. You do not even fit into the frame," I complained.

"Rude!" Sujna shouted, and Ritvik and Krishav booed my comment.

With some difficulty, we managed to click a picture of ourselves, and all of us were looking quite tidy for a change.

Ritvik formally congratulated me on the book's success.

"Come on, Ritvik! I had only a small role to play."

"Of course, I knew you would say something like that."

"Meaning?"

"That's how your brother would have reacted." He smiled.

"Yes, that's how Havish… my brother… would have reacted." I smiled back at him.

He returned to Sujna, who'd been asking him to join her for some time.

"My brother," I whispered to myself, lost in thought, with no one around.

"I am going to get drunk tonight!" Sujna was pouring the third drink for the evening. "Ritvik, let me pour a drink for you too."

"No, ma'am. I've had enough, thanks. My wife doesn't like it when I drink too much."

The two of them were getting acquainted.

I switched on the television and put on *Rick and Morty*.

"*Oh, ho!* Listen," Krishav said, returning to the living room and sitting beside me on the sofa.

"What? You have something to say whenever I switch on the television."

"Mr Sharma and I were speaking."

That caught my attention. I paused the show and looked at him inquiringly.

"Hmm good. I had spoken to him about your romance books. When you and Ritvik were speaking about Havish that day in Delhi, I was trying to tell Mr Sharma that he should look at your stories."

"Oh!" I was surprised.

"He wanted to see how your mystery novel would do and then take a call."

"Really?"

"Yes, and now we know how your book is doing. So I called him up last evening. He said that he will give it a try but that both books need a lot of work, and it may…"

"No, wait, Krishav."

"What?"

"I don't think you should push for it."

"What? Why? I thought that was our agreement when you…"

"Now it's changed. Leave my two romance stories alone for now."

"Oh, okay."

"In fact…"

"Yes?"

"Is there any possibility of looking at Urdu poetry? If need be, I can also translate it to English."

"Where did that come from?"

"Just tell me now."

"It depends on the quality, of course. However, there is surely a lot of market for non-English literature. As you mentioned, if you translate it to English, it will help even more."

"Then, please scrap my two romance novels and focus on this."

"Javed's work, is it?"

I smiled, looking at him.

"Fine, let's give that a shot."

"Thank you!"

"Also, one more thing."

"Dear god! Will you let me watch the show in peace?"

"You are unbelievable!"

"What now?"

"While Mr Sharma was not keen on focusing on your romance books, he has been quite shameless in wanting to explore another series on mystery."

I got up, all excited. "What the hell! Why didn't you tell me?"

"Come on! While he had been hinting towards that for some time, it was only a day before that he spoke about it openly. I wanted to tell you in person and waited for you, but you have been busy with television."

"Has he said anything more?"

"Nope. He just wanted you to warm up to the idea."

"Okay. Only if I can continue writing as Rāghavānka, though."

"Of course!"

"Can I watch the show in peace now?"

"Yes, sure."

"Good." I played the show again.

"Sorry, one more thing."

"*Argh!* What?"

"There are some fan mails. Hope you will respond to them, or even you are like Havish?"

"Huh… what does that mean?"

"Oh, you don't know. Havish hardly responded to his fan mails."

"How rude!"

"Not necessarily rude. He was way too lazy and private. So he didn't entertain them much."

"That is one way I am going to differ from my brother."

"Good. There are some three hundred emails to attend to."

"What the hell!"

"What? That is the fan following you have."

"Woah! Okay. I didn't see that coming. Fine, I will do that. Now, Krishav, I am going to watch the television show, okay?"

"Of course! When did I ever stop you?" Krishav stuffed something into his mouth.

I started with the show.

"One last thing."

"You are dead, Krishav Karunakara!" I pounced on him and held his neck with both hands as all three laughed at me.

Acknowledgements

I'm grateful to my support system, which consists of a few friends and family members. Their scolding, hand-holding, affection, wisdom, and sacrifices, among many other things, keep me going in all my roles.

I'm extremely thankful to the Nu Voice team for trusting my script and toiling to make it a much better novel.

A special acknowledgement to the masters of the mystery universe—Agatha Christie and Sir Arthur Conan Doyle—who continue to impress, influence, and inspire generations with their dedication to the genre.

About the Author

Santosh has lived in Bangalore all his life, dedicating over two decades to corporate roles and making sense out of numbers. In parallel, he has tried his hand as a professional writer for more than fifteen years, experimenting with humour, romance, and fantasy. Recently, he ventured into the realm of mystery with *The Unfinished Mystery*, now *An Author's Secret*, his first book in the genre. He promises to offer more across various genres to his readers in the future. When not working with numbers and words, Santosh enjoys cooking and spending time with his wife and son.